HIS SECRET HEART

A Crown Creek Novel

THERESA LEIGH

❀ Created with Vellum

To the makers of dictation software and the creators of HemingwayApp.com

THANK YOU

If you build yourself up tall you can tell me what the future holds
Will you settle where you stand or keep it to yourself?
Will you go?
Will you go?
Will you go?
Will you go?

Waxahatchee - “Chapel of Pines

I say
You will hit the bottom harder each time
I say
You can leave all of your failure behind
Take it out
Take it out
Take it out on me baby

Waxahatchee - “Takes So Much”

AUTHOR'S NOTE

Finn King is a character with undiagnosed mental illness. As such, this book touches on topics of depression and briefly mentions suicide. If these subjects are at all triggering for you, please proceed with caution.

PROLOGUE

Sky

I unfolded my cramping legs and stumbled from the driver's seat. Steadying myself against the door, I blinked at the sign in front of me. As if I could somehow rearrange the words into an order that made sense.

Blink.

Blink.

But even as the letters swam together in my confused tears, they still formed the same three words.

Lowry Funeral Home.

This was it. This was where my father's funeral was being held.

But what I couldn't understand was... why?

Was it strange that I was stuck on that? Not on the fact that my father was dead. No, his sudden death while I was on the road - unaware that he'd even been ill - was not what was tripping me up.

The loss of my sole remaining parent? The loss of my hope for home and security now that I lost my job? I skipped right over *that*. The shock, the confusion, the grief - it all glanced right off of me without even sticking.

But the fact that his funeral was here? In a town I'd never been in? Almost an hour away from where he'd lived?

That was what my free-falling mind had chosen to grab onto. That was what had taken on the most importance to me. I clung to that question like a drowning woman grips a piece of wreckage after her ship sinks. That question gave me a purpose. A reason not to fall to pieces.

Why was his funeral... *here?*

A stiff breeze blew past, sharply colder than the still-warm September air. It carried the smell of campfire and the promise of autumn around the corner as it lifted my hair away from my face.

Except for the few pieces still stuck fast in the tracks of my tears.

I palmed them away and wiped at my eyes with my sleeves. I hadn't even known I was crying, but it made sense. Grief kept sneaking up on me, sniffing around like a dog in search of a place to spend the night, but I kept shoving it away. I knew that I'd feel the throbbing hurt later, because pushing things to the side was a particular talent of mine. I could *go go go* for months on end, running too fast for the exhaustion and loneliness to catch up. But it always did.

But not now. Now I had questions.

I shut my car door and scanned the cars. As if I'd recognize someone from Reckless Falls. As if somehow I'd find answers immediately. I'd almost hoped to be able to wave an old neighbor down. "How did he die?" I imagined asking one of the Abbott boys. "Was he alone?"

There were no Abbotts here. Or anyone else that might know these things. No one that could tell me why I'd only learned about the swift, merciless cancer once he was gone. No one waiting around to explain why he'd never called his only daughter to say goodbye.

Grief nudged at me again. I shoved it away with more questions, firing them out one after another like a reporter hot on the heels of a scoop. *Who paid for his care? Who sat by his bedside? Who arranged this funeral?*

Why were they holding in a town that didn't know Bill Clarence?

I blinked at the cars again and amended that last question.

How *did so many people here in Crown Creek know Bill Clarence?*

An elderly couple emerged from their pristine Cadillac and shuffled towards the entrance. The old woman clutched a tiny white dog to her chest, and the old man had a paper bag of groceries tucked under his arm. I'd never seen them before. But I was confused and they weren't scary, so I fell in step behind them with a nervous smile tugging at my lips.

They didn't acknowledge me at all, even when we entered the funeral home together. .

The door swung shut behind us, leaving us in a silence so sudden it made my ears ring. I'd always felt a little claustrophobic indoors. Like the four walls surrounded my heart as well as my body, encasing it in concrete so that each beat was a struggle.

I tried to take a deep breath to slow my panic. But my nose filled with the sickeningly fake scent of flowers and I sneezed instead.

I was surrounded by lilies. Lilies on the tables. Lilies on the floor. They lined the walls like an honor guard, waiting for me to start walking.

So I did. The carpet was a deep burgundy the exact shade of dried blood. And it was so thickly padded that it swallowed the sound of my footsteps entirely as it led me down the hall.

I slowed and then stopped in front of the sign set up in the very center.

Once again, it took several tries before I could get the letters to arrange themselves into words. *Names,* I suddenly realized. These were the names of the people for whom the wakes were being held. Mourners for Dennis Ridge should head to the right. And mourners for William Knight needed to go left.

William *Knight?*

A faint, slippery hope skipped across my chest when I saw the wrong last name. I wanted to reach out and cling to it the way I was clinging to the strangeness of the funeral location. *Yes, yes of course!* I wanted to cry with relief. *This was all a mistake! Of course my Dad isn't* dead! *How could I have ever thought otherwise?*

This is all just a very bad dream!

When you try to read in dreams, the words never stay in one place. They skip around the page, flitting like butterflies and refusing to stay put.

I read and re-read the name William *Knight.* If this was a nightmare, it would surely start changing.

When it didn't, I knew this wasn't a nightmare. This was real life. I had arrived in a strange town to attend my Daddy's wake. But the name on this sign wasn't Bill Clarence.

A sick heave of dread turned over in my stomach. I didn't know what it meant that it wasn't the right name, but the hair on my arms was standing up all the same.

I swallowed down the lump of fear in my throat. Then I turned to the left.

Towards the wake of William *Knight*.

My feet sank into the deep carpet as I dragged myself to the room where the casket lay. I could turn around now, and follow a trail of my own footprints right out of this surreal waking nightmare.

But I had to know. Questions raced around in my head, searching for answers I wouldn't get if I turned and left right now. So I forced myself to keep moving forward until I finally burst into the room.

And stopped short.

A throng of people gathered in tight clumps in front of an ornate wooden casket. I searched their faces as I approached, but didn't recognize any of them.

Except the face of the man in the casket.

Lying there, his hands folded across his chest, was the answer to one of my questions. A simple, straightforward answer, but it hit me like a blow to the chest.

Question: Was my father really dead?

Answer: *Yes.*

My breath left my lungs. I staggered to the kneeler and sank down as the strength left my legs. Then I knelt over him and whispered, "Daddy?"

His hair was longer, slicked back from a wasted face ravaged by a disease I didn't even know he'd had. I reached out, wanting to touch him. Then pulled back when I felt the unnatural cold that clung to him. My hand hovered over his face and then I lost my nerve and put it lightly over his hands. "Daddy?"

His hands were icy, the cold piercing and strangely metallic. I snatched my hand away and stared.

There on his left hand was a wedding ring. It was solid and silver and heavy.

And it didn't belong there at all.

My father and mother never married. Before she split, my mother sometimes wore earrings she said were a gift from my Daddy. But her hands - and his hands - were always unadorned.

I swallowed. Then swallowed again. But I couldn't dislodge the terror that stuck in my throat. As I brushed my fingertip over the ice-cold, inexplicable ring, a wave of nausea hit me so hard I had to push back.

Standing, whirling, I clapped my hands over my mouth before I lost everything in my stomach. Frantically, I searched the crowd of mourners, looking for Janet, for Bee, for Harper... Anyone who'd known my father... Who knew me and could tell me... anything...

But in the sea of faces, there wasn't a single familiar one. There wasn't a single friendly one either.

I saw open-mouthed shock. I saw distaste and contempt. I saw pure hatred that I didn't understand on faces I didn't recognize at all. Not a single one - except..,

I stopped short when a man around my age stood up from where he'd been leaning over a sobbing woman. When he looked at me it was with my father's eyes. *My* eyes. The ones that stared back at me when I looked in a mirror. The same deep-set blue framed by heavy dark brows that slashed across his face.

They were eyes that were so familiar I almost smiled at him. But he was a complete stranger.

He stood up straighter when he saw me. Then he stepped back, dropping into a defensive pose like he expected me to spring at him. He dropped his hand down to shoulder of the sobbing woman. It looked like he was trying hold her down. Trying to keep her from turning and seeing... *me.*

"Don't," the man with my father's eyes warned. Whether he was talking to her or to me, I wasn't sure.

But either way...

It was too late.

She saw me.

It took half a breath for me to take her in - same age as me, same hair as mine, same build, same height - and for her to do the same to me. Her face went from sorrow to surprise...

To rage.

With a hoarse cry, she threw the restraining hand off her shoulder and vaulted to her feet. Her face contorted into a mask of such pure hatred that I faltered backwards and nearly lost my footing.

"You!" she shouted. Her voice rang out, echoing off the walls in spite of the deadening silence. She stabbed her finger at me like she wished it was a knife. "You... bitch! How dare you?" I clutched at the kneeler as her voice rose to a piercing shriek. "You have got some nerve, you little cunt! How dare you show your face here? How *dare* you?"

Chapter One

SKY

Eighteen years ago

I am seven years old - though I will correct you if you forget to add the "and one-quarter." It's a bright October day two weeks before Halloween and I've known what I want my costume to be for weeks now. I've already told everyone I know about my plans to be a black cat. "Because they're supposed to be unlucky, right? And my birthday is on Friday the thirteenth too," I'd explain. "But I don't believe in bad luck."

My Daddy would like that. He doesn't believe in bad luck either. He believes - like I do - that you make your own luck. So I know he'll chuckle when I tell him my costume plan. He'll see the significance right away.

I hate that he's going to be the last to know.

I've been saving the news about my costume much longer than I thought I'd have to. Daddy hasn't been home since the end of September, which is longer than he's usually away. But you always save the best for last, right? He's definitely the best. And I forgive him for being away so long.

Just like I forgive him missing my first day of second grade at Reckless Falls Elementary.

Just like I forgive him for saying he'll take me camping over the long, boring summer break and then forgetting.

Missed visits from the Tooth Fairy. Birthday presents weeks after my actual birthday. The class play where the only thing I could see when I looked out into the audience what his empty seat.

I always forgive my Daddy.

Even when he's away for this long, I know, with rock-solid certainty, that he'll always come back for me.

I know he can't wait to come home to his Princess.

And he's coming home today.

Ever since I got home from school, I've been right here by the window, watching. I can feel Janet's disapproving glares every time she moves around behind me. I know she wants me to turn around and see her watching me.

So I don't. I face the window and I don't even turn when she drops a plate in the kitchen and swears to herself. It sounds like she's crying, though why would she cry over something so silly? Just get a broom and sweep it up, and stop making so much noise. Grown-ups are so *weird*. I huff and roll my eyes, blowing out a puff of breath that sends my wispy, too-long bangs skyward.

Janet's the housekeeper. She's not my mom, not my aunt, not my grammy, not that any of those people matter either. She might be the one who gets me off to school every morning and tucks me into bed every night. But she isn't my Daddy.

I know she thinks I should move away from the window. I know she thinks I shouldn't get excited every time I hear the rumble of a semi. But I don't care what she thinks. She's not important.

"You and me, Princess," my father likes to say as he pulls me into his lap and tickles my cheek with his whiskers. "We're a team. You and me."

I always smile and agree. "We're a team," I echo, smiling my gap-toothed smile because I know it makes him happy to see how cute I am. I never ask why, if we're a team, he doesn't stay around more. It's hard being part of a team that's always down one man.

But I don't say that. I know better. I know that his job as a trucker keeps him on the road for weeks at a time. And I also know that I'm his little lady, the only woman that matters to him now that my mom's run off.

She wasn't part of the team. She tired him out, always asking too many questions. Wanting to know what took him so long. Badgering him late at night when he just wants to bask in the sweetness of coming home. Making his life harder instead of easier.

I've got blonde hair just like her, which makes me feel a little bit like a traitor. But I know I've got his eyes and that's the important thing. I've got eyes the same color as my name, he always says. "Sky with eyes like the sky." Then he tugs my braid and I feel proud and special. And I don't even cry when he leaves again. I just stand with my back straight, shrugging off Janet's hand as she tries to comfort me. And I wave until his truck disappears over the hill

To me, that's what love is. Something fleeting that you cling to as you lie awake at night, running over your memories. When he leaves, I go over them one by one, the same way I play with the jewelry in the box my mother left behind. I lie in bed and open the box in my mind marked "Daddy," and select one perfect moment. I play with it, lifting it up to the light and admiring its gleaming shine.

There aren't enough of them to last me the time it takes to fall asleep, so some I take out more than others. I relive those memories again and again, polishing them until they shine with impossible radiance.

But I never let myself stay with them for long. I know I need to put them back in the box, and close it tight. Somehow I know that if I polish something too often, it'll get dull.

And love is a shining, precious, rare thing. It's not the boring, constant, nagging presence of Janet. It's not my teachers hugging me and brightly asking when my dad could make it to a parent teacher conference. Love is not my friends asking me if they can come over to play and then wanting to know why I aways say no.

Those are my constants. They're boring and familiar and that's what I resent most about them. I lose interest in things that are the same every day.

My Daddy, though. He's not boring. He not constant or familiar.

One time in school, my teacher read us a book about the dinosaurs. There was one illustration at the end that I could not tear my eyes away from. It showed two brontosauruses staring up at the sky in alarm as a bright streak tore across it. Seconds away from obliterating them forever.

My father's love was a meteor strike, just like in that book. He streaked in out of nowhere, lighting up my life in a blaze of incandescent fury that lasted only second. He left me scorched and cratered. He hollowed me out and left me waiting for the next time he'd cross my path.

And like the dinosaurs, I was helpless to do anything but watch and wait.

But right now my waiting is over. "That's him!" I shout, recognizing the sound of his truck, its bass rumble vibrating me from far away. It brings me to life, that sound. I leap up, shaking off the malaise, the boredom, the sameness of my life between his homecomings. "That's him!"

Now I am the meteor, streaking out of the house and onto the front porch. With my heart pounding, I watch as my Daddy rolls in. He swing his big red rig into the gravel apron of our drive, and then I am moving.

I fly across the lawn and yank the door open before he even cuts the engine. Then I leap straight into his arms.

He roars with laughter, leaping down to swing me in a circle and then up to the sky. "There's my Princess!" I whoop and laugh, and am convinced I could fly. Like a parched, wilted flower coming to life after a spring rain, I guzzle him up. I soak up his smile, cling to his neck and refuse to let him put me down even when he complains about how I've gotten heavier. "What are you feeding this child?" he calls out to Janet.

"Whatever I can scrape together on the little bit you give me for a food budget, Bill," Janet says darkly. "Since I never know when you're gonna be back, I have to make things that are cheap and filling."

"Is she always this grumpy?" my Daddy asks me with a wink, and I giggle and nod because we're a team. We're united against Janet, against my mother, against my teachers. It's us against the whole entire world.

“Sorry I had to leave you with Grouchypants Magoo over there,” he whispers.

"What was that, Bill?" Janet calls, and I fall out laughing.

My Daddy nods his approval. He likes when I show him how loyal I am. “What do you say we get out of here, Princess?”

“Yeah?” I hold my tongue and don't ask questions. He might change his mind if I do.

“You and me on a camping trip? How does that sound?”

I squeal and fling my arms around him again. I don't love camping as much as he thinks I do. What I love is being the very center of his attention. Just him and me in the woods, with nothing to distract him. Nowhere to run off to. "It sounds good, Daddy," I say, picturing him in his hammock and feeling happy and relaxed. I’ll fetch him his beers so he’ll call me his good girl and tug my braid. And at night when he folds me into my sleeping bag, he’ll sing to me. I’ll fall asleep to the night noises and the sound of his breathing. And once or twice in the night I’ll reach out and poke him just to reassure myself that he is still there.

That's what I love about camping, and his suggestion has me weak with wanting. But I still don't move or get my hopes up about it. “I have school," I remind him, because he most likely forgot. I give him one more chance to take it away from me.

"Fuck it," he says.

I hide a scandalized giggle behind my hands. My Daddy's language is always salty when he comes home from being on the road. My Mom used to get on him about it, but I never will.

He can swear all he like so long as he stays longer than a day.

"Are we going right now?" I don't dare hope.

He tugs my braid. "Yep, right now. Go get your things. Run, Princess."

I run, flying past Janet like she's nothing but a shadow cast by my father's bright light. I can hear her sigh as I pass though. She's always sighing. It's just one more thing that Janet does. Like her grim smiles and syrupy nicknames, her sighs wash right over me. I barely notice them at all.

I rush upstairs, practiced hands grabbing only the essentials. I know I need to be fast, before something else can catch his attention. Before Janet starts lighting into him, the way my mom used to do, and puts him in a bad mood. Before he can say "why do I even bother then?" and hop back into his rig. Before he heads back out on the road without me.

I know he doesn't mean to hurt me when he does this. I know it's just the rest of the world weighing him down. Nobody understands him. But I do.

So I hurry, mentally running down the checklist. And then whirling around laughing because I almost forgot my sleeping bag.

Janet is murmuring at him in a low voice when I get back down to the driveway. It sounds like she's trying to press a point, make my father see her point of view. She's not yelling at him. Yet.

But the second I appear, he turns his attention away from her and claps his hand in glee. "There she is, my little lightning bolt!" I grin, proud of how fast I am, and then laugh when he takes my duffel and sleeping bag with a chivalrous bow.

I don't even say goodbye to Janet as we climb back into his rig. I put her behind me. Just like I do with everything else. There is always a future to hope for. And there is always the now to contend with. I am at tabula rasa, a blank slate, ready for my story to be written by who ever appears in it next. My father impermanence has made a permanent mark on me in ways I'm too young to understand.

But high up in his rig, as proud as a queen on her throne, I don't think about that. Because I'm heading out to camp with my Daddy.

SKY

Now

I threaded my tent poles through the guides. It was a good thing I'd done this so often that my hands moved without thought.

Because the last thing I wanted to do was start thinking.

Once my tent was set up, I paused and looked up. The blaze of bright orange oak leaves stood out vibrant against the darkening sky. Today had been beautiful. And all I wanted to was pretend it never happened.

The smell of charcoal and campfires hit me with a jaw-cracking punch of nostalgia. "Here's how you build a fire, Princess," my dad had said on one of those camping trips long ago. One of those treasured snatches of a childhood spent in concentrated form. "Let me show you how to do this. I used to build the fires, back when I was in Scouts —."

The fires were real, I knew because I'd built one right here at my campsite. Just the way he'd shown me. But those stories he'd tell about his boyhood and the adventures he had. Were those true?

Had he ever told me the truth about anything? Or was my entire life built - from the ground up - on a lie?

Shit. I was thinking again.

I shook my head and looked around, searching for something to capture my attention and take me out of my head.

And then, blessedly, I heard it.

"Fuck."

It was a low voice. A male voice. And he sounded frustrated.

I turned in a slow circle, searching for the source of the voice. Driven more by the need to stay out of my head than by any kind of curiosity.

There, across the road from my corner site, there was the silhouette of a man crouched over a fire pit.

He struck his matches again and again, but all he was managing to do was create a lot of smoke.

An echo of my father sounded in my head. *Look at this joker. What the hell is he doing?*

The man stood back up. Then kicked at the pile of logs, stomping his big boots so hard that I felt the vibration where I stood. My dad's echo was chuckling now. *Come on, Princess. Let's go show him how it's done.*

“Stop!”

I was talking to my father. I didn't realize I'd spoken aloud until the silhouette shifted and turned my way. His face was masked in shadow, but I could sense he was watching me. And I was too grateful for the distraction to feel embarrassed that he'd caught me talking to the voices in my head.

Putting one foot in front of the other would carry me away from thoughts I did not want to think. So I started walking towards him. “Hey, you need a hand?” I called into the gloom.

He was building a fire - or trying to anyway - in the shadow of a huge, boxy trailer, the biggest one I'd ever seen. It stood out as the height of luxury, even in a luxe campground like this one. The curved front almost made it look like a bus. Specifically a rock star's tour bus.

Odd accommodations and piss-poor fire-building skill. This guy was not your usual camper.

“No. I got it,” he grumbled. Growled was more like it. His voice was a deep bass note that went straight to my toes. And it held an air of menace. Of danger. The kind of danger a woman camping alone is usually very much in tune with. If I had been in my right mind, I would have ducked back into my tent and checked that my pepper spray was nearby.

I was not in my right mind. *At all.*

“Fuck it.” I said that aloud too. I was talking to myself now. Or maybe I was talking to my Dad. After all, he could probably hear me, wherever he was. Above me. Or below.

“Let me do that,” I called again, and didn’t give the stranger any time to be all rumbly and threatening. If he couldn’t make a fucking fire, how much of a threat could he be? “You’re smothering it.”

He chuckled darkly and rumbled something else. But as I approached him - alone and in the dark - he stepped back instead of stepping forward. And gestured for me to go ahead.

I crouched down and rearranged the crowded logs in the fire pit. I stacked them up in a neat teepee the way my dad had taught me. “Where’s your kindling?” I asked.

"Don't have any."

"How do you figure this'll catch?"

“Lighter fluid.”

“Pussy,” I challenged. Did I have a death wish? All I knew was nothing seemed to matter. If my Dad was dead… and if what I’d learned today was the truth, then what was the point of being safe? “Lighter fluid? You obviously weren’t a Boy Scout.”

“Nope.” There was that rumble again, but this time it vibrated up my spine.

“You’ve got a deep voice.”

“Yeah.”

“You ever sing?”

A pause. Then. “Yeah.”

I nodded as I struck the match and held it to the neat pile of kindling I'd mounded under the logs. "You'd be a good bass guy in a barbershop quartet."

This brought that dark chuckle again, but I didn't get to think on what it might mean because the kindling had caught. "Ha!" I crowed as the little tongue of flame curled upward and licked at the underside of a log. "See? Now it has room to breathe."

I heard him inhale and then let out a frustrated exhale. "I know how it feels."

A note in his voice made me look up. He was still mostly in shadow. But in the flickering light of the newly built fire, I caught quick little flashes to piece together. He had the high, jutting cheekbones of a model. But his strong jaw disappeared into a beard worthy of scary hermit-axe-murderer. It was wild and ungroomed, but his hair hung in a stylish undercut that had been recently trimmed.

The flames flickered higher, giving me a glimpse of the ironic glint in his eyes. But I couldn't discern the color. Brown? Hazel?

What did it matter? Other than a description to give to the police if he *did* turn out to be an axe murderer, I supposed.

Strangely, just from those glimpses, I had a picture in my head of what the rest of his face would look like. Like he was someone I knew. "Do I know you?"

"Do you?"

"I asked you."

"How the fuck should I know?"

"You're a surly bastard, aren't you?"

That dark chuckle. "So they tell me."

This caught me off guard and I started to laugh. "Who? The woodland creatures that live in your beard?"

"You ask a lot of question."

"You're answering them," I pointed out.

He fell silent and turned away. For a second I thought I'd offended him. Grief was making me run my mouth. All the things I couldn't say, all the questions I couldn't ask. The poisonous anger eating at my insides had me bitchy and itching for a fight.

But not with a stranger. I opened my mouth to apologize. It wasn't this surly asshole's fault that my life was complete shit.

Then he turned back with a bottle of something in his hand. He shook it at me. "You want some?"

"What is it?"

"Bourbon"

I couldn't seem to stop running my mouth. "You trying to get me drunk so you can have your way with me later?"

The fire was stronger now, so I could see the way he rolled his eyes. He looked amused. "No. I'm trying to thank you for making my fire for me." He paused and looked at the bottle. "I'm not so good with people."

He didn't sound surly anymore. He sounded bothered. For the first time today, my heart squeezed with something other than numb, empty grief. "Yeah, me neither." I reached for his bottle and sniffed. "You sure you didn't put something funny in this?"

"You want me to drink first?" He reached and snatched it away with a little too much force and then took a deep swig. "No I didn't slip a fucking mickey in there, see? Besides, it'd ruin the taste."

"I just thought I'd should be cautious since we're both terrible with people." I grabbed the bottle back again.

"Like hell you're terrible with people." His eyes followed my hand up to my face and lingered there like he was noticing me for the first time. "A pretty girl who has no trouble talking to complete strangers? Bullshit."

I laughed as I lifted the bottle to my lips. It sure smelled like bourbon. Strong stuff too. All at once, I wanted nothing more than to down the bottle and burn away the awfulness of today. "Yeah well, I seem to be good at pissing them off." I took a swig and swallowed, letting the burn be the excuse for the tears that were pricking at the corners of my eyes. When I spoke again, there was a catch to my voice. Because the thoughts were catching up with me. "And it seems like I'm not a very good judge of their character either."

His silence stretched so long I snapped out of my reverie and glanced up at him.

If there had been a trace of sympathy in those eyes of his, I wouldn't have said a damn thing. Same with pity. I wasn't looking for a shoulder to cry on, because I didn't want to cry about this. I didn't want to be sad, I wanted to be angry.

But there wasn't sympathy. Just calm, patient waiting for me to finish my thought.

So I did.

I took a deep breath. "Today has been a really, really bad day." Then I took another long drink.

In the shadows, I saw him lift his hand and reach for me and then drop it. Then lift it again.

How fucked up was I that I wanted to go to him? A complete stranger?

But then again, my instincts were shot after today. Everything I'd thought was real and true had been flipped upside down. If something felt wrong right now, it was probably the right thing to do.

So I accepted the invitation of that hesitating hand and stepped forward.

Right into the arms of a stranger.

Chapter Three

FINN

In my life, there are two constants.

The first is the knowledge that I'm *going* to fuck up.

My intentions don't matter. Even when I set out to do some good, I find a way to do the complete opposite.

Leaving was the first good thing I'd done in my life. I was almost — almost — proud of myself.

So of course I had to fuck it up.

I knew better than to start talking to a pretty girl like her. It was the exact opposite of what I'd set out to do here. But I was talking to her all the same. Enjoying myself when I shouldn't have. Flirting instead of pulling back and warning her to get away.

I also knew better than to touch her. Or to try, in some idiotic way, to comfort her.

So of course, I went and did that too.

The second constant?

That's my brother.

Strange to say that when he's the one I most needed to leave behind. I may not be in Beau's life anymore. But he's still in my head.

If I know that I'm going to screw up doing things my way, I try to think to myself, what would Beau do?

Beau would give this pretty girl a hug. Then he'd sit her down and share his whiskey and try to figure out why she sounded so sad. He was a good person. I wanted to be a good person.

Beau definitely wouldn't have kissed her. But see? That's where the first constant comes in. I fucked that up. I'm an asshole, and I always find a way to sabotage my best intentions.

I didn't intend to let her brush against me. I didn't intend to breathe in the scent of her hair.

I didn't intend any of what happened next. There's no excuse for it. Other than this: just like the girl now sitting down at my fire, I've had an astoundingly shitty day.

Chapter Four

FINN

During our quick, awkward embrace I'd gotten a pretty good sense of her slamming body. I kind of wanted to reach out to offer another hug, just to be sure.

Hey, I did tell you I was an asshole.

But she'd pulled herself together and was now sitting and staring into the fire. Her eyes gleamed, but not with tears. No, she was staring into the fire like it had wronged her. Anger burned on her face.

We sat there in silence as I tried like hell to imagine what Beau would say right now. "Shitty day, huh?" I finally ventured. My brother's words in my mouth. "I know how those are."

She glanced up. "You one-upping me?" she challenged.

That was a surprise. "Not trying to," I shot back. Harsh. Sarcastic. Defensive. Those were definitely *my* words.

She leaned forward and reached for a stick on the ground and gave the fire a practiced poke. I'd given her my chair and sat perched on the bench of the slanted picnic table that came with the site. But we were still close enough that her arm brushed my thigh when she sat back again.

I was having a hard time remembering how to breathe. She was distracting as fuck.

It's like when you quit smoking and start seeing cigarettes everywhere. Or when you announce you're going to start eating healthy and your brothers show up with steaks and a case of beer. I'd left a note this morning explaining to my family why it was best that I take off on my own and live in solitude.

And *she* barges in.

Satisfied with the fire, she sat back on her chair and crossed her arms over her chest. Gazing up at the sky, she blew out a long exhale. "Yeah? Well I'll play anyway."

I'd forgotten what we were talking about. "Play what?"

"One-upping."

"I wasn't tryin - ."

"So what happened to you today?" she butted in.

This chick was pissed about something and she wanted to tell me all about it. I didn't need to be Beau to figure that out. "Oh," I minimized with a chuckle. "Well, I couldn't build a fire, so some random chick came over and did it for me, completely emasculating me in the process."

She burst out laughing. "That's the worst you've got?"

"No. But it's you're turn."

She pulled her arms more tightly across her chest. She'd wanted to tell, so badly, but now in the moment she couldn't seem to find the words. Her tongue swept along the inside her her cheek as she opened and then closed her mouth.

Finally she lurched forward and reached onto the ground, coming back up with my bottle of whiskey in hand. "Hey," I muttered, not really making any move to stop her. She drank it down like she'd just crossed the desert and it was the first water she'd found. "Jesus." It was pretty impressive. And disturbing.

She winced and set it down, swallowing and shaking her head. "I went to my father's funeral today," she blurted.

I don't know what I expected, but it wasn't that. "For real?"

"You think I'm lying?" She swiveled her glare from the fire to me.

I shook my head. "No, but it'd be a good way to win."

"Ha! I always knew I was a winner." She grabbed the bottle and took another swallow.

"Fuck," I exhaled. "Hey, slow down." Beau's words. She was a small thing and she was drinking way too fast. "You're definitely drinking me under the table." I lifted the bottle to my lips and took a swig of my own. The edges of my mouth curled up in spite of myself. "So if we're competing, you're winning by a mile."

She leaned forward, resting her elbows on her knees in a decidedly unladylike stance. My sister Claire would be rolling her eyes if she saw it. I wondered if my mystery fire builder was more comfortable in the presence of men.

Then I remembered that I wasn't supposed to care anymore.

"Your turn," she said. Her hand moved so quickly, she probably thought I didn't notice how she was wiping at her eyes.

A crying stranger invading my solitude. It was the sort of thing that I had sworn I'd never allow again. I was poison. Bad luck. The anchor weighing down the people I love.

But I had no obligation to this chick. I just knew she was pretty and getting drunker by the minute. So drunk she'd probably forget this conversation ever happened. What did I have to lose?

Fuck it. "I left a note for my family, telling them not to come looking for me," I volunteered.

"Why?"

"I..." *Fuck it.* "I shouldn't be around people."

"And?"

I licked my lips. "And... they haven't."

She looked at me. I shrugged. There was more to it. But I didn't have the words to explain.

"So, what's bad?" she asked. She asked a lot of questions. Too many. "Isn't that what you wanted?"

I swallowed. Then cleared my throat. Then took another drink from the whiskey bottle. But I still felt like there was something lodged in my throat. "It's what I suspected," I finally coughed. "But it kind of sucks having it confirmed."

Her silence was steady. I've got a sixth sense for pity and have no use for it. My demons are my own, and I keep them close and nurture them well. If the next thing out of her mouth was anything close to "poor you," or worse, "*poor them*," I'd be gone like a shot.

But she just nodded, a small movement that got bigger as she thought about it. “Okay,” she finally said. “So yeah, that’s kind of rough. But I’ll do you one better.” Her voice had softened around the edges and I wondered if she was too wasted to take seriously.

But the next sentence out of her mouth was perfectly clear. “At my father's funeral, I found out I had some brothers and sisters."

"You... Didn't know this?"

"Apparently I didn't know my father!" She said this in a burst of hysterical, gallows humor laughter, then fell against me. Her head came to rest on my shoulder as she laughed on, making no noise except the occasional gasping squeak.

I felt my hand lift. Like I was going to pet her. Would Beau pet her? God, I was so bad at this human contact bullshit. "Okay, that's pretty good. If you're not making that up, I think you win." I let my hand rest on her back.

She shifted. I shifted. My hand slid all the way around her of its own accord. She slid down a little.

And suddenly I was holding her just like a lover.

Chapter Five

FINN

Her hair was tickling my nose but I didn't dare move. If I moved, I'd break this spell.

She inhaled, then sighed. Her head got heavier on my shoulder. She tilted her head up to look at me and I swear I almost smiled at her. She peered at me intently.

"Do I know you?" she blurted.

And there it was.

"Maybe." I tried to shrug her head off my shoulder, but she was either too oblivious or too drunk to get the hint. "Maybe you've *heard* of me. Doubt you actually *know* me."

She pulled back and shrugged. "Fine. Be a dick. But don't forget, I won the 'having a bad day contest' here, so don't be getting too high and mighty with me."

My shoulder felt cold without her there. And my smile was curling up at the edges again. "Yeah, well. I think you cheated."

"I think you're a dick."

"I think you're pretty nosy."

Her head was tilting towards me again. "I think you're probably right you should stay away from people." Her mouth was close now. Her breath smelled of bourbon and peppermint gum.

"I think you're drunk."

Her wide eyes were now heavy-lidded in a way I couldn't stop staring at. "I think you like it," she taunted. "I think you like *me*."

"Yeah, drunk girl? You think I'm that kind of asshole?"

But I was. I was exactly that kind of asshole. I leaned in, catching her lips with mine.

It was a jolt to both of us. She gasped, her lips parting and softening in surprise.

But she didn't pull away and slap me.

I was *looking* for that slap. I *wanted* her to call me names. I *wanted* her to remind me of all the worst things I already believed about myself. Kissing her was a power move, a dick move, and I deserved a knee to the balls.

Instead she was kissing me back. *What the fuck?* I leaned in further, threading my hand around her the back of her neck and pinning her mouth to mine. *Come on. Hate me.*

She one-upped me, nipping hard enough at my lip to draw blood.

My heart beat in my ears. My whole body seemed to pulse at once. Her mouth, her skin, that tangle of hair, that little slipping tongue of hers dancing against mine. She was fucking *getting to me.* When all I'd wanted was to feel nothing.

I was doing the exact opposite of the right thing. Just like I always did.

I growled, pissed off that she wasn't angry with me. I snagged my hand into her hair, yanking her head back and exposing her throat. "You're damn right I'm an asshole," I growled into her neck. "You want me to prove it?"

"Do it." There was a throaty quality to her voice that wasn't tears. She wasn't crying, sobbing, or pulling away.

She was leaning in, exposing her throat to me, pressing her breasts against my chest. I reached up, palming one in my hand, sure that would be the moment that she came to her senses. Or fuck, that I came to mine. I'd come here to be alone.

What was one last hurrah though? Goodbye to this. She wanted it. I could feel her need trembling through her. And I knew, by the harsh, rasping note to her breathing, that if I slid my hands down between her legs, she'd be wet and ready.

The thought brought a groan to my throat. I was pissed at myself for wanting this, pissed at myself for even considering. "You have no idea who I am."

"I have no idea who *I* am," she corrected. There was that jagged laugh again, harsh and desperate, and it was like pouring gasoline on a flame. I pulled her to me and she knelt up on the bench, straddling my lap. I squeezed my hands over her hipbones and she responded by arching again. I heard the sharp intake of her breath as she brushed against me and felt how hard I was already.

"Start with a name," I almost begged.

"Sky," she panted as her hips rolled. She was using me to get off, to feel better about the shitty fucking day she'd had. And no matter how I tried to escape it, I wanted to do this for her. I'd fuck up her mind, but I could take care of her body.

"Sky." I pressed down on her hips, letting her grind into my thigh. "You want me to do something for you?" I slipped the flat of my hand against her mound.

"Make it go away," she begged. "Make me stop thinking."

Chapter Six

SKY

I felt as insubstantial as the ash rising from the fire. Maybe I needed to feel tethered to something. Maybe I needed to hold on to him so I wouldn't float away and disappear like everything I'd ever known.

Maybe it was a desperate need for something physical, something real. And here. And now.

If I could afford a therapist, I bet that would be what she'd conclude.

But I'd bet it was a lot simpler than that. I'd bet I just wanted to punish my Dad. Fuck him. Fuck being Daddy's Little Princess. That shiny little crown on my head was put there by a stranger.

What better way to tarnish it than by fucking another stranger?

Yeah. Maybe it really was that simple. Maybe I was just a painful cliche. I had sudden and serious Daddy issues. So I climbed into a stranger's lap and begged him to fuck me.

He was surprised, but he certainly wasn't unwilling. I could feel that as I ground my hips into his lap. Kissing him was an accident, something I didn't think I wanted, but once I started, it only made me want more. He - whoever he was - was a really good kisser. Taking his time, letting me control it right up until the moment I lost control.

And then he took over, twining his fingers into my hair, and tilting my head to use me as he saw fit.

I let him. I wanted this stranger to mark me. To *bruise* me. I wanted to feel his fingers all over me, raking down my back and sinking into my hips. I wanted him to overwhelm me and silence the crush of thoughts in my head. I wanted to shut off my brain and just be a body. Something mindless and free.

Most of all, I wanted to feel good.

"Make me feel good," I groaned against his mouth.

His answer was to stand, lifting me as he did. I wrapped my legs around his waist and kept kissing him, biting, licking, tasting the ash and salt on his skin. His growl was what I needed. His grunt as I used my teeth to hurt him - but not enough to stop me - was what I craved.

He took the two steps up to the trailer and threw the door open. But he kept the light off. Thank God. If he'd turned the light on, I might have come to my senses. Light would bring me back to reality and remind me that I wasn't the kind of girl who did shit like this. But in the dark, I could pretend I was a different person. Someone who took this kind of risk. Someone whose world wasn't completely upside down.

Someone who wasn't me.

He tumbled us into the bed, and landed on top of me. I let him lift my shirt from my body, and was rewarded with the suck of his lips against the tops of my breasts. His mouth was searingly hot, and smell of bourbon hung in a mist around us.

"Keep going," I urged him, and that low evil chuckle should have scared me. But it didn't. The darkness made it easy to let him pull my jeans down, then my panties. My skin was already humming. So when he traced a trail down my center with his finger, then followed it with his tongue, I was primed for the explosion. Like a rubber band pulled too tight, I snapped.

I reached down, yanking his hair into fistfuls as I ground up against his mouth. Taking. Taking. I screamed out my pain along with the pleasure. Frustration and grief along with the ecstasy.

"Yes!" I was panting now, and tears were falling down my face. "Fuck, that was good."

He pulled back and stood up, a shadow looming above me. I was already aching for more, and I knew he would give it. The no-holds-barred way he'd used his tongue and fingers told me exactly what I could expect to come next. I was shaking with need for it.

"You want me? God you want me so bad. don't you?" I reached up and closed my hand around the perfect shape of him that pressed under his jeans. "Tell me you want me. Say something." I spread my legs wider as I tugged at his belt. "What are you waiting for?"

Even in the gloom I could see his shoulders rise and fall in a huge inhale. And for some reason I could feel tears prick at the corners of my eyes.

When he pressed his hand over mine, pushing it away from his belt, shame heated by face. "You don't want me." It came out like an accusation.

"No!" he shouted. I scrambled backward, but he reached out, and wrapped his fingers around my ankles. Not holding me, not preventing me from escaping. Just applying slight pressure. He squeezed, then swirled his roughly calloused thumbs in circles.

Then snatched his hands away again.

"You'd better believe I want you." He sounded like he was trying to keep his voice steady so as not to frighten me again. "But I know what it's like to make a bad decision when you're hurting."

"I'm fine." I clenched my teeth and lifted my chin even though he couldn't see me in the dark.

I sensed him shaking his head. There was something about this man that made me hugely aware of the space he took up. H changed the patten of the air around him, as if he was some great mountain disrupting the ocean and wind.

"Yeah, maybe you are." He stepped away, then away again, until he had put several feet of space between us. I was instantly colder, and I reached for the sheet to clutch around my shoulders.

"Maybe you're fine," he repeated. "But the fact that I even have to question it means I need to back the fuck up here. I've made a lot of bad decisions and I own them." He let out a long breath. "But I don't think I am too keen on being someone else's."

Hot angry tears were closing my throat. The room lurched and I suddenly felt unhinged. And very, *very* drunk. If I spoke now, it would be in a high pitched shriek. I would shout at him and swear at him and claw at his eyes.

I didn't have much of anything left in the world that I could hold on to except for my dignity. So I kept my mouth shut. I held my head high and kept my jaw clenched, willing the tears to stay away until I was no longer in his presence. I would *not* fall apart a second time today.

I felt around for my clothes, and bundled them against my chest. Then hesitated. I wasn't sure I could stand without falling.

"You don't have to go," he rumbled out from the dark.

"I'm not staying," I snapped, anger steadying my voice. "Not now."

"Suit yourself," he said. "But it's raining."

The world snapped back into drunken focus. I suddenly became aware of the study patter of drops on the roof of his trailer.

"Might be more comfortable here," he went on.

"Fuck." The tears were coming, and I wasn't able to stop them. Shame, despair, and complete bewilderment took over. I fell back onto the bed and curled up in a tight ball, clutching the sheet around my naked body.

The tears fell fast soaking the bed beneath me. I squeezed my eyes shut.

The last thing I felt - before whiskey and exhaustion tugged me towards a dreamless black - was his hand on my back. It was warm, and heavy, and he kept it there, rubbing in slow, hesitant circles until I fell asleep.

Chapter Seven

FINN

I awoke with an ache in my neck and an even bigger ache in my groin. Usually an epic case of blue balls wasn't something to smile about.

But that's what I did.

I'd packed up and left so my brother could have a shot at happiness with Rachel. Giving him the chance to live his new life unburdened by... me - was the only selfless thing I'd ever done.

Until last night.

Last night, I'd brought that lifelong total up to... two. My brother would be proud of me.

I almost wish I could call and tell him.

It was the kind of thing he would've done. It was something a good person did. Definitely out of character for a piece of shit like Finn King.

I smiled and almost felt proud of myself.

And then I remembered what exactly what it was that I was celebrating.

I didn't fuck a drunk chick.

My proud smile shriveled back up again and I cursed. That's what I was proud of? Really? Not fucking her? I'd kissed her, undressed her, and eaten her pussy like a starving man, but I didn't stick my cock in her. Woo hoo. Somebody get me a goddamn gold medal for doing the absolute bare minimum.

That fledgling pride gave way to disgust, which propelled me out of the tiny corner of the bed that she left me.

I stood, and stretched. Then studied the near catastrophe now spilled across my mattress.

From her voice, I knew she'd be pretty. From her eyes I'd known she'd be beautiful. And I'd gotten enough sense of her shape with my hands to have a pretty good idea that she was actually smoking hot. After last night, I'd formed a picture in my head of someone rough. The tattooed bad girl with nicotine stains on her fingers and a "Daddy's Little Angel" tattoo across her chest.

So it was a bit of a shock to see a pale, delicate slip of a thing wrapped in my bed sheets. Her hair was not just blond. It was a fine white gold the same color as the sunshine that spilled through my trailer windows. Her lips weren't just pink. They were perfectly formed and obviously ripe for kissing.

But her pale perfection was interrupted by the startling slash of her dark eyebrows. There was something familiar about that combination of blond hair, and dark brows. I'd seen it before.

But before I could think too hard on what that meant, her eyes fluttered open.

I barely had a moment to take in their startling blueness before she narrowed them at me.

"No fucking way," she breathed.

"Good morning to you too," I said, turning away as she tugged the sheet up above her breasts.

She sounded pissed. Why the fuck was she pissed at *me*? I didn't touch her except to rub her back as she cried and push her over onto her side so she didn't puke. Well, that's if you set aside all the touching I'd done before that, but still. I didn't *fuck* her. My aching balls were a testament to *that*. She'd drunk my whiskey and slept in my bed. How the fuck was she *pissed* at me?

I let the defensiveness wash over me. Yet another case of me trying to do the right thing and fucking it up anyway. I was so used to it, it almost felt comforting. I was always at my best when I had a reason to feel persecuted. "I'll turn around, let you get dressed and everything," I muttered. "You can go now or you can get some coffee, then go. Your choice."

I turned my back and headed to the espresso machine. I'd given Jonah so much shit for having it installed in our tour bus, but now I was grateful for it. I stood at the dials, waiting to hear her reply. I expected another smart remark.

I didn't expect her to burst out laughing.

Dumbfounded, I turned back to the bed. She'd doubled over. With her head cradled on her knees, her shoulders shook in silent, helpless laughter. "At least you're not crying?" I muttered.

She wiped her eyes with my sheet. "Holy fuck," she wheezed. "Ah God, so *that's* why you sounded so familiar."

I was instantly cold. "Do I know you? Please fucking tell me I don't know you." I didn't know her, although her eyes were bugging the shit out of me. Like I'd seen them before. On another face.

"No. You don't." She shook her head and looked away, biting her lip to try to stop laughing. But she didn't succeed, and started laughing again.

This was too much for first thing in the morning. "Please," I sniped. "Let me in on the joke. I could use a laugh. And an aspirin." My head was throbbing now, instead of my dick. "What about you?"

She pinched the bridge of her nose between her fingers. "Yeah, Finn. I could use an aspirin."

I stiffened at my name and sucked in a slow breath. So fucking much for disappearing. "You recognize me?"

"The beard is different. But not by much."

I went rigid. "Are you a fan or something?"

"Like... the complete opposite."

"Re-eally?"

"That surprise you? That a girl my age didn't want to like, marry you on sight or something?"

"Nah. That's more Jonah's thing."

She looked up sharply. "Holy shit, you really are Finn King."

This was getting old. I poured myself an espresso without offering her one. “We established this.”

She looked down at the sheets. “And I’m in your bed.” The wild laughter was bubbling up again. “The only chick on the planet Finn King *won’t* fuck. I should get that engraved on a trophy.”

“What the hell?” I set the cup down before I threw it. Fight or flight, they call it. The panic response. The second she'd said my name, adrenaline surged through me.

I couldn't exactly fight a girl - especially not when she was tiny and naked and lying in my bed. So I started looking for an escape route. Getting ready to walk right out of this trailer and never look back. “You got a problem with me?”

But she either didn’t notice my reaction, or didn’t care. “No,” she mused, picking at the sheet with her fingers. The casual slope of her shoulders made mine relax a fraction. “True, I always thought The King Brothers were shit, but that's not really *your* fault. Hell, you always looked like you belonged more in a punk band than in some crappy teen pop band."

I'd had very similar thoughts. *Many* similar thoughts, many, *many,* times. But I still felt a protective prickle for my brothers' sake. "That 'crappy teen pop' paid for the trailer you slept in,” I retorted. “*And* this fucking espresso machine.” I went back over to it, and grudgingly started setting it up for another cup.

For her.

Because no matter how much I’d wanted to run a second ago, I wasn't going to. Her fragile rage - as well as her wide eyes and that dark slash of brows that gave her an edge I wanted to peer over and into - kept me here. With *her.*

I didn’t want to - no I *couldn’t* - leave her alone.

“So you know who I am,” I grunted, shoving my way through the complicated sequence of levers and buttons to make her espresso. “Can I at least know who you are? I mean, since you’re drinking my coffee and took up seven-eighths of my bed last night?”

She looked down again like she’d forgotten where she was. “Jesus,” she muttered.

“Here.” I handed her the cup I’d prepared. “I’ll go get the aspirin.”

"And my T-shirt?" she asked. "If I'm going to be drinking this, I'd like to be clothed."

"Fair." I stood up and reached under the bed, then handed it to her.

She laughed when I turned my back to give her privacy. "What the fuck?" She didn't sound like she was talking to me, so I didn't turn even though I wanted to. I went to the bathroom and fetched the aspirin, listening to her chant it over and over again, "What the fuck? What the fuck?" She whispered it like a little prayer.

"You decent?" I called out.

"Am I dead?" she blurted.

I peered around the corner. "Are you still drunk?"

"I wish." She sighed. "So this is real then? I didn't die and end up in purgatory?" She glanced around, taking in the inside of the tour bus. "Or some really strange version of heaven?"

"I have no idea how to answer that. Except no. This is real."

"I'm really in a tour bus with Finn King."

I jerked at the sound of my name again. "Yeah, you know my name. Can I at least know yours now?"

She grimaced. "My name is Sky. I told you that."

"Do you have a last name, Sky? Or are you like Cher or Prince or something?"

"Well, now," she sat up straighter and leaned against the headboard. Tucking her legs under her, she folded her hands in her lap. She looked... *demure.* So very different from the wild abandon of last night. I wondered which version was the real Sky. "So here's the thing, Finn." She bit off my name acidly. "That's the funny part. You see, up until yesterday, I would have told you my last name was Clarence."

This cryptic shit was starting to annoy me. "How the fuck does your last name change in the span of twenty-hour hours?"

Instead of answering, she stared me straight in the face with those vivid blue eyes. "What the hell are you doing here? You're like, a celebrity."

Fuck it. If she wasn't going to answer questions, I wasn't going to either. "Camping," I deadpanned.

She glared at me. I glared right back. She widened her eyes and clapped her hand over her mouth.

And then the laughter came again. Helpless and hysterical, it bubbled around her hand until she gave up and let it fall to her side with a thud. She shook her head, blinking those big blue eyes as they filled with tears, then cast them up to the ceiling. But even as she laughed, they began to fall again.

I knew what a breakdown looks like. I'd seen this staring back at me from the mirror, but I'd never watched it in another person before.

I flexed my fingers. The tips itched with the need to reach for something... something I didn't have a name for. I hated feeling helpless, but I had no idea what to do for her. Fucking or fighting, those were the two things I was good at. And I'd already almost fucked this girl. I sure as hell wasn't about to fight her, not when she looked like she was one step outside of the mental hospital.

So I did the only other thing I'm good at.

I ran away.

Sure, I was still right here in the room. You don't have to actually leave to check the fuck out. You also don't have to mean to do it either. The walls come up automatically, forming a barrier between you and the world.

"Fuck," I whispered as I felt it happened. But it happened all the same. No matter how badly I wanted to stay open, I closed myself off. And turned away.

When she finally stopped laughing, she didn't say anything. Maybe she sensed the change in me. Maybe she knew it was useless to even try to explain now. I wouldn't hear it.

The set of her mouth hardened into a thin, grim line. Then with a purposeful squaring of her narrow shoulders, she stood up. The light from the window spilled a broad streak of sunlight diagonally across her back. Throwing a spotlight on the perfect roundness of her ass.

Right before it disappeared into yesterday's jeans.

I ached to tell her how beautiful she was. And how much I'd like to start over again and do this right.

But I couldn't. The walls were too high.

"Thanks for the coffee, bourbon and oral, Finn King. And thanks for not fucking me, I guess." she said without turning. "Have a nice life. And make sure to google how to make fires before tonight."

What more confirmation that I need that my very existence was poison? No one needed me. I didn't need anyone. I didn't need connection, attachment, or scandal, and I'd avoided all that with her.

I'd done exactly what I set out to do.

But the trailer still seemed emptier with Sky Clarence gone.

Chapter Eight

SKY

And on top of everything else, today was my birthday.

I didn't know it when I left Finn's trailer. It didn't even cross my mind when I spotted my sad blue tent still sitting there waiting for me. The way I used to wait at the window for my father to come home.

That perverse thought drew another hysterical laugh out of me. I walked over to my tent, unzipped the flap, and stepped inside, zipping it back up again to seal myself off from the world.

The need to sleep, to let unconsciousness take over, was so overwhelming, I laid down flat on top of my sleeping bag. And I didn't move until the buzz of my text alert jerked me awake again hours later.

"Happy birthday!" it read.

That's when I remembered what today was and almost started laughing again.

My cousin Olivia was the only family member from my mom's side that I still kept in touch with. But even then, it was a sporadic thing. She dutifully sent me a birthday text every year. Tomorrow I'd do the same thing since we were a year and a day apart. We'd called ourselves the 'almost-twins' back when we were girls.

But her family moved away when I was six and she was five. Then they'd moved again, and again, and again. Four times in one year.

I'd turned seven without my birthday twin there to celebrate. And then a month later, my mother split, leaving me in Reckless Falls with my Dad and no one else.

Olivia and I had tried, but we hadn't seen each other in years. I knew the rough outline of her life. Mostly from liking her posts on Instagram.

I knew that she'd landed here in Crown Creek her junior year of high school. She'd gone to community college, never finished her degree, and seemed happy to stay in her small town. I didn't blame her. From the looks of her posts, she had a ton of friends.

Her text jolted me out of my daze and back to reality. I was homeless, jobless and my Daddy was dead. And I had a five surprise half-siblings who were seriously pissed about my existence.

What the hell am I supposed to do now?

One more question to add to the pile. I had quite a stack now. But I hadn't thought to go to my cousin for answers until I saw her text.

As the phone rang in my ear, my hands shook so badly I had to lie down so I didn't drop it.

Livvy was startled when she answered the phone, but covered it smoothly. "There's the birthday girl!"

I could hear the smile in her voice and it tugged at me. I swallowed hard. "Hey cuz!"

My voice sounded much smaller than usual, and Livvy picked up on it right away. "You okay?" she asked. "Not too broken up about being old, right?"

"Hey you're about to join me, I reminded her. Then my voice broke. "No it's... been a weird twenty-four hours."

"Hey where are you?" she wondered. "I saw your post that the tour was winding down."

I sucked in air through my teeth. My old life felt alien to me now. Like it happened to a different person I'd only read about. But now I remembered that I'd just finished a nine month gig running wardrobe for a second string Broadway touring company. Which really meant I was a glorified laundress.

Usually life on the road meant that the cast and crew became family. But the dynamic had been off for this one from the start. The lead actor's diva-like behavior made all of us - cast and crew alike - miserable. He seemed to take particular delight in throwing tantrums about his costume. I hadn't been sorry about the end of this show. I'd been looking forward to coming home - back when I'd thought I had a home to come to. "Yeah we wrapped four days ago."

"Do you miss everybody?"

"I don't miss getting a basket of dirty socks dumped on my head by a tantrumming actor, that's for sure. "

"No way!" my cousin squealed. "That didn't happen."

"Oh, it did." I remembered when that seemed like the biggest problem I had.

"What did you do?"

"I sewed fishing line into the toe of his sock for Act III," I declared matter-of-factly. When my cousin's silence told me she was trying to figure out what that meant, I elaborated. "You clip it after sewing the seam. It's basically invisible, but you can feel it. And with any luck, you get so irritated that you flub your lines and end up getting booed at curtain call." I bit my lip to keep from laughing.

"That's absolutely diabolical," my cousin said, sounding half awed and a half scandalized.

"Don't fuck with the people who keep you clothed, you know?"

"I think it's better if people just don't fuck with you at all," Livvy corrected.

"That's the whole idea."

"So are you back at home? And what are you doing on your birthday?"

"I'm not at home." I tapped my fingers on my knee. I'd called her hoping to get some answers, but now I wasn't even sure I wanted to ask the question. What if she *did* know? Did I want to find out she'd been keeping it from me? We weren't as close as we were when we were kids, but I thought there'd be leftover loyalty.

For what felt like the millionth time in as many minutes, shame clawed hot streaks across my face. If she was keeping a secret, she was no better than my dad. But after living a lie for so long, how could I duck the truth any longer? Wouldn't keeping his secret for him just end up exonerating him?

Fuck it. He didn't deserve my protection. Not anymore. "I'm not home." The result in my voice startled me. "I'm sitting in a tent at a campground just outside of Crown Creek."

"What? You're here?" The open happiness in her voice encouraged me.

"I came here for my Dad's funeral."

There was a long silence. "Oh, Sky. Shit. I am so sorry."

I waited. Waited for some admission, some inkling that she knew more than she was letting on.

But after she drew in a long breath, the next thing out of her mouth was innocent confusion. "Wait? You're here in Crown Creek for your Dad's funeral? Why here?"

"It was at the Lowry Funeral Home," I said.

"Why?"

"Because." There was no way to sugarcoat it. There was no way to explain it other then by saying the truth. "Because Olivia, my father lived here in Crown Creek with his family."

"I don't understand," she answered immediately.

"Let me ask you something?" I sat up straighter.

"Okay?" She sounded confused, but I heard no lie in her voice.

"How long have you lived here?"

"Since junior year in high school."

"It's a small town right?"

"A little smaller than Reckless Falls. We definitely don't get all the tourists you guys do."

"So would you say you know pretty much everyone here?"

She laughed. "I'm shit with names, that is for sure. But, if I forget somebody, I can always ask my friend Claire. She... I swear she has full genealogical histories memorized for every single resident of this town."

I was getting impatient. "So, you know the Knights?"

She hesitated. "Yeah, I know *of* them. But they're a little scary."

"Yeah." I exhaled. I felt like I needed to rush to get all the answers, and also slow down. Before I found out something *else* I didn't want to know. "But, what did you *know* about them?"

"Just that they live outside of town, and they work on cars, I guess."

I could hear a tapping sound and wondered if it was her nails on a table top or a pen. I didn't know her well enough to picture either. "Um, a couple of the brothers drive motorcycles, those really custom shop jobs with the loud ass motors. I know *that*. Oh and the oldest guy? Rocky or Rocco or something, he likes to get in fights. Well, more like cause fights. He's always getting thrown out of the bar. But he always manages to escape getting charged with anything. Because everyone's scared of their dad."

My heart sank. "*Their* Dad?"

"He's like this mythical figure," she went on, innocent to the nausea her words inflicted on me. "Bill Knight, *ooooh* spooky right? Everybody knows a guy who knows him. But I feel like everyone's more scared of his reputation than anything he ever *did*. Remember *The Princess Bride*? How everyone talked about the Dread Pirate Roberts, but nobody knew who he actually was?"

I rested the heel of my hand against my eye, digging in half to soothe the pain there, half to make it worse. "So you've never actually seen him?" I asked.

"No way. I try to steer clear of those people."

"Do you know what he looks like?"

"I can ask Claire. Why?"

I had to fight to keep from screaming in frustration. Livvy was my cousin. She lived here in Crown Creek. She knew the Knights. She was the only link between my past and my nightmarish present...

And she couldn't help me.

"Never mind," I said, suddenly irritated with everything. A rush of wind made the tent walls bow, closing me in. "Happy early birthday, by the way."

"Uh, thanks?" Livvy sounded confused. "So you want to get together? Since you're here in town - ?"

"Not for long," I interrupted. "Sorry."

"Uh, okay then! Hey sorry about your Dad, Sky, seriously. I know it's been a long time, but I always thought he was such a great guy."

"Yeah," I whispered. "So did I."

Chapter Nine

FINN

Once Sky left, I tried to shrug. "Crazy bitch," I said aloud. But the words didn't sound right at all, and I immediately hated myself for saying them.

She wasn't a bitch. Whether she was crazy or not... I was in no place to judge her for it. I felt pretty close to insanity myself.

I shrugged again, trying to shake loose the strangeness of last night. I showered. Made the bed. Fried up a couple of eggs in a ton of butter and then sat down to eat them.

The trailer rocked gently. Outside the wind was kicking up and dark clouds were moving in, heavy with the promise of rain. I sat there at the table where, in another life, I'd sat with my brothers. The four of us ate breakfast right here as we crossed the country on tour after tour.

Sitting here was like eating with their ghosts.

I scraped my fork across the plate and shoved the last bite of egg into my mouth. And tried to shove those memories down with it.

It was over. I'd done it. I'd cut them loose. I'd left a note right there on the refrigerator. It was tucked underneath a magnet stamped with the hours of the Crown Creek library. Where my mom worked.

The actual letter itself was short. You'd never know how many drafts I went through before giving up and angrily scratching out the truth.

Beau,

You're my brother. The best man I've ever known. And you found the best woman too. I know you want to marry her and I want you to be happy together. But you'll never have peace as long as I'm around, so I'm leaving. Don't worry about me. Don't try to call me. Please believe me when I tell you that you're better off without me. Please believe that this is the right thing for us all.

- Finn

Leaving was the best way I knew to be as good of a brother to Beau as he had been to me. I wasn't cutting him off.

I was setting him free.

In a way, it was my engagement gift. The best one I could give him. I was the albatross around his neck. I was an anchor weighing him down. He'd never cut me loose, so I did it for him.

I tossed my plate into the sink with a clatter. I resolved to wash it before the egg hardened onto the plate but knew that I wouldn't.

Then I raked my fingers through my hair and glanced at my phone charging in the outlet by my bed.

I'd told him not to worry. I'd told him not to call.

I knew him well enough to understand that the first part was impossible.

Maybe it was dumb to believe the second one was as well.

It was two full days now since I'd left the note on the fridge and changed my number. What did I expect would happen? Did I think he had superpowers? That he'd somehow know to call me here?

No. I'd freed him of his burden and now Beau was moving on. The rest of my family... well, I could just imagine their relief.

I looked down at the table where I'd sat with my brothers. I dragged my fingers over the shiny formica. Then pressed them down flat and braced my weight against the table top.

Yes. Alone. Peace and solitude. That's what the clamor in my head craved. It's what the blackness in my heart required.

I spent the rest of the morning at the table. I alternated between trying and failing to read a paperback, and staring out the window. The clouds were rolling closer.

Late in the afternoon, my stomach complained about missing lunch. I stretched and stood up again, then went to the refrigerator.

Unless I wanted eggs again, I was shit out of luck. I'd been surviving on a carton of eggs, and the bland, tasteless sandwiches from the camp store.

"Fuck," I sighed and grabbed my coat.

The clouds were right overhead now, but the rain was holding off. I pulled up my collar and hurried out into the damp chill.

When I'd arrived here, I handed over a fistful of cash to the owner. She'd been more than happy to give me six spaces all to myself to avoid neighbors. I figured this would be temporary. After all, since I cut myself free, there was nothing keeping me in Crown Creek.

But instead of leaving the next day, I stayed glued here, not quite willing to leave yet. I felt stuck in the orbit of the place where I had grown up, unable to break free of the tug of home. Every morning I told myself that this was it, the day I would leave, and then I'd find a reason to stay.

Yesterday, it had been Sky.

Today? Well, today it looked like rain. It was a piss-poor excuse, but I grabbed on to it anyway. Who wants to drive to a new life in a rainstorm? Not me.

I hurried along the road, waiting to feel the wet smack of raindrops on my face. That'd be a sign I'd made the right decision by staying.

The campground was set up in a series of concentric circles. My trailer sat out on the far edge, closest to the wall of pines that formed the border. Dirt roads, like spokes on a wheel, crossed over the circles at regular intervals. They all lead to the center buildings. A lounge that, as far as I could tell, no one had used since 1972. A laundry facility. The office building. And an general store of sorts. That was where I headed now.

The summer renters had all packed up their monstrous RVs and headed back home. I knew they'd be gone by now. It was why I chose to leave when I did. It would have been a special kind of hell to be in the middle of all happy vacationers.

Now the mostly empty camp was home to a different kind of camper. Desperate, weird loners just passing through.

Like me.

I vaulted up onto the front step of the camp store. It was half stocked with useful provisions, half with tatty tourist crap. I immediately headed over to the useful part.

The woman behind the counter slid off her stool as I approached. She was the owner, near as I could tell. She wore a pink sweatshirt printed with cartoon flowers. Her graying hair was scraped back from her face and tucked into her collar.

And even though I'd been in here four separate times since moving in, I hadn't noticed she did that with her hair until just now.

"How you doing today Mr. Prince?" she asked brightly.

Yeah, I'd given her a fake name. And a stack of fifties for not asking to see my license. I thought I was buying her silence. I didn't realize I'd just piqued her interest.

I looked up at her. "Fine," I said. Then - when that didn't seem enough - I gave her a polite smile.

She stared in wide-eyed shock and I wondered if this was the first time I'd actually looked her in the eye. Then she smiled right back. "Hope you have a wonderful day!" she trilled as she pushed my meager bag of provisions across the counter.

There was something I needed to say... I could feel it. A bit too late I summoned the words, “You too,” in an effort that felt almost exhausting.

She smiled again, and I nodded before retreating back out the door.

All through the walk back to my trailer I replayed that strange exchange over and over in my head. Wondering why it had felt so significant. Why today felt different. Why being alone now felt less like solitude... and more like loneliness.

The threatened rain finally came late that afternoon. I looked up from the book I was barely reading and watched the first fat drops hit the window of the trailer.

I'd parked the bus at an angle, far back from the central dirt road that looped around the perimeter of the campsite. I'd paid for the privilege of solitude and space, but I didn't mind the view either. I could look out one window and see nothing but looming pines stretching straight into the darkening sky.

But if I looked out the other window, I saw the rest of the campsite. That's the one I was looking out now.

I wasn't sure what I was searching for until I found it. The neon blue tent across the road there, set up on a tiny lot perched right by the roadside.

That had to be her tent. She'd come from that direction last night, and she'd gone back in that direction this morning. It was raining like crazy all of a sudden, and Sky was there in the middle of it. If that was her tent. Which I was pretty sure it was. Except I wasn't sure at all.

Fuck, why did I care?

All of a sudden, I was pissed. I smacked my palm against the glass. Who knew she was even there? Who knew if that was even her tent? *Not me.* Why was I straining so hard to catch some glimpse of movement that I was giving myself a headache? I'd had one strange night with her, and then we'd said goodbye.

Or, more precisely, she'd left without a backward glance. I didn't owe her anything.

There was a distant rumble of thunder and suddenly I was on my feet and moving.

The biting rain slashed at my face, soaking my shirt to my skin in seconds. I was pissed at myself first. And then I was pissed at her for being the reason I was doing this.

"Sky!" There was no door, obviously, but I knocked against the blue nylon wall all the same. "Are you in there?"

I didn't hear anything from inside. No movement, no answer. And then I wondered what the hell I was doing.

I turned to leave.

Then, underneath the noise of the rain, the lash of the wind, and the now constant rumble of thunder, I heard something else.

A sniff.

And then a stifled sob.

I dropped down to a crouch before I knew what I was doing. "Hey," I called staring awkwardly at the bright blue wall of her tent. "It's fucking raining like a bitch out here. Don't you want to get out of it?" When there was nothing but silence I raised my voice higher. "Sky! Come on, it's a fucking thunderstorm, are you insane?"

The tent zipper shot up so fast it was a blur, and suddenly Sky was there. Her face was wet, and for a second I wondered if her tent was leaking. Until she I saw her red rimmed eyes. "Are you crying?"

"Goddamnit leave me alone!" she shouted, reaching for the zipper and starting to pull it shut again.

I shot my arm out, stopping her. "You're sitting in a tent crying in the rain? Are you like, *actively* trying to catch pneumonia and die here?"

"It's none of your damn business what I do."

"You're right it's not, but too bad. If you wanna die of pneumonia, don't do it on my watch."

I was startled to hear those words coming out of my mouth. *You want to kill yourself, don't do it on my watch.* How many times had Beau said that to me?

I shook my head and glared at the girl in the tent. Since being myself sucked so much, maybe I should keep this going. What would Beau do? "Come on." I softened my voice so that it sounded much more like my brother's. "Let me help you. Come on and get warm."

Chapter Ten

SKY

He was right. I *was* cold.

But getting mad that he was right warmed me up fast. "I'm warm enough, thank you," I retorted, reaching to close the tent flap again. "I'm fine."

"Liar," he said softly.

I froze mid-zip. "What did you call me?"

It was a full body reaction. Starting with a clenching pain my stomach and a ringing in my ears. I started to shake my head, slowly at first, the faster. "No. I'm not a liar. I never lie." *Not like him. I'm nothing like him.* "Don't call me a liar."

Finn watched me steadily, waiting until I had to pause to take a breath before he clarified. "Look at your hand," he said mildly.

I looked and saw that it was shaking. I was shivering that hard.

Chastened, I drew it away. "I'm not a liar," I protested.

"Sure you're not."

"Why are you being nice to me?"

"Am I?" He smiled. "Huh. Weird. No idea. It's never happened before." He stood up, brushing the dirt from his knees and then reaching out his hand. "Come on. You built me a fire last night. Consider this me paying you back."

I lifted my hand, then hesitated. He rolled his eyes and snatched my wrist, yanking me up and out of the tent so fast I went airborne. Then, with a whoop, he half led, half-dragged me across the dirt-road-turned-streambed, and up the two-step ladder into his trailer.

The warmth hit me first. Inside of Finn's luxury trailer, it was so deliciously warm that the tips of my fingers tingled. I hadn't even realized they were numb. I lifted them to my lips and blew on them as I looked around.

This morning, when I'd woken up in that very bed, I'd been so wrapped up in shame and disbelief that I'd barely registered my surroundings. Now it was like I was seeing everything for the first time. "This is yours?" I asked, completely nonsensically.

Because Finn, for all of his surly grumpiness and unruly beard, was a fucking rock star. He and his brothers, they'd played the soundtrack to my tween years. Whether I'd wanted to pay attention to them or not was a moot point, because they were *literally* everywhere back then. They toured non-stop for years. Toured in *this* very bus.

This morning I'd wondered if I'd died and gone to heaven. This trailer was heaven.

Finn raised a sardonic eyebrow. "One-quarter of it, yeah," he corrected before walking down the central hallway to the back.

At the rear of the bus curved a full kitchen, complete with marble topped counters and stainless steel appliances. Including the espresso machine he'd used to make me coffee this morning. Built into the wall across the central aisle was a table with four chairs. They were all bolted into a central beam underneath the table so they could swivel freely as the bus moved. The middle of the bus was an open area outfitted with a fluffy shag rug that made me raise my eyebrow. "We'd practice here," Finn explained, as if reading my thoughts. "See the plugs on the wall?"

I licked my lips, nodding. It was beautiful in here, and it made me feel small and shabby to be dripping all over the floor the way I was. "Nice," I said, and tried to suppress a shiver.

I was keeping myself deliberately turned away from the bed that took up the front of the bus by the driver's seat. But when he saw me looking over my shoulder at it, Finn shrugged. "I took out the bunks."

I nodded. “I guess it makes sense that all four of you didn’t sleep there. Even though it is a really big bed.”

He jerked a little, like he’d touched electricity. “No.” Then he stalked past me and knelt at the drawers built into the wall across from the bed. Wordlessly, he handed me a old T-shirt, and a pair of basketball shorts. "These are definitely not your size," he said making the awkward, obvious joke.

I tried to smile, because he was being nice. Because this was very kind. Something I wouldn't have expected from him.

"You're really Finn King,” I said.

"Nah, I'm Beau,” he said, yanking a towel off a rack by the bathroom and holding it out for me to grab. Then he skirted past me and heading towards the kitchen.

I raised my eyebrows. Okay. That was weird. I filed it away to ask about later. Once I gave him back his clothes.

"You want some hot chocolate?” he called, keeping his back to me so I could change.

"You have hot chocolate?" I asked. That was surprising.

"I like hot chocolate," he grumbled. "I can spike it if you want."

“Ooh, manly hot chocolate.” I pulled his shirt over my head before wiggling out of my wet one. “Hot chocolate befitting a rockstar?"

He glowered at the counter and wouldn't look at me.

I wrung out my hair into the towel he's given me and twisted it up into a knot at the top of my head. Warm and dry, and surround by the scent of him, I felt like I was back on stable ground. More like myself. “You’re not Beau,” I pressed. “We already went over this. Why are you lying?"

His shoulders rose and then fell. “Because you seem to hate the idea of Finn King.” He turned with two mugs and walked over to hand me one. “Not that I blame you.”

I accepted the mug, feeling guilty. But I shook it off. Because I was realizing as I stood here, that maybe Livvy wasn’t my only chance to get some answers. “So let’s see if I remember my King Brothers lore. You’re from around here, right? Crown Creek?”

"Born and raised." He lifted his mug to his lips. Lips I could very clearly remember the taste of.

I pushed that thought aside. I had a mission. “Do you know the Knights, then?”

One eyebrow arched over his green-hazel eyes. “The Knights?” For a moment I thought he was going to deny it. Then he shrugged. “I mean, yeah. Everyone knows them.”

That wasn’t what I needed. “Do *you* know the Knights?”

His other eyebrow rose to meet the first one. “I said everyone knows them, didn’t I?”

I took a deep, steadying breath. I wrapped my fingers around the mug and tried to draw strength from the warmth. “Okay yeah, I suppose you did. So you know Bill Knight then?”

"Yeah?” Finn sounded confused.

I gripped the mug tighter to keep my fingers from shaking. “Nice guy?"

Finn was watching me warily. “I’ve never actually talk to him face-to-face."

"You're being careful."

"Yeah."

"Why?"

"Because I don't know what you're getting at."

No more dancing around. I lifted my chin, ready to tell him, but the words felt too big to fit my tongue around. It took several tries before I got it out. “Bill Knight is my father.”

Finn’s eyebrows dropped into a scowl. “You’re one of the Knights?” The way his emphasis landed heavily on the last name confirmed my suspicions. The Knights were infamous in Crown Creek.

I shrugged. “So it would appear.” A small, mirthless laugh escaped my mouth.

He narrowed his eyes. "I don't remember you," he said before shaking his head. “And you said your last name is Clarence.”

“I said I *thought* it was Clarence.”

Finn stepped back and paced a tight, frustrated circle. “You know you sound like an absolute lunatic, right?”

“I feel like one too,” I exhaled.

That stopped him short. “Start again?” he hissed through clenched teeth. “At the beginning, please, I’m not that bright.”

His eyes snapped so sharply green at me that I felt unsteady. I closed my eyes, and found it was easier to form words without having to see them. “Up until about twenty-four hours ago, I knew who I was. I was Sky Clarence. Only daughter of long distance trucker Bill Clarence of Reckless Falls.” I opened my eyes and locked on to Finn’s hazel ones. “But it turns out that single dad Bill Clarence of Reckless Falls is - was - actually respected husband and father Bill *Knight* of Crown Creek. Bill Knight had a mistress there for a few years, it seems.” I spread my hands. “Resulting in... me.”

“Shi-it,” Finn drawled.

“Yeah. I’m not his daughter. I’m his dirty little secret.” I paused, clenching my teeth. "Or I *was* his dirty little secret. Until I showed up for his funeral. Now it's not so secret anymore.”

I watched Finn carefully as I said this. I didn’t know why it was important to me that he believe me. Except that it was.

His expression was cycling through every emotion in the book - surprise, sympathy, amusement - until it finally settled on one. The worst one possible.

Disbelief. “That’s one hell of a story there, Sky.”

“You don’t believe me?”

“I didn’t say that.”

“But it’s true.”

“I’m just saying it’s a little much.” He smirked. “Don’t you think? I mean, I already told you I knew the Knights. You could have picked any other family in town, someone I don’t know. That would have made it seem at least a little bit less far-fetched.”

His disbelief was a punch in the gut. How could I make him believe me when I could barely believe it myself? “You think I'm lying?”

He shrugged.

And just like that, I knew something for certain. Something that I would hold myself to for the rest of my life. I lowered my voice, and fixed him with my gaze, forcing him to look me in the eye. I felt the weight of the declaration settle around my shoulders like a blanket I could wrap myself in. "No,” I said. “I don't lie. I always tell the truth.”

I sniffled and then drew my shoulders back. I looked at Finn like I was seeing him for the first time.

I saw a man with secrets. I saw a man in denial. I saw a man who didn't want answers. Who, like my dad, didn't even want to hear the questions.

And you know what?

Tough shit. Because I didn't work that way.

Not any more.

Chapter Eleven

FINN

"I'm telling the truth," she repeated.

This chick was out of her goddamn mind. I held up my hands. "Okay psycho, you don't lie. I *get* it."

"I don't!"" She said it with such conviction I could tell she believed herself. I had to hand it to her. However insane her story was, she believed it."

"Fine, you don't lie. Now I know." I turned away, ready to be done with this conversation.

"And what about you?"

I turned back. "What about me?"

"You're Finn King."

"You keep saying that like it's the name of some infectious disease."

She ignored that. "What the hell are you doing in a campground?"

"I told you. Camping."

"By yourself?"

"Is that weird? I mean, you're doing the same thing."

She rolled her eyes. "I'm not famous rockstar."

"You sure about that? Maybe you should add it to your story. You can be Bill Knight's long-lost secret rockstar daughter. That'd be fun."

She glared at me murderously. "Does anyone know you're here?"

"Sure." The owner of the campground did. Not a lie.

"Really?" she probed.

"What do you care?"

Her impossibly blue eyes flicked back and forth across my face like she was reading me... and I was several steps below her reading level. “No one knows you're here,” she declared. “Why are you hiding?”

I turned away again. “Are you done with your hot chocolate?"

"Stop avoiding the question."

"Stop *asking* questions.”

She drew up taller. “I am alone and vulnerable in a strange man's weird trailer,” she said. “And I just drank some liquid he handed me too -.”

“It’s *hot chocolate*. And I’m starting to regret offering it in the first place.”

“- So I feel like I have a right to know what brought him here."

I blew out a long, whistling breath. I’d never met a more frustrating person. My head was spinning and I couldn’t decide between laughing at her or strangling her. “I dunno, I guess I thought this was the best place to start my new career as a serial killer.” When her eyes widened, I rolled mine. "Calm down. Haven’t I already proven I'm not a bad guy?"

I glanced at her. I’d asked it like I didn’t care at all what she thought. But I did want to know.

I didn’t get why I wasn’t throwing her out of here. She was pissing me off. My blood was boiling.

And I liked it.

The more she got under my skin, the more I wanted to keep her there. I was angry, yeah, but anger was something I hadn’t felt in a long, long time. She had me laughing and shouting when up til now I’d felt nothing but numb detachment. She had me wanting to kiss her hard and then take her over my knee. Last night, when we’d gotten together, it was because I was thinking about what Beau would do.

Now I was thinking about what I wanted.

Her.

Those snapping blue eyes. That tangle of hair. That challenging sneer on her perfect little mouth. "So what is it?” she scoffed, one hand on her nicely rounded hip. "Are you running away from your problems?"

I leaned against the kitchen counter. "No," I stonewalled, enjoying how red her face was getting. "I'm camping."

"Ha! I'm right, aren't I? You're having one of those breakdowns that the tabloids are always talking about. What is it?" She smirked. "Exhaustion?"

"I'm getting pretty goddamn tired of questions, so yeah, maybe it is."

"Poor you," she deadpanned. "Hiding from your problems in the woods."

"Seems to me you're doing the same thing," I pointed out.

She made a hissing sound. "I don't have to take this." And headed for the door.

"You do if you wanna stay dry," I pointed out, moving to intercept her.

She rolled her eyes. "Some kind of camper you are." She gestured around the trailer. "Can't even give up your luxury for one second can you?"

"You're taking advantage of this luxury right now, Sky Knight."

The new last name seem to hit her like a smack in the face. Her eyes widened, then narrowed. She was close enough that her warm breath traced a path across my face. We were both breathing hard, the heat of our frustration filling the entryway. I stepped down one step and blocked the door. She lifted her chin so we were nearly eye to eye. "Fuck you," she hissed.

"I already told you I wasn't going to do that," I growled back. But I lowered my lips, noting the way that she tilted her chin up to match the angle of mine.

"Yeah? Well you missed out."

"I learned long ago not to stick my dick in crazy. It would be pretty fucking crazy for me to fuck one of the Knights. Dirty little secret or otherwise."

With a gasping cry, she yanked her head back, but I matched her movement on instant and caught her lips.

Her mouth seared to mine. Rough, hot and angry, it was a war in the form of a kiss. She attacked first, raking her nails down my back hard enough to make me hiss. But I countered by tangling my fist in her hair and yanking her head back. "So this is it?" I growled as I nipped her earlobe. "This is what I have to do to get you to stop asking questions?"

"I *knew* you wanted me," she spat back.

Cursing, I covered her mouth with mine again. "I just want quiet," I hissed against her lips, then hissed again when she bit me. "Goddamn..." I cupped her ass and lifted her up. She wrapped one leg around my waist, then the other.

My blood rushed in my ears, hot and dangerous. This was bad, the worst thing I could do. I needed her to stop me. But she was urging me on, grabbing my hand away from her breast and shoving it down between her legs. The heat of her made me dizzy. I unzipped my jeans and pressed her against the wall, lifting her higher. My old basketball shorts were already too big on her. All it took was one head-spinningly sexy shimmy and she was open to me.

"Tell me to stop," I warned her.

"Don't you dare stop."

"Fucking hell," I swore as I sank into her.

She was hotter and tighter and sweeter than I could have ever dreamed. This was dangerous. I didn't know her and even as I thrust into her again and again, some alarm bell went off inside of me.

"Turn around." Without waiting, I pulled out of her and spun her around so that her breasts were pressed flat against the wall. "Come on," I groaned, reaching around to the front of her and finding that hot space with my fingers. I gripped my cock tight with my other hand. "You'd better come for me. I want to feel you on my fingers, you hear me? Come on my fingers like a good girl. I'll even let you ask me more questions."

She keened, arching against me as I moved my fingers, and then reached behind her to close her small hand around my cock. I was still slippery from being inside of her, and the combination of her fast-moving hand and the feel of her clenching around my fingers as they slid in and out of her had me at the edge in an instant.

When I slid my thumb over that tight little nub of her clit, her head fell back. She rose onto her tiptoes, crying out.

The blood roared in my ears and I pulled back, catching myself just before I lost control completely.

She staggered and I caught her around the waist with one arm. Her eyes were still heavy lidded, but not closed. She was watching me. "You didn't..."

"It doesn't matter." I was throbbing, aching, out of my mind crazy to just let go... and what? I closed my eyes and pictured painting myself on the smooth rise of her ass cheeks. It would be so easy to use her to get off, the way she had just done to me.

Why had I stopped myself? "I'm fine."

Color rose to her cheeks. This was the second time I'd held back with her. I didn't know how she felt about that. I didn't know how I felt about it either - except it was the strangest combination of satisfaction and shame.

Satisfaction I'd made her come. Satisfaction because she'd lost control but I hadn't.

Shame because she deserved better than this. A rough, sloppy finger-fuck against the wall of my trailer? How low had I sunk?

For a fleeting second, I allowed myself the fantasy of laying her out on my bed and making love to her. Slowly and properly.

The way a good man would.

Not an asshole like me.

The thought made me loosen my grip on her. "Fuck," she panted as I lowered her back to the floor again.

"Yeah, that's what happened." My mind was still reeling.

She pressed the heel of her hand to her eye . "I can't believe I just fucked Finn King," she murmured, as if to herself. "Again."

"I can't believe I just fucked Bill Knight's secret daughter."

She glared at me, fire in her eyes. "Asshole," she breathed.

I nodded, unable to look her in the eye. "I warned you."

Chapter Twelve

SKY

The ground felt especially hard that night.

I thrashed and turned, squirming inside of my sleeping bag. Every rock and pebble, every rut and divot in the uneven ground, seemed to be right underneath my body. Poking into me and denying me sleep.

And I was already sore to begin with.

I flopped back onto my back and threw the cover off. And just laid there, panting.

My skin felt too tight - bruised and swollen, like an overripe peach. The chill of the cold night air soothed the burn of my overheated skin a bit. But not enough to make it go away.

The marks his fingers had left on my body still smoldered. Waiting for me to notice them so they could blaze up and remind me of everything I had just done. If I closed my eyes, I knew Finn's face would be right there. I just didn't know what expression it would wear.

Would it be the one of open, desperate yearning? The one I saw right before I broke apart over his fingers, coming so hard I was sure I'd lost my mind?

Or would it be the closed off, angry one? The one I saw right before I ran the fuck away, sprinting across the wet grass with no shoes and only the one sock I could find before shame made me bolt.

I had no idea. And frankly, I didn't want to see either one.

So I kept my eyes open.

That was the second time he'd pulled back like that. And why? The first time it had happened, I'd thought he'd changed his mind. That he'd regretted the idea of having sex with a fuck-up like me.

But then he'd done it again.

I knew he wanted me. I saw it written in every tense line on his face. And I knew I wanted...

Well..

What *did* I want?

The cold air on my skin was clearing my head. Enough that I could see the sobering truth.

I wanted to lose myself. It didn't matter where. Or how. Or with who. I wanted to numb the pain. And Finn was better than any drug or drink I could find.

He was also as dangerous

It was clear he was shattered. A broken man hiding away from the world and the wild success he'd been a part of. He dodged my questions and made up stories until I had no idea which one was true. He was maddening. Frustrating. He was sarcastic and moody and evasive. A mind-fuck wrapped in a mystery.

He was the living embodiment of my turmoil.

And I kept going back for more.

I rolled to the side and drew my knees up to my chest, suddenly cold. "What the fuck is wrong with you?" I whispered into the dark.

Self hatred was seeping in. I yanked the cover back over me and closed my eyes, expecting to see Finn's face waiting for me. It would make sense that I'd dwell on him, since tomorrow I would be packing up and moving on. Where, I had no idea yet. But there was no way I could stay here. Not when he was so close by. Not after I'd left my dignity in his trailer along with my other sock.

I closed my eyes. But instead of his face, it was the funeral home that leaped out at me. Like it had been lying in wait, holding off until I was still and alone. The picture snapped into focus with crystal clarity and I whimpered.

There had been five of them. Four men and a woman, all around my age. My brothers. My sister. All of them with my father's eyes staring at me with pure hatred.

It was my sister - my *sister,* I had a *sister* - who'd done the talking.

She'd known about me.

My brothers didn't. I don't know how it was that came to be the case.

But she was aware of me. She just didn't want to think about me. And I'd denied her that.

The funniest part was her surprise. Did she I wouldn't come to the funeral? She'd definitely hoped I wouldn't. But she should have expected me. When my Dad confessed to her in whatever fit of deathbed honesty he'd been seized with, she had to wonder about my whereabouts. Right?

Or had she'd hoped I'd fallen off the face of the earth, never to be spoken of again? Whatever her hope had been, it was dashed when she was confronted by my existence. A real, solid, living, breathing result of father's infidelity.

Her delusions, like mine, had fallen to pieces the moment we locked eyes in front of our father's coffin.

I'd been shocked.

She'd been *angry*.

And probably still was.

I didn't go to the cemetery. I didn't see my father's casket lowered to the ground. They'd - she'd - denied me that closure. Just like I'd been denied the life she was angry at me for disrupting.

I whimpered again. It was too much to think about. Too enormous to take in. Once again my mind skipped over the full extent of my father's betrayal and settled on something easier.

Jealousy.

Without thinking, I brought my knuckle to my mouth and bit down. Hot anger was pushing away the chill of gut-wrenching sorrow and I was glad of it. Because jealousy was easier. I'd much rather be pissed off than crying. And rivalry with the siblings I'd only just found out about? That was an easy thing to get pissed about.

Everywhere I'd looked in that room, I'd seen the evidence of the life of stability he'd bestowed on them. He'd lived in their house with them nearly full-time. Along with the wife he'd loved dearly, if the obituary was to be believed, and who'd died only a few years back. My brothers, my sister, they'd grown up with two parents who were well-known and well-regarded. He'd given them roots.

I'd had none of that. He'd given them everything and me only moments. Little pieces doled out carefully and stingily. Out of that, I'd tried to build a life. I'd tried to grow roots, but the ground underneath me wasn't solid enough for them to take hold. I'd tried to build an identity out of the leftover scraps thrown my way. But it was like trying to weave cloth out of cobwebs.

Was it any wonder, then, that I was doing the same thing right now? Grasping at something thin and breakable, something I knew had an end date? Finn was unstable.

Of *course* I was clinging to him.

I hugged my knees tighter.

I knew how this would end. I saw it clearly, because it had happened so many times before. And in so many forms. I'd weave these scraps of fulfillment together and wrap myself in them like a blanket. It would be tattered, and full of holes, too thin and insubstantial to ever keep me warm. But I'd stay under it, shivering and clutching it tighter and tighter around me until it fell apart.

And I'd call it love.

Shame nipped along the edges of this hard-won clarity. It heated my cheeks and urged me to do something self-destructive. I *wanted* Finn. I wanted him like I wanted junk food and bourbon. I craved a cheap, destructive hit. I wanted to ride that familiar roller coaster of drama and upheaval, and pretend that pain was love.

I wanted chaos.

How many times had I done this before? I brought up the old memories, flipping through those scraps of fleeting connection. An actor just before he was leaving for the West Coast to try his hand at Hollywood. A lighting tech with an ex-wife and a gambling problem. A musician who crashed with me any time our tours overlapped.

I chose the ones who were only passing through. Who could never give me all of themselves. Impermanence was my permanent state.

And not just with men. With my life too. I spent it touring. Living life at full throttle while on the road. The all day, all night, all consuming schedule. Driving twenty straight hours until I was sure my eyes would bleed from exhaustion. Hopping from company to company. Always the new girl. Always reinventing myself. Always the one on the outside. I formed wild, beautiful friendships that ended the second the curtains came down and the tour was over. And I had to scramble to find another one before I went broke.

Connecting with people and then losing them. Over and over. My phone contacts were clogged with the people I'd lost.

This was the legacy my father had handed me. Chaos I'd mistaken for a life. Chaos I'd mistaken for love.

But I didn't have to live with the scraps anymore. I could stop the chaos right now, and free myself from my father's shitty legacy.

I just had to figure out *how*.

Chapter Thirteen

SKY

I must have slept, because I woke to the screeching of some very pissed off blue jays and the growling of my own stomach.

I groaned and sat up, rolling my shoulders around and testing my body. I was sore. But more importantly, I was hungry.

And needed coffee desperately.

After searching through the detritus strewn across my tent, I managed to cobble together an outfit warm enough to venture outside in.

"Now," I muttered. "Where the fuck are my shoes?"

I clapped my hand over my mouth. And then groaned anyway when I remembered where they were.

Kicked under Finn's bed.

"Fuck," I hissed. Did I dare go over there and knock on his door?

I shook my head. After last night, I'd already filed him away. He was another entry to the file marked 'Bad Decisions' to be boxed up and never thought of again. I was leaving today anyway. I would get another pair. Somewhere.

First though, coffee.

I found that if I ran fast and on the balls of my feet, I didn't feel the cold as much. So I sprinted down the dirt road, past the mostly emptied out lots, to the main building at the center of the camp.

"Hi!" I burst in to the store, startling the woman behind the counter. "Do you have coffee?"

"Honey, where are your shoes?"

I pasted a blithe smile on my face and looked down at my bare dirty feet. "Oh, I hate shoes. I try to wear them as little as possible, you know?"

"Oh for sure, I do that too. But in the summer. There's frost on the ground out there, honey!"

"Is there?" I turned around and looked. As if I hadn't noticed. As if I hadn't felt the the cold with each step. "It doesn't bother me."

The lie burned in my stomach. I didn't lie anymore. This was crazy. All I needed to do was go knock on Finn's door and demand he give my shoes back before I left.

The woman shook her head. "You guys are a hardier breed than me. Out there in only your tents when the season is over. You're the one in Lot 43, right?"

I nodded and she slid her finger along a pad of paper. "You're checking out today?"

"I am. Gotta pack up yet, but I needed some coffee first if you've got it." I pulled a crumpled dollar bill out of my pocket.

She filled a Styrofoam cup from a carafe and handed it over. It was weak and bitter, close enough coffee to satisfy only the worst addict's craving. The polar opposite of the smooth, rich mellowness of what Finn had served me.

I winced as I sipped, then forced a smiled.

"So where are you headed now?" She ran her finger down the paper again. " - Sky? That's a pretty name. I'm Dinah."

"Thank you. I don't know yet, actually." I took another sip and wiggled my toes. "I don't have much of a plan yet, Dinah. Not much of one, anyway." Lingering here meant I would have to hustle to pack up and break down my tent before check out. And I still didn't have my shoes.

Dinah smiled. "Whatever way the wind blows, right?"

I winced again. And this time it had nothing to do with the coffee.

"Usually." The coffee was jumpstarting my brain, and the warmth was making me relax. "Can I ask you something?"

"Sure, honey."

"Are you from around here? Crown Creek, I mean?"

It was a long shot. A very long shot. But she looked the right age, maybe a little younger. If she had known my Dad...

Her face fell a bit. "Not exactly." She narrowed her eyes. "How much do you know about it, round here?"

"I grew up in Reckless Falls, actually."

She nodded. "So not far. That's a pretty area. Got some friends that moved there recently."

I finished my coffee and tried to summon some happy memories because I knew it would show on my face if I didn't. "It was tough in the summer with all the tourists," I confided. "But after Labor Day it started to feel like ours again."

She nodded, pressing a strong, thick finger to the center of her chin. In the long pause that followed, I had time to take in her faded pink sweatshirt and jeans cut for a man. A long brown braid shot through with streaks of silver was tucked into her shirt collar. Her brows were bushy and she had a spray of light hair over her top lip, but her eyes were kind and looked like they'd seen a lot. I had the strongest, strangest urge to hug her. "Well now," she asked, her voice carefully nonchalant. Like she wanted to downplay the importance of her next question. "You ever see any of God's Chosen down that way?"

The name rang the faintest of bells. I wracked my brain. "Oh, the cult?" I asked.

I immediately wanted to eat my words. The long braid was a dead giveaway. "Oh. Oh my God, I'm so sorry. That was such a terrible thing to say."

She blew out a heavy sigh. "No, you're right on, it's definitely a cult. I'm not part of it anymore." She lifted her heavy braid and let it fall alongside her. "I cut it off first thing, but felt naked without it so I let it grow back. Keeps me tied to it, you know?" She dropped her voice to the point where I had to lean in to catch what she was saying. "I got a lot of family still in there. Feels like I should stick around close. In case they need me." Her eyes brimmed with sadness, and an almost unbearable hope.

"That's kind of you," I faltered. Her intensity was making me uncomfortable.

"Family is family."

"I wouldn't know." I lifted my hand in farewell, taking a huge step back so I didn't have to say anything. Just in case my voice started shaking.

I walked slowly enough back to my tent to feel the cold seep through my feet. But I couldn't help it. I felt weighed down by Dinah's words. She was from here. She had roots she wasn't willing to let go of, no matter how poisoned the tree turned out. She kept her ties.

Unlike me. I was about to pack up and leave - with no destination in mind - for no other reason than that's what I did. I didn't even want to, but felt compelled to anyway.

I walked slower and slower, until I came to a dead stop in the middle of an empty dirt road.

I was an addict. Chaos and upheaval were my drugs of choice.

And the only way to break myself of the habit was to go cold turkey.

I spun around and faced the office building again. A campground is hardly a permanent place. But packing up and moving on right now would only feed my addiction.

"One month." I said it aloud. Sternly . The way Janet would have done. Giving me a time limit at the window. Putting some structure around my chaos.

I rushed back to the office and burst into the door for a second time. "How much for a month's rent?" I panted to Dinah.

"Well now, honey, hang on. Its off-season, so I bet I could give you a good rate."

I nodded and leaned against the counter. One month. The very idea made my scalp itch and I felt myself already struggling against the order. Trying to wheedle it down. Bargain for my freedom. The way my Dad would have.

"Fuck," I mouthed. That settled it. If I could stay rooted here for one month, it would prove I could build a life with more than just the scraps I'd been handed. When Dinah told me the price, my resolve almost faltered. Until she agreed to only take a deposit now, with the full balance due later.

And just like that, I was living in Crown Creek.

"Hey, one more thing?" I asked Dinah before she went back to the safe.

"Yes, honey?"

"You know the area, right?"

"I do, yes."

I looked down. "Can you tell me where I can buy some shoes?"

Chapter Fourteen

FINN

When the windows lightened from black to gray, I gave up on ever falling asleep.

It wasn't for lack of trying. I'd utilized every trick in my dirtbag arsenal. Two beers sat heavily in my stomach, doing nothing but make me feel uncomfortable. The first hit off the joint left me so paranoid I chucked it down the drain.

And when I closed my eyes and tried to jerk off to the memory of the sounds Sky made when she came, I couldn't do it. It seemed like a betrayal of... something. Some principle I was unaware I possessed.

It was frustrating as fuck.

Especially when I was pretty sure last night was goodbye. People came and went in this campground. Always a rotating cast of happy vacationers - or sad refugees from real life, like Sky. And me.

"Fuck it." I sat up and propelled myself out of my bed. For the first time, leaving actually seemed possible. Necessary even.

I suddenly could think of nothing else.

The motivation that had eluded me for a nearly a week was now switched on full blast. I took a big step, ready to finally be on the move.

And fell right on my ass.

"Ah, what the fuck!" I rubbed my shin. I'd tripped over... something... and stumbled right into my bedframe before landing on the floor. What the hell had I stepped on? I looked around, and then down...

And stared at the unlaced sneaker on the floor.

I had a fuzzy memory, more like a dream than anything, of it digging into the small of my back as I thrust inside of her. I'd yanked it off and thrown it over my shoulder, where it had landed out of sight.

Where it had stayed. Along with the other one I fished out from way under the bed.

Did Sky have any other shoes? I had no idea. Leaning over, I looked out the window and saw the glitter of frost still clinging to each blade of grass. It was cold out there. I hoped she had boots.

Did she have boots?

I went down on my hands and knees and peered further under my bed.

"Ah, fuck me." A fitted white sock lay there. Right next to a pair of white panties.

She'd run out of here last night with no intention of coming back. What did I owe her here? Disappearing without a trace and stealing her shoes and panties in the process?

Or being a decent fucking person and giving them back?

I could be an asshole and walk them over to the lost and found at the camp store. I could leave them on my doorstep and hope she'd notice.

Or, I could be like my brother.

I stood up and yanked a shirt over my head. Then pulled on my jeans and a coat. And boots too, because the morning looked cold as fuck. Then I headed out to face a person who probably hoped she'd never have to see me again.

Jesus. Being a good person was a pain in the fucking ass.

Chapter Fifteen

SKY

Armed with the directions Dinah had given me, I hurried back to my tent.

Why did I choose the lot the furthest from the camp store? I was so far off, it took a second for my bright blue tent to come back into view.

And for me to see the silhouette of the man crouching next to it.

A flutter of fear - *it's one of my brothers, what does he want? how'd he find me?* - made the hair on the back of my neck stand up. I stopped short and stared.

He was behaving... oddly. He shifted and bounced on the balls of his feet. His hands moved like he was having a conversation with the front of my empty tent. I inched closer at the same time the sun finally broke through the heavy clouds.

Leather jacket. Light brown hair. Big beard a shade darker than the hair of his head.

"Finn!"

He jumped to his feet when he heard me, and then did a comical triple take between me and my tent. "You weren't in there?"

"Clearly not."

“Oh.” He rubbed the back of his neck. “I thought you were just ignoring me.”

“What were you even doing?”

“Trying to give you these.” He held out my shoes.

“Oh my God. Thank you” I grabbed them, yanked out the sock he’d tucked into one and pulled it onto my foot. Then I yanked the other sock out and -.

It wasn’t a sock.

“Oh for fuck’s sake.” I quickly shoved the panties he’d returned into my pocket. But not quick enough to stop the blush that flared on my cheeks.

He looked down and away. But not before I saw that he was blushing too. “You’ve been running around barefoot?" he grumbled. "It’s freezing.”

“I have. Why does that make you mad?”

“I'm not.”

“You sound mad,” I pressed.

He shook his head. “I’d hoped seeing me again was preferable to frostbite. I guess it isn’t.”

“It wasn’t that.” Or was it? “Yeah it was. I guess I'd chalked them up to a lost cause.”

He took a deep breath and blew it out.

I took a deep breath as well. “Look -.”

“Yeah?”

I shook my head. “No, go ahead. Were you going to say something?”

“I wasn’t, you can...”

I pressed my lips together and we both went silent. I thought miserably of the deposit I’d just put down with Dinah. Forcing me to stay here instead of fleeing like I’d wanted. “Look,” I said. Slowly. Because these were words I’d never said before. “I’m sorry. I think we might have gotten off on the wrong foot.”

“You mean, we fucked on one foot.”

“Is that supposed to be funny?”

“I don’t know.” He rubbed the back of his neck. “I... don’t know.”

“Okay. Well.”

"Can we maybe...?"

"Start over?" I supplied.

He looked relieved that I'd suggested it. "Yeah."

I tapped my fingers against my thigh. It was one thing to arrive at conclusions in the privacy of your own tent. It was another thing to put them into action. Especially when the focal point of your chaotic cravings was standing right in front of you.

"I don't want..." How could I put it into words? "The last thing I need is... I don't even know what the fuck is going on..."

"I don't want anything from you, Sky," he said in a rush.

I looked up in surprise. He shifted his gaze like it was uncomfortable to look back at me, but with a great effort he kept his gaze direct.

"Everything is... " I was doing a terrible job at this.

But he nodded like he understood. "So, you're leaving?"

"Why?"

He shrugged and looked away.

I swallowed. "No. I'm not."

He looked back at me.

"Do you think I should?" I pressed.

"I don't think you should do anything."

"I'm not going to do the walk of shame here, Finn. So we had some... so we... So we *fucked*." His eyebrow shot up. "And maybe we both regret it a little? But fuck it. I'm not going to run away from my regrets any more. I'm staying here. I just paid for a month's rent."

"You're going to freeze."

"Yeah, probably. But I have to prove to myself that I can do it. So if it's gonna be awkward, well, tough. I'll stay away from you if you want. I can ask to move to a different lot. But I'm not going to disappear just because you don't want to see me anymore." Was I talking to him or was I taking to my father's family? I wasn't sure. "I'm not your dirty secret or your worst regret. I'm a human fucking being."

Finn blinked. "Jesus." He licked his lips. "Sky. You've got it all wrong."

"Do I?"

"I don't want you to disappear."

"You sure about that?"

"I don't know why you think these things about me, but you're wrong. You don't know me." He drew a deep breath and held up his hand when he saw me ready to snap at him. "I don't know you either. But what I'm saying is, I'd like to."

"What?"

"I was coming over here to... well I was giving you your shoes back but also... I wanted to give you my number too. If you were leaving I wanted to... stay in touch."

"I thought - ." He'd cut himself off from his family. From everyone. Why me?

He gave me a look like he understood what I was thinking. "Maybe I want to prove something to myself, too."

"I can't..." I cleared my throat. "I'm not going to fuck you."

He nodded. "That seems like a good plan."

"So how are we...?"

"I can just be your friend?"

Something slid into place. "Can you?"

"Maybe not." He shrugged. "But I'll at least attempt it?"

"So. Starting over... as friends?"

"Yeah."

"Should we... shake on it?"

"Okay." He held out his hand. As it closed over mine, I felt the echo of his touch on my skin. The roughness of his callouses, the strength in his fingertips. These were the same hands, but now he held me gently. The strength was something solid I could hold on to.

Without meaning to, I squeezed, which seemed to startle him. He stiffened and jerked his elbow, but with the same effort he was exerting to hold my gaze, he kept his hand in mine.

"Why is this so hard for you?"

"Asking questions again?" This time he drew his hand back.

"We're friends. We're talking."

"You're talking."

"You talk just as much, you know." I pointed out. "You're not the stalwart, stoic silent type you seem to think you are. You were downright chatty last night."

Mentioning last night made us both stiffen and this time, I was the one who looked away. "So we're friends now." I needed to remind him, I thought. And myself. "You must not have had too many friends growing up, right? Because you spent so much time on the road?"

He shrugged one shoulder. "I guess."

"I wish I'd made more of an effort," I exhaled. "I made friends easily but then things just... *fizzled*. Because my focus was on when my father was coming back next."

I shook my head, looking at the ground. For a moment, the feelings were too overwhelming.

I saw Finn's boots shuffling in the dirt.

And then the solid weight of his hand as he rested it on my shoulder and squeezed. "That sucks."

I laughed and then nodded. "It does."

"I hate when people try to give you that positive bullshit. Finding the goodness in the bad shit that's happened to you."

"I don't see how I can find any goodness here."

"So don't," he said. "Be pissed. You have the right. What he did to you? It's wrong and unfair. It shouldn't have fucking happened."

"You're damn right it shouldn't have, my friend.

I looked at Finn. He looked at me.

And we both smiled.

Chapter Sixteen

FINN

And just like that, I had a friend.

Me. The unlikable asshole who got in fights like it was his job. The one whose brother had to drag him along to anything and who sat in the corner, pissed off about it the rest of the night.

I'd done basically everything I could to drive her off, but Sky was still here, four days into our reboot. Making fun of my pop-star beginnings, but still. She was here.

"Oh my God," she groaned. "I remember those suits!" She handed me the ear of corn she'd finished husking and I wrapped it in foil to put on the grill. "How did you let that happen?"

I didn't like talking about my brothers. Not now. But I liked to see Sky's smile so I answered her. "The label wanted to play up the twin angle. You can be sure it wasn't our idea. Though I was a lot more resistant than Beau was. I think that's because he got to wear the blue one."

"While yours was a lovely shade of -."

"Puke green," I finished, which made her laugh harder.

"Ugh, you poor thing." She handed me another ear and then stood up and wiped the corn silk from her lap. "They were ridiculous. But sadly not the worst costumes I've ever seen. I once worked a production of *The Glass Menagerie* where the costume designer put these silver, elbow-length gloves on Laura. Her dress was pure twenties glam, but her gloves were straight out of a disco."

I blinked at her. "I'm afraid I don't know what the hell you're talking about."

"*The Glass Menagerie*? Tennessee Williams? Didn't you read it in school?"

I snorted. "I didn't go to school. I did have a tutor who didn't give much of a shit about his job, however. And he never mentioned it."

"So you've never seen *The Glass Menagerie*?"

"Seen? Read? Heard of? No to all of the above."

She looked scandalized. "How about *Cat on a Hot Tin Roof*? Come on now, you're alive, right?"

I closed the lid of the grill. "I'm alive and apparently uncultured, Miss Theatre Snob."

"Oh, can it," she laughed, batting at me with her hand. "I'm hardly a snob."

I struck a dramatic pose. "Oh, but you work in the the-a-tra!"

"Yeah, doing laundry for divas." She rolled her eyes. "But don't change the subject. This is an emergency. You're missing out on like, the building blocks of cultural expression."

"You ought to talk with Jonah," I muttered. "You two would hit it off immediately." My oldest brother was the kind of Type-A control freak who was perfectly functional on three hours of sleep. I was sure he'd know what she was talking about. And be thrilled to share his opinions about it, too. I picked up the tongs and opened the grill again to turn the corn.

"Jonah's not here. And you're the one who needs an education on the classics." She stomped up the stairs into the trailer and poked her head in the door. "Hey, you have a DVD player in here, right?" she bellowed from inside.

"Yeah?" I was a little wary about where this was going.

She laughed and shook her head as she stepped back out again. "Course you do. How could I forget? You're 'camping.'" She made air quotes with her fingers. "But it's perfect. We can get started tonight. After dinner let's head out to the library."

I dropped the tongs.

"Five second rule!" Sky swooped in and picked them up again. She was grinning when she held them out to me, but her face fell when she saw my expression. "Hey, what's up?"

What was up was that my mother worked at the library.

Sky's eager suggestion nearly caved my chest in with longing. Mom might even be working tonight. It would be so easy to walk in there - like I had a million times before - to say hello.

"I'm not going to the fucking library," I growled.

"Jesus." She stepped back. "Fine then. Have a tantrum about it."

I finished flipping the corn and slammed the lid of the grill down so hard it rang out. And made Sky jump. She turned away from me and busied herself setting out the hamburger buns on our paper plates.

Shit. She'd been really excited and I shut her down. And for some reason I cared about the things she cared about. "You could go?" I heard myself say. "Maybe? I wouldn't know what to get, anyway."

Her little pink tongue flicked out and I watched her mouth as she tried to hold it in a frown. And then failed. "Are you sending me on your errands, Finn King?" she smirked.

I relaxed. "Sure am. And we need more cereal too."

"That's because you eat a whole box in one sitting."

"I like cereal." I shrugged. Then gestured for her to hold out her plate.

"I guess I need some things too, now that I'm staying." She held her plate up to her nose and sniffed. "Nice work. You're better at grilling than you are at making the fire itself." She laughed when I gave her the finger. "But I'm a little freaked out about going into Crown Creek, to be honest."

I slid onto the bench across from her. "Are you worried about running into your family?"

"They're not my family. They made that amply clear."

"Well, don't be too stressed out. I know the Knights, and you're not likely to find them hanging out near the library."

"What about somewhere else?"

I bit into my burger and chewed thoughtfully. "They keep to themselves," I said after I'd swallowed. "And besides, what do you think they're going to do, anyway?"

"I don't know," she sighed. "You're the one who knows them, not me."

I took another bite. I did know them. J.D. was fairly reasonable, but the rest of them? Prickly. Quick to find insult. Rocco was no worse than me in the temper department, which made him bad enough. Maddox, though. He was a wild card. And Lennon actually *scared* me.

Their sister Grace? I didn't know her except in passing. But her brothers seemed to defer to her in a way that Claire could only dream of Jonah, Gabe, Beau and me doing for her. If a scary motherfucker like Lennon found Grace intimidating, she was probably the worst of the bunch.

Poor Sky. I knew what she was up against. But I didn't want her to be scared either. "You're not anyone's dirty secret," I reminded her. "Remember how you said that?"

Her smile was pure sunshine. I swore it warmed me from the inside out.

And I wished like hell I could fix things for her.

But I knew that was a fantasy. So far I'd fucked up twice with Sky, but I seemed to be doing well right now. In spite of myself. I watched her eat, and then laugh, those eyes of her widening as she told me stories about life in theater.

Friendship was something I wasn't good at, and I'd only make things worse for her with my good intentions. But the thought stayed there, lodged in my brain. Twisting like a worm on a hook.

You could fix this for her.

But how?

Chapter Seventeen

FINN

"Guess what I did!" Sky burst into my trailer without even bothering to knock.

I looked up from my book. I'd been sitting here trying not to think about what she was doing for the past forty-five minutes. All kinds of dark suspicions had crowded into my head.

But when I saw her again, I could only smile. "I have no idea. You jumped up and yelled about having something to do. And by the looks of it, it wasn't learning how not to be a slob." I stooped to pick up the bag she'd dumped at her feet.

"Nope!" She reached into it and pulled out a small blue card.

I licked my lips. "You went to the library?"

She nodded. "Turns out the month's deposit I put on a campsite qualifies me as a resident of Crown Creek." She tapped the card against my shoulder. "I put an absolute shit-ton of DVDs on hold too, so prepare yourself."

"Fuck," I complained. But I wasn't really mad. How could I be when she looked so damn excited to share something with me? "I thought I was safe because you were worried about seeing the Knights in town."

She pressed her lips together. "Well, you told me they didn't go to the library, so I thought I'd be okay."

A strange warmth filled my chest. *She trusts me.*

"Yeah, you're fine," I grunted, turning away. "So, since tonight is my last night of freedom before you start putting me through your culture classes, how about we do a bonfire?"

"Sure. Let me run to my tent real quick and then I'll make it for us."

"You don't have to!" I shouted at her retreating form. "I know how to build a fire!"

"No you don't!" she shot back from across the road.

I laughed as I watched her stooping into her tent. Half her shit was still over there, strewn around in a messy pile.

The other half was strewn across my trailer. I pushed her bag aside on the counter and poured us both some drinks, then headed outside.

Tonight was the perfect night for a fire. A cloudless sky meant we could see the stars and with the sun setting, the chill was coming on fast. I gathered up our paper plates from earlier to put in the fire pit and held my lighter to them.

The flame caught. Then fizzled.

"Fucking seriously?" I complained.

Sky bounded over with her hands shoved in the pocket of a hoodie advertising some two year old Broadway tour. But when she saw me crouched over the fire pit, she folded her arms over her chest. "Are you seriously trying to make a fire when I'm right here?"

"You know? I would have gotten it if you'd just given me a minute."

She tapped her foot. "Minute's up."

I huffed and rolled my eyes and pretended not to enjoy watching her ass as she bent over the flames. "Honestly, you're like a newborn baby," she complained as the plates finally caught. She looked around appraisingly. "We need more wood," she said, planting her hands on her hips.

I gestured to the logs I'd had delivered yesterday. "Right there."

"Those? That's not firewood. It's too huge."

I planted my tongue in my cheek. "Why thank you."

"Fuck off." She rolled her eyes as I laughed. "No, the firewood, dumbass. We can't put that on the fire. It'll smother it."

"So I'll go buy a bundle from the camp store." She was looking at me. "What?"

"Buy it? There's wood right here."

"You said it was too big."

"Hey Einstein, you know how you make wood smaller?"

"Have you ask a bunch of questions?" I crudely supplied. I liked how she was getting all lathered up. Mad Sky was freaking cute. "Fine," I relented when she started sputtering. "I'll chop us some fucking firewood."

The storage compartment under the bus used to hold our band equipment. Now it was a jumble of random shit I'd thought I might need in my new life. Including the axe my great-great-grandfather had used to build the first house on what was now my parents' property. I hoped my Dad didn't miss it too much.

I also hoped he knew why I needed it.

When I pulled it out, Sky pressed her hand to her heart. "You know how to use an axe?" she gasped, faking a swoon.

"I do indeed."

"Bullshit."

"Oh, you want to try?" I held it out to her. "Go ahead."

With a smug look on her face, she reached out and grabbed it.

And promptly let it drop down, "Hey!" I warned, snatching it back up again before she chopped off her leg. "Watch where you swing it."

She was pale. "It's... heavy."

"Yeah, no shit."

"You can lift that?"

"I lifted you. Only needed one hand, too."

I didn't mean to keep bringing that night up. It's just.... I'm an asshole.

She blushed and looked away, and I knew she was remembering it too. I took a step away from her. It was the only way to stop thinking about the way she'd bucked against me as my fingers slid inside her. "Stand back," I grunted. "I don't want to hit you."

She stepped back and watched with an expression of mute respect as I made my first cut. The pent up adrenaline I'd stored up trying not to want her made quick work of the first log. I handed her a piece I'd split. "Is this a good size?"

She took it gingerly. "It's good." She was staring at me open-mouthed.

I grinned at her. "What? You like what you see or something?"

She recovered enough to give me a look. "I'm impressed. Didn't think you had it in you."

"We have a wood stove, you know."

"Who does?"

I swallowed. "Me and Beau. In our house."

She went quiet. I didn't look at her. I hefted the axe and then split the next log in one go. Then the next. Then the next.

"Hey, killer," she whispered, interrupting me before I yanked the next log from the pile. She spoke softly. Carefully. "That's plenty. You can sit now."

My knees gave out, and I sat.

After a moment, Sky slid closer. She put her arm around me. "You look like you need a hug. That's what friends do. Right? Hug each other?"

"Wouldn't know," I grimaced, but leaned into her embrace anyway. She put her hand on my face and tilted my head until it was resting on her shoulder.

She moved her fingers in idle, soothing traces. Across my brow and down my cheek, the up to my ear. When was the last time I'd been touched like this? Gently? Affectionately?

I couldn't remember.

My eyes were nearly closed when she startled me by clearing her throat. "So. I saw your mom today."

I stiffened.

"I know it was her. Her eyes. They're the exact same color. You definitely got her bone structure too. Damn, I hope I look that good when I'm her age."

I said nothing.

"She helped me get signed up. And I stood there having to make chit chat with her the whole time she was putting in all the holds for me." Sky let her hand fall from my face. "Finn, I felt like I was lying to her."

I said nothing. I had nothing to say.

She twisted until she could see my face. "You know I don't lie."

I gripped my knees. "So you said something?"

"No." She watched me unclench my fists. "No, I wouldn't do that. You have your reasons, whatever they are."

"I do."

She went silent again. "You really do look like her," she said finally. "People always said I looked like my mom."

Some of my tension eased to have the spotlight off of me. "Do you?"

"I guess. I felt bad about it too. Guilty."

"Why?"

"Because my Dad was the one who raised me. My mom split when I was seven."

"I thought your Dad wasn't around?"

"No. He wasn't. Not really, anyway." She sighed and laughed. "Jeez, I keep having to do that. Adjust how I talk about these things." She grabbed a stick and poked the fire, sending up a shower of sparks. "It wasn't just that he lied to me. It's that I lied to myself."

"Your mom left -."

"When I was seven."

"And your Dad would be gone -."

"For weeks at a time."

I felt myself leaning in closer to her. "So who took care of you?" I wondered. "You were a kid."

"Janet." She shrugged like this was was self-evident.

"An aunt?"

"Not even. I think she was a neighbor?"

"And she watched you?"

"She started after my mom left." She blinked rapidly. "Funny. I never think about her. But she was there. Every day. She was the thing that was constant. She was the one I could count on." She shook her head. "She lived down the street from us, but somehow she'd be there in the morning when I got up, and there in the night to put me to bed.

Then she'd sleep on the couch. Fuck... she didn't even have her own room and I never wondered *why*." Sky trailed off as her eyes suddenly filled. "She tried so hard to give me something solid and real. But then my Dad would come in and fuck it all up. Pulling me out of school for a week to go camping. Letting me stay up as late as I wanted. Ice cream for dinner." The corner of her mouth tipped into a lopsided frown. "He undermined everything Janet did for me. And I worshipped him for it. And *hated* her."

It was my turn to stay silent.

"Shit. I treated her terribly." She looked alarmed. "I don't even know if she's alive or dead." With a sudden cry, she buried her face in her hands. "Jesus. I'm an asshole."

I moved on pure instinct. Wrapping her in my arms, I pulled her tight to my chest.

I had no idea how long I held her. It might have been only a minute, but it was a minute I felt so keenly that it stretched into forever. With her body in my arms and her hair brushing my cheek, I felt something I'd never known in my life.

Peace.

I could have held her forever, rubbing slow circles on her back every time her shoulders quivered. But she finally stirred and pulled away.

Then she leaned in and pressed a soft kiss on my cheek. "Thank you."

"For what?"

She smiled. I closed my eyes as she traced her finger over my brow. "So what was that?" she asked. Her warm breath on my ear made me shiver. "Before? When you got all... choppy?"

My head was spinning. Instead of answering, I tilted my head up.

Her lips parted in surprise when I caught them. She drew back. "We doing this again?" she chided gently.

Immediately, I burned with regret. "Don't friends kiss each other?" I joked.

"What kind of friends do *you* have?"

I sat up. "Sorry Sky."

"No. It's my fault too."

"You didn't kiss me."

She pressed her finger to my cheek. "Yeah I did. Did you forget?"

"That's how my grandma kissed me."

"You saying I kiss like your grandma?"

"I dunno. Do it again so I can be sure."

A moment blazed between us. Then she looked away, two spots of color on her cheeks. "The fire is dying," she announced and jumped up.

I brushed my hands down my thighs. I'd come close. So close to fucking everything up with her. I counted backwards from ten, and then backwards from twenty. "Good thing the fire-expert is on the case," I said.

It was a test, and I'd passed. My voice sounded normal enough. You'd never guess I was two seconds away from sabotaging the best thing I'd had in a while.

"It's a good thing too." Sky's voice sounded strained too, but some of her sass was coming back. Thank god. "Honestly. You're like a babe in the woods with this."

I couldn't help but grin at her when she stood back up, cheeks pink from the flame. "Which of us is the babe again?" I wondered.

"You, Mr. Pop Star." She touched the tip of my nose with her finger.

"I'm more than just a pretty face," I protested. "I have skills."

"Yeah?" She looked skeptical. "Like what?"

I was not about to remind her about how I'd made her come all over my hand. "Chopping wood. And. Um." I pretended to wrack my brain. "Fishing."

She stared at me. "Fishing," she said levelly. "Bullshit."

"I don't tell lies," I mimicked her, grinning.

She tried to stomp on my foot and I yanked it away laughing. "I still call bullshit!" she said.

Relief flooded my veins. I hadn't ruined anything. We were back to normal.

"Yeah?" I challenged. "Care to make a wager?"

"You have more money than me." She arched an eyebrow at the trailer. "You have more money than God too."

"So don't make it money."

"What else is there?"

"If I catch a fish before you, you have to run my errands for a week."

She wrinkled her nose. "And if I catch one before you?"

I pretended to grimace. "I'll watch whatever movie you want without complaining." She goggled her eyes at me and I amended. "Too much."

"And if neither of us catch anything?"

"Not gonna happen." I struck a heroic pose to make her laugh. Which she did. Big and loud and full-throated. The kind of laugh that made me smile right along with her. Relieved because, in spite of everything, she was still here.

I hadn't lost her. Yet.

Chapter Eighteen

SKY

"Hey."

I muttered and rolled over, marveling at how soft the ground felt. I'd really toughened up these past few weeks. I was totally rocking this sleeping in a tent thing. I was a bad ass, no doubt.

"Hey!" Something jostled me side to side.

"What the hell?" I protested. I blinked in surprise to see that I wasn't staring up at the familiar blue nylon roof. *Huh,* my sleepy brain noted. *I'm inside.*

Then I rolled over and buried my face in the pillow.

"Okay fine. I'll go fishing myself and you can do all the errands. Including my laundry."

I opened one eye. Finn was standing next to the bed. I was in a *bed*.

When he saw me stirring, he chuckled. "Morning, sleepyhead."

I jolted awake and rubbed my eyes. "Where did you sleep?" I squeaked.

Finn's lip curled in a smile. "Where do you think?"

"Uh." I didn't want to say what I thought. I also shouldn't have glanced to the side of the bed next to me.

The covers were undisturbed. And the pillow was missing. I

spotted it over there on the couch, along with a rumpled tangle of blankets.

He'd let me stay in the bed last night. "You didn't have to do that," I muttered, struggling to free myself from the sheets. "I could have moved."

Finn's face showed a trace of disappointment. "There's no room for me anyway," he grunted, walking away from the bed. "You sleep diagonally and like to have fights with the covers."

"I do?"

"And you talk in your sleep too."

I swallowed. Another man, maybe a year ago? He'd said the same thing. I'd laughed it off. Now it made me feel vulnerable. "Did I say anything weird?"

"Something about shampoo being in the toilet and this not being your exit," he said with a solemn look. I gaped. He snorted. I threw a pillow at him. He ducked. "We're going to miss out on the best fish," he warned. "Come on and stop stalling!"

"Who's stalling? I'm gonna wipe the floor with you." I jumped out of bed, skirted around him and shut the door to the bathroom, laughing as he complained outside the door. "And I'm going to use all the hot water!"

"I'm going to give you decaf!" he called back.

"You wouldn't dare!"

Finn first let me use his shower three days ago. "The hell do you think you're doing?" he'd grumbled when he caught me gathering my toiletries before running to the main building for a shower.

"What does it look like?" I'd shot back.

"Looks like you're being pretty dumb. Give me that." He'd snatched my towel off my shoulder.

"Hey!"

"I have a shower right here. And you know that."

"Yeah but I didn't think you'd want..."

"Why not?" He'd pinned me with those hazel eyes of his.

And I'd showered in his trailer ever since.

He was maddeningly confrontational. And it seemed physically impossible for him to be polite.

But in his own roundabout way, he took care of me.

I smiled as I lathered up, making sure to use liberal amounts of his pine scented soap in the process. I liked it when he got all put out about it, for one. And also because my own, more feminine scented soap was back in my abandoned tent and going out to fetch it felt like it would be disrespectful. I didn't want to scorn a single bit of Finn's generosity, no matter how roundabout it was.

I sort of liked letting him take care of me. Even that care came wrapped up in a bad attitude and frequent cursing.

Yeah, there were doors that Finn wanted to keep firmly shut. But his walls weren't as high as he thought they were. And I felt like I was starting to get a toehold. One day I'd climb high enough to peer over the top.

As I rubbed the cloth over my body, I brushed against a tender place. A chafe mark still lingered on my lower back. From where his belt buckle had rubbed against me as he...

No. Don't think about it.

But I traced my hand over it anyway. I ran my finger over the mark with an idle fascination. The pain was kind of pleasant now, like scratching a deep of itch, and with it came the flood of... well, memories.

I twisted the faucet off a little too viciously and threw back the curtain with way too much force,

Because that's what they had to remain. Memories.

The door swung open. I yelped and dove for the towel as Finn swiftly turned around again. "Sorry, I thought you were still in there."

We caught eyes in the mirror, over his shoulder. He was watching me. I slowly lowered my hands from my breasts, transfixed by the fire in his hazel eyes.

Then we both snapped back into focus. I grabbed the shower curtain and wrapped myself in it. "Get out!"

"Sorry!" he laughed, shutting the door behind him. "If it makes you feel better about showing me your tits," he called through it. "It didn't do a damn thing for me."

There is was. The crudeness along with the care. "Oh yeah, I feel so much better now," I scoffed.

He might think he was throwing me off. But I was pretty sure I could handle Finn King.

When I emerged, he was still standing there with his back to me. "Are you decent?"

"Jury's still out on my decency." Two could play this game. "But yes, I'm dressed."

He turned and grinned. "Well played."

"Thank you."

"I'll be out in a sec," he said, squeezing past me so he knocked into my hip. Even though there was plenty of room for him to get around. "You see, I don't take quite so long in the bathroom."

"You might want to try it. Maybe you could trim your beard while you're in there."

"Never!" he called from the other side of the door.

As I laughed, I caught my reflection in the window. Dawn was still a few minutes off, so I could see myself. Pink cheeked and bright eyed and smiling like crazy.

It felt like I was hiding. And it felt good to hide. To play and tease and have fun with my friend. Like this trailer was our clubhouse. Our fortress with a sign hung on the door that read *KEEP OUT WORLD*.

The darkness was still hanging over us, over me. But I hadn't run.

And right now I was really, really glad I'd stayed.

Chapter Nineteen

SKY

He'd actually been pretty quick in the bathroom. And once he handed me a half a bagel and the cup of espresso I was now completely dependent on, we headed out through the woods.

I didn't ask how he knew about the fishing pond he was leading us too. He was from around here, after all. And as much as I wanted to make some crack about him leading me off into the woods to have his way with me, it didn't feel funny to joke about it any more.

Not when I kind of wished it was true.

"At least I'm getting my cardio in for today," I cracked instead. "How much longer?"

"About five more steps," Finn sighed. "Anyone ever tell you how unobservant you are?"

I went up on my tiptoes. "Oh!" Then I smacked his arm. "You're too big. You blocked the entire path and I couldn't see!"

"I'm not sure how you could miss *that,*" he said quietly as he gestured towards the water.

Morning mist hung over the pond, making it look like a steaming cauldron. Heavy clouds scudded across the sky, their bottoms still tinged with dawn-pink. There was a snap of cool to the air, but the dampness still held traces of summer's heat.

Finn's mouth was always moving. Frowning, smirking, his tongue poking against the side of his cheek as he tried to figure out what to say next. But as he tilted his face to the sun, it stilled and his face took on an expression I'd never seen on him before. Quiet. Not smiling, but peaceful.

He closed his eyes and inhaled.

The simple sight of his shoulder rising and falling tugged at me in a way I didn't quite understand. I was suddenly very warm and shrugged off my jacket. "Nice morning," I commented, not knowing what else to say.

His hazel eyes flicked over to me and then down to his feet. We both stood stock still for a moment. The air between us crackled with electricity.

Fuck. Not this again.

Finn recovered first by taking a big step away from me. He held out one of the poles he'd brought with him. "You can use this one."

Sarcasm seemed like the easiest way to come back to myself. "Why? Because it's the crappier one?"

He rolled his eyes. "No. It's lighter."

"Give me the heavier one," I insisted. "You're not cheating me out of the better equipment."

With a mighty sigh, he handed over the reel. I held it gingerly, trying to look professional and failing miserably. "So I just throw it in now, right?"

"Sure, you could do that. But unless you think a fish is going to come up and impale itself on a bare hook for no reason, you might want to use bait."

"What bait?"

Finn knelt down and shook the coffee can he'd brought with him. I'd pictured us sharing a cup by water when he grabbed it, and hadn't thought to ask what was inside. Now I looked in and nearly retched to see the wriggling red worms. "I'm never drinking your coffee again," I grumbled.

He chuckled and plucked one out. The way his fingers moved... It was another one of those moments where his past was written all over him. I didn't like seeing it, because it reminded me I had a past too.

But there was no way I could look away when his quick musician fingers worked so cleanly.

I'd felt the skill in those fingers.

I shifted from side to side. I was getting turned on by a guy putting a worm on a hook. Just one more thing to add to my growing list of "*what the fuck*" moments with Finn King.

"Your turn," Finn said once he'd finished with his hook.

"You want me to - ?" I swallowed back my horror. He grabbed my hand and dropped the worm into my outstretched palm. It wriggled piteously. "Oh God, I'm so sorry little guy."

Finn laughed. "I didn't think you'd be able to do it."

"What?"

"I knew it." He knelt to the tackle box and pulled up a shiny beautiful lure. "Let the worm go, Snow White, and use this instead. It's my best one." He tied it to the end of my line and once again I was captivated by the skill in his fingers. I was watching them so intently that I didn't realize he was done until he stepped back. "Got it?"

"Oh!" I snatched the rod back before it clattered to the ground. It felt like the mist over the lake was gathering in between my ears. "Got it, yeah." I struck the pose of a mighty warrior. "Now what?"

"Cast."

"You go first."

He sidestepped until there was more distance between us than I wanted.

But from way over here, I could see him. All of him. The easy, wide-legged stance he took. The settled way his weight gathered on his heels, like he was planted into the ground. He drew his rod back, and then with an easy flick of his wrist, he sent it flying out into the water. It landed with a faint 'plop.'

The red and white bobber sent ripples expanding ever outward on the tranquil surface of the pond. That same tranquility rippled out from Finn. His expression was one of casual concentration. Both fully present and somewhere else entirely.

I felt like I was intruding. I wanted to call off the competition. Concede that he'd won. I wanted to dissolve away and leave him to his peace, because I knew how badly he needed it.

Then he glanced over at me. When he saw me standing there, still fiddling with the reel, he grinned. "Chickening out on me?"

The spell was broken. "You wish," I cackled. I stepped back and tried to mimic the casual flick of his wrist that sent his line flying.

My line flew all right. Right into the tangle of cattails that lined the bank.

"Oops, don't pull, you'll break it." Finn handed me his rod to hold and stepped into the muddy water without hesitation. "Wanna try that again?" he asked when he'd recovered my line.

He stepped behind me.

I braced myself. Instantly, I was back in his trailer, my chest crushed against the wall as I came apart on his fingers. As he reached around to my front, I sucked in a ragged breath, remembering how he'd reached around from behind me to slide his fingers...

But his hand landed on my wrist. Only my wrist.

"Gently now," he murmured, drawing my hand back. "It's not a big movement, but everything moves together, feel that?" I felt it. I felt *all* of it. "Now," he instructed, as he stepped back. "Just flick it."

The space between us was enough for me to recover a little. "Like this?" I lifted my middle finger, flicking him off."

"That's awfully brave of you, considering how close you are to the edge," he warned. "I could throw you right in."

"You wouldn't dare."

"Wouldn't be the first time I got you wet."

My ears burned because I'd been thinking the exact same thing. "Hey!" I sputtered.

"Sorry, sorry."

The back of my neck itched. I cast out my line just to give me something to do, something to look at besides my feet. Finn moved away from me and picked up his own line, but I was still acutely aware of him.

"Hey!" Finn's cry snapped me out of my turmoil.

I looked up and saw my bobber dancing frantically. "Ha!" I shouted. "I won!"

"You won!" He was grinning.

I did a strutting victory dance. "Told you! You totally suck at fishing, by the way."

"Are you going to dance or are you going to reel it in?"

"Um, dance?" Finn laughed as I clumsily tried to reel in my line. "Jesus, this thing is a monster!"

"Don't give him slack! Here."

And Finn was behind me again.

I moved my hand a little too slowly and his fingers brushed mine. I snatched it away and gripped the rod with all my strength, white knuckling it. Not because the fish was heavy but because I had to hold on to something.

Finn didn't seem to notice. His eyes were on the skittering line and he reeled and reeled and....

"There's my fish!" I held up the line and brandished the flopping trophy at him. "Look! I caught a fish!"

"You did!" He was grinning. "Now toss it back."

"What?"

He slipped the hook from the gasping fish's mouth. "It's too small. Throw it back."

"No way. You're trying to deny me my victory."

"You have your victory," he sighed as he walked down to the bank and knelt down. "Here little buddy," he said gently.

As soon as the fish slid beneath the surface it seemed to shake itself. "I think it just said 'what the fuck, dude?'" I observed and we both watched it shoot away in a flash of green gills. "There goes my trophy," I sighed.

"So get another one."

"What? I already won!"

"Win again."

I rolled my eyes in a mock huff, but went to my rod readily.

"You gonna get tangled again?

"Not a chance."

"Good." He walked over to his rod.

He was so goddamn distracting that I flubbed my cast, again. I looked over to see if he'd seen it. If he was going to tease me again.

And then caught my breath.

The tip of his line was dipping down. "Hey! You got something!" I yelled.

"Ssh," he hushed me.

He furrowed his brow. I watched, transfixed, as he started reeling it in. The corded muscles of his forearm played under the surface of his tanned skin in a way that made my throat go dry. I licked my lips. "You need help over there?" I squeaked.

"No." He grunted and stepped back with fluid grace,

Out of the water shot a massive green and gold fish. I had no idea what kind it was, other than the pissed off kind. It fought and twisted, but Finn was relentless. And in another breath he lifted it in triumph.

He was out of breath and grinning. His hair flopped into his eyes and he blew it upward, treating me to the full force of his hazel gaze.

And even though I'd won, I was completely lost.

Chapter Twenty

FINN

She'd won by catching the first fish. I caught three more after that, and kept expecting her to grab her rod again just to spite me.

But Sky seemed content to sit on the bank and watch me.

And only *occasionally* shit talk.

"All that and you just let them get away," she marveled after I released the second one. "Seems like a pretty futile hobby to me."

"It's catch and release."

"What do you think it thinks about all of this? Does it just go back into the water with a sore mouth going 'what the fuck was that about?' Or do you think it brags to its fishy friends about how it fought the big, bipedal weirdo and won?"

"Who are you calling a big, bipedal weirdo?"

She laughed.

When the sun was high enough in the sky to burn off the mists, I packed up my tackle box. "I smell like fish breath," Sky complained. But I could tell it was just for show. I felt like we'd shared something. Something a lot more significant than the sharing we'd done with no clothes on.

When we got back to the trailer, she immediately sprinted past me. "Where are you going?"

"I won," she reminded me.

"Oh fuck, I forgot," I groaned.

She grinned evilly and ran over to her battered little hatchback. "Prepare yourself for culture!" she called out of her open window, then bumped down the dirt road with her middle finger held aloft the whole way.

I walked back into the trailer and realized I was alone for the first time in a while.

And I wasn't sure I liked it.

The space felt too big without her in it. Too silent without her questions. Too sad without her smile.

I stripped out of my fish-smelling clothes and hopped into the shower, thinking about Sky.

But when my hand strayed to my cock, I snatched it away.

Her smiles. Her teasing. Her laughter. They didn't mean what my cock wanted them to mean.

This was friendship. We'd made a pact. It felt disloyal to think of her like this. With my hand moving faster and faster now.

"Fuck." I pulled away. I couldn't do it. I couldn't give myself that moment of release.

I was an asshole.

But I was trying really fucking hard not to be.

I twisted the knob all the way to the right and stood under the frigid stream until my teeth were chattering and my blood had cooled.

I emerged from the shower with aching balls and a decidedly more somber frame of mind. She was my friend. And I was jerking off in the shower over her.

But I'd stopped myself.

Again and again I had stopped myself with this girl. I'd shoved down my worst impulses, my raging demons. All my terrible instincts were still there. I wasn't kidding myself into thinking I'd somehow gotten over them. But I was resisting them.

I was denying myself the comfort of fucking things up.

It was new. It was strange. I'd never felt this before.

My stomach growled, reminding me it was lunchtime. I slapped some cheese between two tortillas and put it in the microwave.

Then I thought for a second and made another one.

“Honey! I’m home!"

I jumped. And when I saw her climbing up into the trailer, my heart jumped too.

Then I told it to calm back down again. Because whatever my body thought of Sky, it didn't matter any more. Friends. We were just friends.

"What did you get?" I asked as I sank back down into the sofa, hoping I looked casually disinterested.

Her grin was all teeth. “It’s a surprise."

"Oh joy."

"Settle down," she admonished with grin. "And get your lazy ass up. I have stuff I need you to carry."

"What stuff? You went to the library."

But as I stepped out of the trailer into the gravel lot and saw into the trunk of her hatchback, I widened my eyes. It was filled with grocery bags. "Really?" I arched an eyebrow at her.

She rolled her eyes and looked away for me. "There, okay? I ran your errands. And I didn’t even run into any of my evil half-siblings.” She blew out a sigh. “Now we're even. Now you can't hold it over me that you caught the bigger fish."

I shoved my hands into my pockets. I wanted to tell her how proud I was of her for facing her fears, but I thought it would sound pretty hypocritical coming from me. “I wasn't planning on it,” I said instead. “But cool."

“And!” She held up a warning finger. “I demand a rematch."

"At *what*? You *won*."

She screwed up her face in concentration as we carried the groceries into my trailer. I made a mental note to slip some money to her. Somehow. Although I wasn't sure how I do it, or even if she'd let me. Stubborn little thing.

"I'll think of something," she announced, dropping the paper bag onto the counter.

I took out the cereal. “Whatever you want.”

She slammed the fridge shut. “Just name the time and place.”

I grabbed the two plates I’d prepared and went over to the couch.

"How about right here?" I asked with a grin, patting the cushion next to me as I sat down.

"Dork." But she plopped right next to me. Her thigh wasn't touching mine, but it was close enough for me to feel the heat rising off of it. Which reminded me of the other places I'd felt her heat.

I roughly pushed those thoughts aside and shifted a fraction of an inch away from her. Away from that distracting heat. "So what are we watching?"

Her grin was truly evil. "My Fair Lady first. And it's my copy too, so we can watch it over and over again until you properly appreciate Rex Harrison's talk-singing."

It sounded vaguely familiar. "There's singing?"

"Oh loads." She rubbed her hands together. "And British accents too."

I brandished the plates of half-assed quesadillas. "I have half a mind to eat your lunch for this. Here I was trying to be nice."

"You're not nice," she reminded me. "And gimme, I'm starving."

I jumped back up and grabbed a bottle of hot sauce. "Trust me, you're gonna need this to mask the taste," I warned as I passed it to her. "I'm good at coffee and terrible at cooking."

She delicately shook out three drops and then passed it back. "Here."

I widened my eyes. "That's it?"

"What?"

I upended practically the whole bottle onto mine. "Pussy," I scoffed.

Her eyes went round when she saw how I'd doused it. "Are you insane?"

"This isn't even hot!" I dipped my finger into it and tried to brush it on her lips. "Here, taste it! See?"

"No!" She fell back, flailing her arms as I made stabbing motions at her with my finger. She pressed her lips together and twisted her head from side to side. Then reached out.

"Hey!' I yelped as she squeezed my side.

"Ha!" She scrambled up and then tilted her head. "You have a hole in your shirt."

"No way. I'm not falling for that."

"No you do." Her eyes were on my side. "Right here." She wiggled her finger into the seam at my armpit.

"Hey!" I yelped again.

"Oh my God!" The mother of all evil grins was stretching across her face. "You're ticklish!"

She pounced on me. "Stop!" I crossed my arms over my chest and tried to roll away, gasping as she tickled me. I hated getting tickled. Hated it with a passion.

But I didn't mind Sky's hands on me at all. I was getting harder by the second. I rolled away to hide the evidence.

"Shit, I made it bigger."

I whipped around to look at her, wondering if she'd read my mind. It took me a minute to realize she was referring to the hole in my shirt.

"Shit," she said. "Sorry."

I took the moment to slide away from her and put some distance between us. "No problem. It's not like it's a favorite or anything. I'll chuck it later."

"Chuck it?"

"Throw it away? What, do they not use that expression in Reckless Falls?"

"Ugh," she huffed. "You are such a spoiled little rich boy. Just sew it up! It's right on the seam!"

"Sew it?"

She spoke in a sing song like she was talking to a toddler. "Sew? You know? Like the song? A needle pulling thread?"

When I gave her a blank look, she rolled her eyes. "Okay, I'm adding *The Sound of Music* to our watch-list," she sighed.

Then, to my surprise, she got up and went stomping out of the trailer. She returned with a little kit in her hand. "Give it," she ordered.

"Give what?"

"Your shirt, Finn. Give me your shirt."

This was a part of friendship I wasn't sure I could trust. A true test of just how much of an asshole I was. Or wasn't.

I licked my lips.

And then I lifted my shirt and handed it to Sky.

Chapter Twenty-One

SKY

That was a bad idea.

I didn't realize what I was doing until it was already done. Finn lifted his shirt and handed it to me and I nearly fainted dead away.

How was this the first time I was seeing his skin? He'd been covered both times that we'd... that he'd....

"You have a tattoo." I said dumbly.

"Good eye," he smirked.

It stretched over his left shoulder and down to his pec. Two blackwork figures standing opposed to each other with their arms linked. It twinged some memory. "What's that about?" I leaned in closer.

He stepped back. "I liked it."

"Does it mean anything?" It was a symbol I recognized. But I couldn't place it.

He folded his arms over his chest, partially covering it. "It means you're doing that thing again."

"What thing?"

"Where you cross examine me like I'm on trial."

I shook my head. "Sorry."

He looked away, the set of his jaw betraying his sudden anger. But he swallowed it down. "So you carry a sewing kit around like some grandma?"

I licked the end of my thread and got it through the eye of my needle on the first try. "I work in costuming. This is my job. You never know when something will rip."

"So this happens a lot?"

"What?"

"Guys standing around shirtless waiting for you to do your thing?"

The twinkle in his eyes brought me back to myself. "Yup, you've got it. I've got shirtless guys lining up for my skills."

"Makes sense to me. You know how to work it." He glanced at my fingers as I stitched the hole back up again. "You're good at this."

"You ain't seen nothing yet."

"Yeah? What's the best you got?"

"Are we having a sewing competition now, big man?"

"No way. You'd mop the floor with me."

"Damn right I would."

"Wait. I thought you did laundry."

"I'm a woman of many talents." I grinned. "Ask me about the time the lead actress in *Little Shop of Horrors* ripped out the entire back of her dress five minutes before she was due back out on stage."

"Do I have to?" But he was grinning.

"Do it."

He rolled his eyes. "Hey Sky. What did you do when the lead actress in Little... uh... her dress..." He shrugged, feigning boredom. "I forgot the rest."

I stuck my tongue out at him. "I made her stand over the sewing machine in the costume shop and I sewed it back up again."

It took a moment for him to register shock. "With her in it?"

"Yep."

"She... let you do that?"

"She didn't have much choice. It would have taken too long to take it off."

"Yeah, and we know how disruptive that can be."

I looked away. After a beat, I heard him cough. "Sorry, Sky," he said. "I'm an asshole."

I looked at him. "Yeah. You told me. Can't say I wasn't warned."

"We're friends."

"That's right."

"That's all." He was very near me.

"Yup."

"Me being this close to you has no effect on you whatsoever."

I looked down at his shirt in my hand. "You should put this on." When he didn't move to do it, I reached up and lassoed him around the head with it and yanked it down to his shoulders. "Don't make me stab you with this needle."

"Now why would you want to do that?"

"Because you drive me nuts."

"You drive me nuts too, Sky."

"How?" I licked my lips.

His eyes went right to them. "By doing shit like that."

My blood was thundering in my ears. "What does it make you want to do?"

"Kiss you," he said, without hesitation.

I felt faint. "Go ahead."

"Yeah?"

I swallowed. "Because we're just friends. It won't do anything for me."

"Me either."

I looked down at his jeans.

He snorted. "Purely a reaction to friction darling."

"Oh please, so if I do this?" I leaned in and flicked my tongue on his earlobe. *What was I doing? Why was I fucking with our equilibrium?*

He held himself stiffly until I'd finished. And then shook his head. "Nothing. And if I do this?" He bent his lips and brushed them against mine.

I curled my toes to keep from sagging. "Nothing," I shook my head.

He pulled back. "Good. We're better as friends."

"Right."

He pulled his shirt on the rest of the way. And when he turned his back, I drank an entire glass of water. But it wasn't enough to cool the fire that burned inside of me.

That night, after we'd finished the movie, Finn went into the bathroom first. As soon as he closed the door behind him, I jumped up and grabbed his laptop.

I listened to make sure he was still running the water, then quickly typed my suspicion into the search bar. Then hit Image Search.

I clapped my hand over my mouth and sat back heavily. I'd been right.

His tattoo - the two opposing figures facing each other with their arms linked? It was the symbol for the star sign Gemini.

The Twins.

Chapter Twenty-Two

FINN

Sitting as far away from her as possible - and mercilessly mocking her taste in movies - seemed to put us back on familiar ground. I made it through *My Fair Lady*. And by the end of *The Breakfast Club*, I was no longer afraid that I would spontaneously combust.

"You want to go in first?" I asked when it was over. Sky was very possessive about her pre-bedtime rituals.

"You go," she'd yawned. "I'm too comfortable.

That made one of us, anyway. "Fine. But don't complain if I 'take too long.'" I made air quotes. "I *did* ask."

"I know better than to interrupt your half hour skin care routine," she teased me.

"But look." I pointed to my cheek. "Flawless. Not a pore to be seen."

She laughed sleepily. I snuck a glance at her one more time. Just like I'd been doing all through the movie. No wonder it'd made no sense to me (and why did those 'teenagers' talk like grown ass adults with mortgages?) She was distractingly cute there, curled up in the corner of my couch. She'd put her usually wild hair up in a high topknot that made the idea of kissing her neck run on repeat in my brain.

I pushed myself up and away from her before I gave in. "You snooze you lose," I announced.

But I was careful not to take too long. I was pretty sure I was in there less than five minutes. So I expected her to still be in her place on the sofa when I emerged. Possibly asleep.

Not sitting at the table with my laptop in front of her.

A wave of pure hurt hit me so hard I almost staggered. And with it came the sudden, perfect conviction that *this was it*. The moment it all went to shit.

In a way, it was almost a relief to know it was here.

"What the hell are you doing?" I asked. It was a struggle to keep my voice steady because every emotion was hitting me at once.

"I wanted to look something up." Her voice quavered a little. She sounded guilty.

Which made the betrayal I was feeling even worse. "Who said you could use my laptop?"

"I didn't think you'd mind." She sounded confused. "I mean, I use your *washcloth*."

"This is different." I stalked over and slammed the laptop closed.

She jumped back. "What the hell is wrong with you?"

"What were you looking at?" I roared. A tiny voice inside of me whispered that I sounded irrational. Like a paranoid asshole. But it was drowned out by the louder one that chanted, *she knows now. She knows what a piece of shit you are. She finally knows.*

You could click any result that came up when you searched my name. The evidence was all right there. The fights. The breakdowns. The rambling, incoherent interviews that abruptly ended when I got up and walked out. The breathless tabloid headlines about my family's terror accompanied by a picture of me looking unhinged. "The Kings' Secret Shame," one had labeled me, while the other declared I was the, "The Poison Pop Prince."

It was all there, right back to the articles from fourteen years ago. Gallons of ink were spilled in speculation over what had driven ten-year-old star Finn King to attempt suicide. They'd quoted Beau in one of the less tawdry articles.

I'd read that quote over and over again. It lingered in the back of my brain my whole life. And in the weeks leading up to leaving, I'd dug it back up again to remind myself why I needed to go.

"My brother is going to be okay," my twin had told the reporter. "Because I'm going to take care of him. He's *my* responsibility."

"Did you Google me?" I growled through clenched teeth.

"Calm down, psycho." She took deep breath and suddenly her eyes were filling with tears. "I'll tell you if you promise not to get mad."

I wasn't mad, I was grieving. Sky was... well she was mine. She liked me. She enjoyed being with me for some reason. I'd always known I was living on borrowed time with her. That the time would come when she'd come to her senses and realize I was too broken to waste her time with any more.

I just didn't think it would happen so soon.

"I'll try," I said, deliberately stepping back.

"Your tattoo," she said. "I was trying to see if I was right about what it symbolized."

Icewater flowed in my veins. I couldn't seem to figure out where to put my hands, so I balled them into fists at my sides. "And were you?"

She blinked up at me. A tear tracked down the side of her cheek, single and perfect.

And I knew I'd lost her.

"Gemini," she said softly. Her voice was filled with pity and it set my teeth on edge. "The Twins, right Finn? For you and Beau?"

That was it. I couldn't look at her anymore. I turned away and went to the dark window, staring into nothing.

"Finn?" Sky followed me. She tried to put a hand on my shoulder but I ducked away and sidestepped her. "Does he have the same tattoo?" she asked.

"No," I choked out. "And it's none of your goddamned business."

"I don't get it."

"It's not anything you need to get."

"He means so much to you," she went on, as if she hadn't heard me. "So much that you inked it right into your skin." She reached out again and I stepped around her, evading her touch. "Right over your heart Finn. So why are you in the woods, hiding from him?"

"I told you."

"Yeah, but why? Why do you think you're better off without him?"

"He's better off without me!" I exploded.

Sky's mouth snapped shut. There was too much on her face for me to handle. I didn't want her concern, her worry, her pity.

I didn't want to be a burden on her too.

"Look," I said, after the silence had stretched on too long. "Just forget it, okay? You want the bed or the couch tonight?"

"Why do you believe that about yourself?" she whispered.

"Leave it, Sky."

"Finn, listen to me -."

I whirled on her. "Why? Why are you doing this?" I paced away from her but no matter how far away I got there still wasn't enough distance between me and her worry. "Do you ever listen to yourself? Why why why? Questions questions questions! Christ, you're like a dog with a bone! Why can't you leave well enough alone?"

"You're my friend, Finn - !"

"We're not friends!"

She reeled back. "What the fuck?"

"Are you seriously that deluded? I want to *fuck* you, Sky." The hurt on her face had me nodding because *yes. This was it.* The inevitable was happening. I had a good thing and I was *finally* fucking it all up.

"Yeah," I hissed, moving closer to her. "Every minute of every day, I think of all the things I want to do to you. It's taking everything I have not to rip your clothes off right now."

"So fucking do it," she snarled, lifting her chin. Tears streaked down her cheeks but her eyes were pure challenge.

I gripped her shirt, balling it in my fist to yank her to me. Her lips were right there for the claiming. In one heartbeat, I was harder than I'd ever been in my life, already picturing how she would feel from the inside.

And Sky wasn't fighting me at all. She curled her lip in fury.

And then she sniffled.

The spell broke. I fell back, releasing her. "Go," I said, turning away.

"What?"

"I'm not fucking a girl while she cries. Jesus Christ, what do you think I am?"

A long silence. And then her small, sad voice. "I have no idea, Finn. I have no fucking idea."

I wanted to disappear. I wanted the earth to swallow me up.

I wished to hell I'd never met her so I'd never have to lose her like this.

Chapter Twenty-Three

SKY

Morning came way too quickly. I laid there staring at the blue nylon ceiling, gearing myself up to emerge from the warm cocoon of my sleeping bag and into the frost-tinged morning. And as I did, I kept waiting for the pain to hit me.

But instead of feeling hurt and angry at Finn, I felt only a numb kind of sadness.

I'd made another close connection, only to have it severed in an instant. This was what happened over and over. Why should I lose time grieving it?

That's what I told myself as I made a mental list of what I needed to do next. After weeks of depending on Finn for my food and ways to spend my free time, I'd need something else to do.

I'd need my own food, first off.

Yes. A grocery run. I'd done it a bunch of times for the two of us. I shrugged on a sweatshirt, and took a deep breath before unzipping my tent.

The sight of Finn's trailer made me freeze. The familiar sleek line of it was a gut punch. It had been my home - *he'd* been my home - and now I was homeless again.

This is what happens, the rational side of me whispered. *This shouldn't surprise you.*

Yes, I know, I murmured back. *But I didn't want it to happen with Finn.*

Was he watching me from the window? He could look right out of the one by his bed and see me. Was that his shadow right there?

Fuck. I turned away with my heart lodged in my throat. I couldn't stay here. I wasn't going to run, I rationalized. I just needed to get my tent away and out of sight of that trailer. As far away from my dashed hopes as I could get it.

Angrily, I got into my car and drove out of the campground. There was only one road out. I could turn left and I would be heading away from here. Putting it in my rearview the way every instinct I had demanded.

I turned right.

I cursed all the way to the grocery store and made my way through it like I was traveling through a tunnel. The voices of the other shoppers were nothing more than background noise. I even forgot to be afraid of running into the Knights again.

I returned to the campground with my meager collection of crackers, instant coffee, and a whole lot of peanut butter. Then my phone rang, jolting me out of my tunnel. It still had battery left over from charging in Finn's trailer last night. Before everything went to shit.

I picked it up and stared at the caller ID. "What the?" My cousin never called me. "Hello?"

"Sky?" She sounded put out.

"Hey Olivia!"

"This might sound crazy but." She paused. "Did I just see you?"

I licked my lips. "Um. No?"

"Just now, a second ago? You weren't at the IGA? I kept staring at this woman in the cracker aisle, thinking 'nah, couldn't be. That's not her hair.' But then I went onto the Facebook page of the show you were just working on and saw you're wearing your hair wavy now. That *was* you, right?"

Guilt wiggled in my belly like a slippery fish. I opened my mouth to explain, but Livvy had already seized on my silence. "Oh my god, Sky! Seriously? That *was* you!"

If I lied I'd be the thing I hated most. "Yeah Livvy. That was me."

"You're in Crown Creek?"

"At the campground."

"Still? What the hell, Sky?" The hurt in her voice was palpable.

"Why are you... what are you upset about?"

"That you're camping instead of staying with me!"

I blinked. I hadn't even thought about Olivia. Not once, in this whole time I'd been in Crown Creek had I thought about visiting my cousin.

What kind of person was I? I dragged my hand down my face. "I'm sorry. It's been a... little bit weird."

"You said you're at the campground? Jesus, it's freezing outside."

"It's definitely colder than when I first came here."

"When you first came?" she echoed. "You mean you've been here since your Dad -?" She cut herself short. "You know what? I don't care. This is silly. I have my own place and the world's most comfortable couch. I'm coming to get you."

"Livvy."

"Sky, come on. We're family."

My breath came out in a rush. I'd forgotten. I'd been drifting, unmoored, all this time, when land had always been in sight. I wasn't alone in the world, and Livvy was someone who knew my past. She knew this town.

And she also knew my dad.

Suddenly I wanted to kick myself. I kept saying I wanted the truth but obviously I didn't want it as badly as I'd pretended. I'd been avoiding it, hiding from it, content to let my secrets stay buried. But I, of all people should know that buried secrets were like a land mine. You never knew when they would go off.

Better to dig them up first.

"Yeah," I breathed. "Okay, you know what? That actually sounds wonderful."

"Yeah? Good, because I'm already getting in my car. I should be there in ten minutes."

It took less time than that for me to break down my tent and pack up all my worldly possessions. Clothes, shoes, my sewing kit...

And my DVD of *My Fair Lady*.

I opened up the case and let out a long sigh. The DVD itself was missing. Still sitting in Finn's trailer, no doubt. I licked my lips, feeling a strong sense of deja vu. It was the shoe incident all over again.

I looked at the trailer.

Finn was inside. Shut away from the world. I couldn't be his girlfriend. I couldn't even be his friend. We kept coming at each other from the wrong angle, reaching out and then missing each other. It was maddening.

I'd been using him. Using him for a place to stay. Using him to distract myself from my real problems. It wasn't fair, what I had done. It was no more fair than how I'd been treated.

I turned when I heard the sound of a car pulling up. "Hey!" My cousin waved out of her window. "Sky! Hey!"

"Hang on!" I shouted. "Just one more thing!"

Livvy watched me as I ran over to the trailer. I lifted my hand to knock. Then thought better of it. I knelt down and put the DVD case on the step.

It was his now. I hoped he'd take care of it, but I was pretty sure he wouldn't. Not when he wouldn't take care of himself.

Not when he wouldn't let anyone care about him.

Chapter Twenty-Four

FINN

I could see everything outside of the window.

The car. The girl driving it. She was one of Claire's friends - Libby or Liddy or something. I knew her immediately. How did Sky?

When they hugged tight, I clenched my fist. I wasn't sure what I was feeling. Jealousy? *Hey, that's mine!* She was her own woman. And I'd fucked things up irreparably enough to know that it was best to cut her loose. I was good at it, after all.

But that wasn't what was screwing with my head. It was what happened before they hugged. When Sky had come rushing across the road.

Towards me.

My heart stopped. I stood stock still, frozen. Rehearsing the apologies I'd make once she burst in. Hoping like hell she wouldn't knock and make it awkward. This was her space too, now. And she had every right to come careening in and yelling at me. I really fucking hoped she would.

But she didn't knock. She didn't careen.

She rushed away from my door again, hair flying, and hugged Whatshername. Then she got into her packed car and the two of them drove away.

Sky disappeared from view slowly. It wasn't a cinematic moment. I had ample time to rush out the door after her. Claire's quiet friend was driving so slowly down the rutted, pitted road, that I could have easily caught up to her.

But I didn't.

It wasn't until she was gone, until she was fully out of my reach, that I was able to move again. For the first time in a month, I opened the front compartment and sat in the bus's driver's seat.

Why? Did I think I going to follow her? I was still hooked up to water and electric. It would take at least an hour for me to go anywhere.

Numbly, I went to the door of the trailer and opened it.

Her absence was heavy around me. Even the birds seemed silenced by the weight of it. I stepped down and my foot brushed up against something.

It was the case for her *My Fair Lady* DVD. I opened it and saw it was empty, then turned, remembering that the shiny silver circle was still sitting on top of the DVD player. She'd left me the case so I could watch her favorite movie again. And keep it safe when I was done.

I tried my hardest to feel nothing. Even anger would be preferable to this other thing.

Gratitude. Shame. Clarity.

Something that felt a lot like devotion.

Desire.

Love?

How could I love her? I didn't even deserve her. Sky Clarence Knight deserved a far better man than I could ever be.

But she also made me want to try.

Chapter Twenty-Five

SKY

The kitchen was dim. "I just moved in," Livvy explained, hitting the light. It didn't do much. "The tenants before me left the place a wreck. I was only working part time back then, so Mr. Grant - he's my landlord - gave me a deal on rent if I did the cleaning myself." She grimaced. "And then literally that very week I found a full time job. So I haven't had a chance to... well..." She gestured helplessly

Grime coated the windows. Dead bugs were scattered in the light fixtures like grisly confetti. "It's going to look really nice when you do though?" I said, brightly. Unable to bring myself to lie and tell her it was fine.

She gave a one-shouldered shrug. "I don't know when I'm going to have time. The woman who ran Dr. Fenton's office before had a terrible coke problem. The files are like..." She shrugged again. "Well they're like this kitchen, honestly. Dr. Fenton is letting me work all the over time I can handle trying to match billing records. Which is great for my bank account. And terrible for my living situation." She looked sheepish. "You're the first person I've ever had over."

"I'm family," I replied. It still felt weird on my tongue.

"That's right." She smiled. "Now come in and tell me what's going on."

I followed her into the living room, feeling like I was walking towards my own execution. Shame sent heat crawling up my cheeks and down my neck to my chest, and tied my tongue in knots. But when I sat down and looked into her eyes, I took a deep breath. "Do you remember my Dad?"

She raised an eyebrow. “Barely," she said with a sigh. "Maybe if I saw a picture? But it's more like impressions you know? We were so little when he split with your mom."

"Livvy, my Dad is Bill Knight."

It came out in a rush. And maybe that was on purpose. Maybe I wanted to blindside her the way I've been blindsided when I walked into the funeral home.

"No he's not." I heard the skepticism there. And I knew that she didn't believe me. Why should she? This was the kind of story that was truly unbelievable.

“When I went to the funeral home, I saw my father's body lying there, but there were people I’d never met before mourning him. Calling him Daddy.”

“Jesus,” Livvy whispered. She kept shaking her head again and again. "Wait, no, but, no, but...”

"I didn't even know he was sick, because he didn't dare get in contact with me from the hospital. Because he didn't want them knowing that I existed."

"Sky, Jesus. Are you serious?“

"My mom?” I choked. “Your aunt? She was the other woman."

"Bullshit."

"He was *married*. He had a *family*. Here. In Crown Creek. All those trips he would take? Going on the road? Not being home for weeks at a time? It's because he was *here*. With *them*." My voice was rising in hysteria. A month later it was still hitting me as hard as it had the day of. “I walked into the funeral home, and they kicked me out. I couldn't even say goodbye. I didn't know about them. And they didn't know about me. No one knew anything because my father... Daddy... Daddy was lying to us all."

When my voice broke, Livvy’s grimace of disbelief broke too. She stood up and enveloped me in a giant hug, then went over to a closet.

"Get up a sec?" she asked, then she set about stretching sheets over the couch cushions.

"What are you doing?" I sniffed.

"You need a nap," she said firmly. She pointed at the makeshift bed. "Now lie down."

"What?"

"Lie down."

"It's the middle of the day."

"You look like you are ready to drop."

I wiped my eyes with my sleeve. "I'm not though."

"You've been sleeping on a sleeping bag on the hard ground for how long now?" She handed me a tissue.

Not as long as you'd think, I didn't say. I just blew my nose loudly.

She gave me an encouraging smile. "Come on, cuz."

I shook my head, balling the tissue with fretful hands. "I have too many things to do," I protested. The month I'd spent hiding away from the world suddenly seemed like a lifetime. "I have to find a job, find a place to live, call a lawyer... God, do I need a lawyer do you think? I can't afford one."

Livvy clapped her hand on my shoulder. "You can do all these things after you take a nap." She gave me a gentle shake. "And don't think you're doing them all alone, either."

Chapter Twenty-Six

SKY

I climbed into the makeshift bred grudgingly. Just to make her happy. Because she was doing me a favor and I barely knew her well enough to know how to defy her.

"It's comfy, right?" She looked at me. Pleased. Hopeful.

"Yeah." It actually was. I shifted and rolled to my side.

She leaned over and patted my pillow. "I'm going to run a few errands. When I get back, we'll talk more, okay?"

I figured I wouldn't sleep. The strange house. The strange turn of events. They should have kept me awake.

But the tears had exhausted me and I fell into a fitful sleep. The kind where outside noises seep into your dreams. There were voices, hushed and whispering. *My parents are fighting again.* I pulled the covers over my head, ready to wish that my mom would stop being so hard on my dad.

But with the logic of dreams, I suddenly flipped sides. Now, it seemed like my mom was the one in the right. Her anger at my Dad seemed justified. And he'd always had me believe she was the one who caused the problems.

It was him. All along it was him.

The realization jolted through me and I blinked my eyes open, startled. The voices were still murmuring.

I rolled over. It was coming from the kitchen. Not voices. A single voice. My cousin's quiet, calm one as she spoke into her phone. "Uh huh? Yeah maybe, I don't know."

I felt bad eavesdropping on her phone call. But if I moved then she'd know I was listening too. I froze and closed my eyes again, feigning sleep.

"But we're family too," Livvy was saying.

With a start, I realized she was talking about me.

"You could try that, I guess." She paused, listening to whoever was on the other end of the line. "Ha! You know I'm never going to remember that. Text it to me."

What was she planning? I gripped the sheets. For a moment I longed to be back in Finn's trailer. In the little make-believe fantasy world where we were the only two people who existed.

Would he watch the DVD? Or had he thrown it out after our fight? Did he know I was gone? Was he pissed that I hadn't said goodbye?

It had gotten ugly in the end. But he'd done so much for me before that. Livvy was family and felt obligated to take care of me because of it. But Finn had taken me in for no other reason than we were friends and he cared about me. And he'd done it in such a low-key, unceremonious way that I been able to take it for granted.

Just like with my mom. Just like with Janet.

I was *just* as selfish as my father,

The realization made my whole body jerk like I'd touched a wall outlet. The shock was painful, and electric and filled me with revulsion.

No. I wasn't going to be this way anymore.

It was time to stop floating through life unconscious of the things people did for me every day.

Time to be grateful. Time to give back.

Time to stop being a selfish dick like my father.

I stood up and started folding the blankets neatly at the bottom of the couch.

"What are you doing?" My cousin was in the doorway.

"Making my bed."

"Don't worry about it."

"Hey Livvy?"

"Yeah?"

I went to my cousin. It had taken hitting rock bottom to pierce the bubble of childish self-centeredness. "Thank you. I mean it. You've done more for me already than I deserve."

"You're family," she said simply. But hugged me back.

I squeezed her tightly to me. "What am I going to do, Liv?"

"I'm not sure. What do you want to do?"

I took a deep breath. "Get answers."

"Even if they're hard to hear?" Livvy wanted to know.

I swallowed and nodded as I pulled back and stared at my feet. "I feel like I have to rewrite my own history," I said as I watched my toes wiggle. "Everything I thought I knew about myself is turning out to be a lie."

Livvy looked at me. "That's gonna be hard to do. Where do you even start?"

I shrugged. "No idea."

She nodded, then touched my shoulder lightly. "I'll be right here when you do."

Chapter Twenty-Seven

FINN

It was the second day in a row that I'd awoken to frost glittering on the ground.

Out of habit, I drank my espresso while staring out the window. If you'd asked me what I was looking for, I would have said nothing. Just enjoying the view. But if you watched me for longer than a minute, you would have known I was lying.

Because my gaze was fixed on one thing only. The rough, scraggly patch of dead grass that had recently been covered a bright blue tent.

It was still empty. She hadn't shown up somehow in the middle of the night.

Not that I wanted her to. I mean, I *did*. But not until I was ready.

Not until I could confess my love and feel worthy to ask for hers in return.

I took another sip and then rested my cup on my leg.

That's what four days without Sky in my life had given me. A dogged determination to be the man she deserved.

I'd started the only way I knew how. By sitting down with my laptop with my credit card in hand. I clicked through a bunch of articles, scratching notes on a piece of paper until I'd made a pretty good list. It might not have been the 'cultural touchstone education' Sky had planned for me, but it was a start.

The box full of old paperback classics arrived yesterday. Amazon will deliver anywhere, apparently. Including a campsite at the very edge of the middle of nowhere.

The DVDs were arriving one at a time from dealers. They'd been coming in fits and starts. Which was fine. Because tonight I was going to re-watch *My Fair Lady*.

When the old dude sang, "I've grown accustomed to her face," I kind of understood what he was talk-singing about.

With her gone, I'd spent my days learning the things she'd wanted to teach me. Today I planned on starting *The Great Gatsby* after breakfast.

If I could stop waiting at the window.

What the hell was I doing? It wasn't like her tent would just appear there, springing up like some bright blue mushroom. With a grunt of annoyance, I dragged my eyes away from her site, and forced myself to scan the rest of the campground.

It was unusually crowded for the last day in September. I'd thought the cold weather would keep driving people away. But there were a few more tents scattered across the grounds than yesterday.

I looked up at the sound of car wheels crunching across the gravel. It was an older station wagon that looked familiar. I watched it bump closer and remembered where I'd seen it before. At the front of the camp. Parked in front of the owner's cabin.

I leaned forward... Then stood straight up when it came to a stop. Right next to Sky's lot.

A bearded man jumped from the passenger seat and opened the back door. He held out his hand, helping a woman climb out of the back seat.

As she emerged, her long braid swung behind her. The same kind of braid Rachel wore back when she and Beau first got together.

I'd hardly started making sense of this when she reached into the car and hefted a tiny child into her arms. She turned and looked at the man again. Her posture was one of, 'what now?'

Her answer - and mine - came when the driver's side door opened.

I'd seen the pink-sweatshirted woman from the camp store several times. But she'd always been behind the counter. I was perversely surprised to see that she had legs. I was even more surprised to see that her hair was braided in the same way as the woman holding the child. It swung behind her as she walked around to the young couple.

She hugged the woman first, gesturing with her hands and nodding repeatedly. The young woman looked down and nodded. Then shook her head and looked at the young man, who crossed his arms over his chest. The woman from the camp store touched his arm, and then went to her trunk and pulled out a faded green bundle. He looked at the young woman, and then rushed around to collect the bundle. The young woman jiggled the baby on her hip, then stiffened like she'd heard something. The baby was barely old enough to walk, but she set it down before reaching into the backseat again.

She emerged cradling a tiny bundle, swaying and soothing. The baby on the ground tugged at her skirt and then plopped down on its butt. The young mother fluttered a second, then bent and scooped the bigger one up with the smaller one.

I was impressed. I wondered if my mom had looked like that with Beau and me once Claire came along. That kind of kid-juggling was usually a two person job. But the guy she was with was over wrestling with the green bundle.

With a sickening jolt, I realized it was a tent. The camp store woman was pulling away, leaving the young couple at Sky's site. They had two babies and were about to spend a night - that would no doubt dip into freezing temperatures - in a faded old Army tent.

Instinct propelled me out my door and right across the road before rational thinking made me stop and raise my hand in greeting. "Good morning!' I called.

The woman turned first, fear written all over her face. "Cute kids!" I called. "You guys just getting here, huh?"

This was stupid. What the hell was I doing besides freaking her out even more? Back the trailer, I'd thought she was older than me. But now I could see she was Claire's age. Maybe even younger.

And though his beard aged him, the guy was younger than me for sure. He glared at me, glancing between me and the woman several times. Then abandoned his tent-erecting and came over to stand right next to her. He crossed his arms over his chest like a knight guarding his castle.

I swallowed. "Have a good day, then," I called, getting the message loud and clear. With another wave, I went back into my trailer.

But they stayed with me the rest of the day, that small family. I found myself drawn to the window again and again, watching that faded green tent see if they'd come out again. Trying to engineer a way to "bump into them" and offer something hot to drink. What were they doing out in this weather with such little ones? And did that braid mean what I thought it meant?

I finished The Great Gatsby in record time - and without absorbing a single word. I was too distracted by checking out the window every five seconds. Were they okay? How would I know if they weren't? They wouldn't talk to me. They seemed terrified to even look my way.

It dawned on me. Slowly at first, because this 'caring about others' thing was still new to me. But when I finally figured it out, I smacked myself in the forehead.

Sure, *they* wouldn't talk to me. But the woman from the camp store? Talking to me was her very favorite thing in the world.

Maybe I could finally put that endearing personality quirk of hers to good use.

I walked briskly past the faded tent. I could hear voices inside, too low to understand, but they went quiet as soon as they heard my footsteps.

This young family, with two tiny kids, was crammed into a single person tent. In the middle of a cold snap. And being really sneaky about it too.

They had to be hiding from something.

But what?

I hurried on to the camp store with questions circling in my brain. I hoped like hell the woman in the pink sweatshirt would be there and feeling chatty.

She was, except her sweatshirt was blue now. And she was wearing a name tag over her heart.

Wait, had that always been there and I only noticed now?

"How are you today, Mr. Prince?" she asked with a bright smile.

"I'm good, Dinah, thanks."

She looked startled that I'd called her by her name. I wandered around, picking up items at random.

And then my curiosity got the best of me.

"So. I see I have some new neighbors?"

Dinah gave a tight, cautious smile. "They're not going to bother you," she said quickly. "They won't be here more than a couple days."

"I'm not worried about them bothering me. I was just curious if you could tell me anything about them."

"Why do you want to know?"

It was a fair question. I've never showed an interest in any of the other guests. "The little kids. Do they need coats or anything?"

Dinah's mouth twitched. "They might."

"And the mom, um. Her braid?"

Her face went as rigid as a stone. *Why do you care?* a voice inside of me screamed. *It's not your problem.*

Because this is what a good person would do. I had no idea if that was the case, but it seemed right.

"It's just," I went on. "It reminds me of my future sister-in-law's." I looked up at her. "Yours does too."

Her eyes widened. She ducked her head and covered her mouth with her hand so that I had to lean in to hear her. "Is your sister-in-law Chosen?" she asked in a tight whisper. Then glanced behind me as if she expected someone to be listening.

Startled by her fear, I nodded, dropping my voice to match hers. "She grew up there, yeah. But she left, uh...." I wracked my brain, trying to remember Rachel's story. It felt wrong that I couldn't remember the exact dates, because I was certain I had heard them before. Was I really so wrapped up in my own mental breakdown that I had forgotten? "Three years ago," I said, with a sudden rush of triumph. "She left because she couldn't have kids."

"You mean Rachel?" Dinah gasped.

I pressed my lips together, uncertain about whether I should be say anything further. But Dinah was nodding faster and faster. “Then I’ll tell you, because you’re family.” She licked her lips and lowered her voice some more. “After the season ends, you know, after it clears out from too many eyes, I let them use it.”

“Who?”

“Families that want to escape. I give them a place." She gestured. “They can use it as a way station.

I could not have been more startled if she reached across the counter and slapped me in the face. “You do that for them?”

She nodded and lifted her braid. “Family is family,” she stated in a way that made me certain she’d said those words before.

Before I knew what I was doing, I’d grabbed my wallet. "Here," I said, pulling out every bit of cash I had left and dumping it on the counter in front of her.

She looked startled. "What is this for?"

I looked down at it. “Get them started. Help them make a new life. They deserve a fresh start."

“I can't accept this." She was shaking her head with her hands lifted, like she was afraid to touch it.

“If you won’t give it to them, then I will.”

"Maybe you should," Dinah said with a little glint in her eye. "I haven't seen you talking to anyone since that blonde with the pretty eyes left. I was getting worried about you. Couple times, I almost knocked on your door."

"Yeah." I swallowed hard.

"Have you heard from her?" Dinah pressed.

I shook my head. “No."

"You want me to ask if anyone knows where she ended up?" Her grin was proud. "I've got a lot of people.”

I licked my lips and looked at the drift of bills on the counter. It wasn’t enough. But it was a start. And maybe it could be a start... for *me*.

“Not yet,” I told Dinah. “Soon.”

Chapter Twenty-Eight

SKY

When Livvy got home from work, she stopped dead in the middle of her kitchen and gaped. "Oh my God!" she cried.

I jumped up from where I'd been kneeling by the sink and stretched the cramp from my neck. Then wiped away a piece of hair that was stuck in my sweat. "You're home? Shit. I thought I still had another hour. It's still a mess."

"No. It's not." Livvy looked around her, open mouthed.

I brushed my hair back again and smiled as I watched her take in my efforts.

Phase one of project 'stop being a selfish asshole' was well underway. I'd spent this morning tackling the massive cleaning project Livvy hadn't managed to get to yet.

Starting with the kitchen. I'd opened all the windows and washed the streaks from the glass. I'd scrubbed the dead bugs from the screens and washed the grime from the windowsills. I'd mopped the floor, and then mopped it again. I'd emptied an entire bottle of scouring powder into the sink and scoured it until it shone like new. I'd pulled everything out of the grubby cabinets and washed every single shelf. Then I washed all the dishes for good measure.

It was like a new place... if I did say so myself. The dusty gloom had lifted and light was now streaming in through the windows. What dirt I couldn't get up with fevered scrubbing had been thoroughly doused in bleach. Janet used to call that 'clean dirt.'

"Holy crap, Sky. You cleaned my kitchen. It must have taken forever!" Livvy stepped into the center of the linoleum floor and twirled in a full circle. "It's not gritty under my feet anymore!" she laughed. "It must have been so gross!"

"Now you can have people over," I said, and then laughed when she squealed and hugged me.

Then she pulled back and wrinkled her nose. "Oof, girl. You need a shower."

I laughed and nodded. "Like I said, I thought I had another hour. I was gonna take one once I finished up."

She grabbed the sponge from my hand. "You're finished. Come on, go get cleaned up."

"What's the hurry?"

"We're going out."

"Out?"

"It's Thursday." She said this like it was significant.

"What's Thursday?"

"Just come on!"

I still smelled like bleach, but at least I was cleaned up. Because it turned out that Thursday was the night Livvy met her friends at the Crown Tavern, a bar right smack dab in the middle of town.

It was a wood-paneled, comfortable place. The reassuring scent of a million spilled beers rose from the wide-planked floor. I walked in and let the heavy door swing shut behind me, my eyes quickly adjusting to the homey dimness. The front end was given over to a small stage area where an acne-riddle teenager was strumming his guitar for a few uninterested patrons. But the back end was scattered with mismatched tables and chairs, and that's where we headed.

A bearded, barrel-chested man who looked like he ate a dozen eggs every morning glowered at us from behind the bar. Livvy gave him a cheerful wave. "That's Taylor," she explained. "He hates everything and everyone, so just ignore him."

"*She's* not ignoring him." I gestured to the girl perched on a barstool. She had her elbows planted on the bar and was staring Taylor down with a serious expression on her face.

Livvy called out to her. "Sadie! Hey! This is my cousin Sky."

Sadie turned with that same serious expression on her face. She looked at me so long I felt like she was inspecting me with X-ray vision. "Your eyes are like your name," she finally announced.

I blinked at her directness. "You're right."

"Was that intentional?"

"Not by me."

She leaned in and pressed her finger to my wrist. "You should own it," she whispered.

"Hey!" A loud voice rang out across the bar. Sadie, Livvy and I all turned to see a tall woman with a short, blonde bob approaching us. She was dragging a reluctant looking guy behind her. "That's Claire," Livvy whispered to me. "Don't let her scare you. She's all bark and no bite."

I grinned and nodded.

"Is this her?" Claire bellowed, pointing to me. "The cousin?"

I opened my mouth to agree with her, and then froze.

Claire was close enough now for me to see her eyes.

There was no one else on earth with hazel eyes that matched Finn's in intensity.

Except, possibly, his sister.

As I stood there, frozen to the spot, Claire finished dragging the guy forward. "This idiot actually thought he was staying in tonight," she announced for the group. She stared him down.

"That's Ethan," Livvy jumped in to explain. "He's cousins with Taylor, which is why she's dragging him along like this. Whenever he comes out with us, Taylor lets us drink for free."

"And he thought he could get out of it, too," Claire laughed.

I couldn't help staring at her. I felt like I needed to shake my head over and over again, just to keep it clear enough to make sense of her.

Her expressions were the same as Finn's, right down to the

eyebrows she could arch one at a time. She had his same intensity, no doubt, though hers was definitely less brooding. And more bossy.

I knew all this because I'd spent time with her brother. More recently than she had, I knew that too. And the sheer heavy guilt of it weighed me down like I was holding a bowling ball.

What did I owe him? What did she know? If mentioned a guy at the campground with eyes like hers, how would she react? Would she be happy? Angry?

Or maybe she already knew and I'd be butting into her family's business for no reason at all?

I'd just started over in this town. Could I afford to have enemies already?

It was that thought that had me pressing my lips together and swallowing hard. "You okay?" Livvy murmured when she saw me standing there like my feet were stapled to the floor. "I know, Claire can be a bit much. But once she's on your side, there's no one better."

"Yeah, I'm a ride or die bitch," Claire piped up, clearly eavesdropping.

"Emphasis on the bitch," Ethan muttered. When Claire socked him in the stomach, he smiled like it was a kiss. "What? I told you I needed to stay home tonight! I have a paper to do."

Claire leveled him with her gaze. "You're boring and annoying and I only use you for rides."

I blinked at Claire's rudeness. But from the way Ethan was looking at her, I got the feeling that this how she always talked to him. And he loved it. And loved her too.

"So *anyway,*" Livvy interjected. "Sky's crashing on my couch for a hot minute." She looked at her group. "You guys remember me talking about Sky, right? My cousin who worked on Broadway?"

"Off-Broadway," I corrected, even though I was touched she'd bragged about me. "And the show closed the second night."

"Are you an actor?" Sadie asked as she floated over from Taylor to join us.

I shook my head. "Costumer. Wardrobe, mostly."

"Wait!" Claire raised her index finger for quiet, then pointed it at me. "Are you the cousin from Reckless Falls?"

I lifted my chin. "Yeah, I grew up there."

A hush fell over the group. Claire looked at Livvy, who looked away. Sadie stared at me. Ethan looked up at the ceiling.

"What?" I asked. Then it dawned on me. "Did you tell them?" I demanded of Livvy.

"Not all of it!" Livvy protested, looking guilty as all hell. "But, like, remember how I told you you didn't have to do it alone?"

"Ride or die," Claire added with an emphatic nod.

I was shaking my head. ""How can we ride? I don't even know where were going yet?"

"When the times comes, though. We'll be ready."

I opened my mouth to tell her than I wasn't 'ride or die,' I was 'run and flee.' Then I closed it, my cheeks burning. I was embarrassed and touched at the same time. I was mad at Livvy for spilling my secrets. And thankful she'd gathered her posse on my behalf.

The posse got bigger as the night wore on. We were joined by Livvy's friends Naomi and Ryan, who acted just like a couple in spite of everyone protesting that they weren't. Then tiny, petite Ruby showed up and enveloped me in a giant hug when Livvy introduced me. She waved to Jonah, who could only be related to Finn and Claire and laughed when he swung her around in a circle. Curly haired Willa popped up behind them with her blue-eyed man Cooper in tow, and both of them acted like I was a long lost sister. Which I guess I was. Just not to them.

All through the night, I was alternately teased and hugged. Ethan brought over rounds from the bar and made sure I got first pick. Claire gave me the dirt on everyone sitting with us. Sadie quizzed me on my zodiac sign. Ruby made me a new playlist. Willa promised to teach me how to cook.

I left that night with my face hurting from laughing so hard and a whole bunch of new numbers programmed in my phone.

And for some reason, I was certain that even if I lost touch with these people, like I always did, they would not lose touch with me.

It was all very confusing.

Chapter Twenty-Nine

FINN

"Bless you, honey," Dinah sighed as she took the cup of espresso I'd handed her.

She glanced at the door and I chuckled. "No one's going to catch you," I reassured her.

"I feel guilty, you know?" She took a sip and closed her eyes. "Getting to drink this while my customers have to drink that swill?" She jerked her thumb at the carafe of coffee that always seemed to be filled to the exact same level. "It ain't fair."

"It's plenty fair." I nodded as she pulled out a stool and patted it. Then sat down beside her.

This had become our little morning ritual. I'd bring her a decent cup of coffee, and she'd me sit behind the counter. She always made sure to fill me in on the comings and goings of my neighbors. "And fifteen A is finally leaving today," she told me between sips of her drink. "I thought I was going to have to call Jim at the police department."

"Are you going after fifteen A for the rent?" I asked.

She waved her hand. "He needs it more than me. And honestly, it's a blessing he even decided to leave. Did you know he planted a garden? He was thinking *long-term*." She widened her eyes comically.

I laughed along with her, but inside I was shaking my head in amazement. Dinah's open-hearted generosity never failed to bowl me over. I'd always thought that my brother Beau was the only good person in the world.

Then I'd met Sky. Then Dinah.

I took another sip and tried not to think about how wrong I'd been. About so many things.

The wind caught the door as it opened, sending it flying back against the building with a sharp bang. Dinah nearly spilled her espresso. "Merciful heavens, Adam! You sure do know how to make an entrance!"

I stared at the man in the doorway. Adam. So my neighbor in the faded green Army tent was named Adam.

He looked between me and Dinah and then back to me, his expression unreadable. "Hey man," I said over the rim of my cup.

He looked pleadingly at Dinah. She gestured at me. "Adam, this is my friend Finn - ."

"King," I finished. Before she could use my alias. I felt Dinah staring at me, but I kept my eyes on Adam. "I'm Finn King. And my brother Beau is engaged to Rachel Walker."

Saying it felt like some kind of battle cry. I hadn't taken ownership of the simple fact of my family connections in a long, long time.

Rachel's name had the exact same effect on Adam as it did on Dinah. The tension eased out of his shoulders, though his expression was still wary. "Hello," he said, with a small wave.

It was a start.

"Dinah?" he asked, turning to her. "Is there any food in here that doesn't need to be heated up? Our wood is wet."

"Sure honey, you can check down that aisle right there," Dinah started to say.

But then jumped again when I leaped from my stool. "Merciful heavens," she complained, wiping at the drop she'd spilled on her sweatshirt. "You move way too fast."

"Sorry, Dinah. But Adam?" I called across the store. I had to say it before I lost my nerve. "Do you need to cook tonight? Come over to my trailer. I'm right across the way."

My sister, Claire would never be caught dead deferring to a man. But if she did, she'd be subtly bossy about it.

Exactly like Adam's wife, Esther.

"Sit down," she ordered me for the second time. "I'll have it out in a second."

I hovered at the edge of the kitchen she'd banished me from. My own kitchen. "You need help finding anything?" I asked.

"Sit!" she barked.

I turned and looked at Adam, who was already sitting at the table with a giant grin on his face. He caught my eye and shrugged, and his grin got even wider.

If ever there was such thing as aggressive deference, it would be what Esther was practicing. We were the men, so by God she would cook for us. Even if she had to shout at us until we let her.

"She's happy to have a kitchen again," Adam explained in an undertone as I sat down across from him. "It's been bothering her."

"I can see that," I said as I watched Esther. She moved in double time, fixing a meal for all five of us - right down to mashing peas for little Charity who was currently toddling across my floor towards my boots. And she did it all with tiny Hannah slung over one shoulder.

She served us with Hannah in place too, and then went off to nurse her in the bathroom while Adam and I ate. Adam hefted Charity up into his lap and tried to force some peas into her mouth, but she wailed until he set her back down again. "She's not used to me feeding her," he explained, watching Charity with sad eyes. "The men usually have nothing to do with the care of children."

"Did that bug you?" I asked. He was staring at his little red-faced daughter with an expression of pure love. "Is that why you left?"

Adam looked up. I turned to look where he was looking.

Esther had emerged from the bathroom adjusting her top. Hannah was passed out in her arms.

She looked at the two of us. "Go on," she said to Adam with an encouraging nod.

Adam took a shaky breath. "Being pregnant with Hannah nearly killed her," he said, watching Esther the whole time. "When we were matched, I couldn't believe my good fortune. I was blessed beyond all comprehension. I remember getting down on my knees, thankful that I could spend the rest of my days with the woman I loved more than anyone else." He brushed a finger down Hannah's cheek as Esther lowered her into his arms. "Except you, maybe," he cooed to the infant. "Our little miracle."

"Are you okay?" I asked Esther.

She looked at Adam again.

"Hemorrhage," he told me. "It happened with Charity too, but this was so much worse. She needed so much blood." He shook his head and squeezed the infant tighter. "How could I put her through that again?" he cried. He seemed to be asking me, truly wanting to know. "How could I do it, and leave my daughters without a mother?"

Slowly, I pieced it together. "She's on birth control."

Esther ducked away, heading back into the kitchen where she felt safer. I looked at her, then back to Adam. "Did they kick you out?"

"No." He shook his head. "We left together." His voice dropped to a whisper. "She's still adjusting. She's not sure about it. But I tell you, we're not going back." He shook his head and raised his voice again so Esther could hear. "I'd rather suffer eternal damnation than murder my own wife."

Chapter Thirty

FINN

Sky brushed her fingers down my face. I smiled in my sleep, tilting my head up to her and sighing. I was so glad she was back. How could I have ever let her go?

I rolled over. "Good morning," I murmured to her.

She poked me in the eye.

I jerked awake. Two curious eyes inspected me and a chubby finger was being aimed at my eye again. "Oh," I said, pulling my face back out of toddler range. "Good morning, Charity."

Charity stared down at me as I stretched and sat up. Then shivered. I was in the faded green tent, I remembered. Adam and Esther had slept in the trailer last night. "What are you doing here?" I asked the toddler.

"Buh," she informed me and yanked on my beard.

"Eesh, yeah you got some good finger strength there. You should play bass."

"Charity!" Esther's panicked voice carried across the whole campground. I scrambled to my feet and poked my head out of the tent flap, impressed that a kid who could barely walk had managed to unzip it. She definitely had future bass-player fingers. "She's with me!" I called across the road.

"There you are!" Esther flew across the road in a flurry of skirts and scooped up her daughter, shaking with relief. Charity let out an indignant squawk. "I thought they took you," she whispered against her daughter's cheek. Then she turned to me. "I'm so sorry, she's been going on these little adventures lately."

Then Esther suddenly recalled herself. Her eyes widened and she stared at me.

I looked down and realized I wasn't wearing a shirt. "Sorry," I muttered. But she wasn't running away. That was... progress? "And don't worry about it. She's gonna conquer the world someday," I said, tugging on the toddler's fat little foot.

Esther's smile was pure pride. "That's what I'm hoping," she said shyly. Then she looked at me again. "Thank you for letting us sleep in your trailer. It was nice to be able to stretch out." She jiggled her daughter up and down. "Even though this one takes up half the bed."

"I can imagine." I reached into the tent and pulled out the waffle-weave Henley I'd been wearing last night and pulled it over my head. "And you guys are welcome to it again tonight, too. Keep these little toes warm." I tugged at Charity's foot again and she giggled and kicked.

"Thank you, but it's not necessary." Adam had come across the way to meet us. "She's asleep," he whispered to his wife after kissing her cheek. "I put her on the floor between some pillows."

"It's fine, man," I told him. "I actually slept really good out here. Fresh air and everything. The girl who was staying here before you guys, she got on me a lot about not properly roughing it. She said I wasn't really camping at all, so I can't wait to tell her she was wrong."

"Is she coming back?" Esther wondered.

I snapped my mouth shut. What the hell was I telling them about Sky for? "I don't know." I crossed my arms over my chest. "I hope? Maybe?"

"Thank, Finn. Sincerely. For everything." Adam hesitated and stretched out his hand. "But it's not necessary."

I accepted his handshake. "What do you mean?" I started to ask.

But trailed off when my answer came in the form of Dinah's staton wagon bumping towards us. I swallowed hard. Without thinking, I reached out and squeezed Charity's foot again, a lump forming in my throat. "You guys are leaving?"

"Dinah found us a place to stay," Adam explained. He lifted his chin towards her approaching car, and all four of us watched the car bump towards us.

"Mornin'," Dinah called, once she'd shut off the engine. "Oh, Finn, you're here too? How are you doin' today?"

"You're moving them?" It came out more aggressively than I meant it, but I couldn't seem to let go of Charity's little foot. I was having the strangest feeling of unwanted deja vu.

Dinah narrowed her eyes. "Of course. They can't be staying in a tent forever."

"Is it safe where they're going?"

"As safe as I can make it."

"Where is it?" My heart was racing like a panicked horse. My fist itched to fight something and I dropped Charity's foot before I inadvertently hurt her. "In town? You can't know that they won't come after them there." Rachel's sister had walked all the way to her house just to shame her into returning. It had broken my brother when she'd gone back. "What about security?"

Dinah's wise eyes shone with surprise, and understanding. "There's a house we use," she explained. "It was donated to us by a secular family. We use it as a way station for times like this." She turned and addressed Adam. "One of the bedrooms opened up, but there are still three other people staying there right now. It might be a little cramped, but it'll be better than staying in a tent."

"Finn let us stay in his trailer last night," Esther said softly.

Dinah gave me another one of her understanding looks. Like she was seeing something I wasn't yet aware of. "Did he now?" was all she said. After a heavy pause, she nodded. "Right, let's get you going, okay? Best to do this before too many of the paying guests wake up and wonder what's going on. There ain't too many of them still hanging around, though, so that's good."

"'Cept me," I reminded her. "I'm seeing everything that's going on."

"You don't count, Finn," Dinah chuckled. "You're different."

"I —."

"Help me get this tent loaded up?" Dinah asked.

Esther handed Charity to Adam, then knelt to gather their meager possessions. She folded everything into a cardboard box Dinah had brought with her. Adam returned to the trailer with one daughter and re-emerged holding them both. Both he and Esther chatted excitedly with Dinah as they loaded first the boxes - and then the babies - into the station wagon.

And all the while I broke down their tent, unable to say anything around the lump that clogged my throat.

What had I hoped? What did I want to say? Why did I want to thank them? Why did I feel they'd done something for me that I couldn't have done for myself?

Half formed sentences and clumsy explanations twisted together into an impossible knot in my head.

So I said nothing. And in no time, they'd packed and were ready to go.

I stood with my hands shoved in the pockets of my sweatpants as they climbed into the car. "Good luck," I managed to croak out as Dinah started the engine. Then held up my hand. "Wait!"

I raced back to the trailer.

Dinah was watching me with that look in her eyes when I rushed back up to the car, the wad of bills waving in my hand. "Take this," I urged Adam, opening the passenger side door and shoving the money at his chest.

He looked down at it in shock. "I can't -," he faltered.

"Finn?" Esther stepped out of the back seat.

She took two steps forward. And hugged me tight.

I went stiff. And then wrapped my arms around her and hugged her back.

"You're a good man," she whispered urgently. "They tell us you're all evil. But you're not. There's good in the world." She pressed her hand to my chest. "And there's good in your heart."

I stared at her. Then choked and looked away. She waited a moment. Then nodded and went back to the car. "Please try to remember that," she said, before climbing back in. "Please. Try."

Chapter Thirty-One

SKY

The Chit Chat Cafe was a low-slung, yellow-sided building with a roof that bowed in the middle. Inside, the floor sloped at such a steep angle that I stumbled when I first walked in.

Livvy looked back. "Oh whoops! Yeah, sorry. Should have warned you, this place is like a funhouse. I don't think there's a right angle in the entire building."

"You seem fine though," I observed as I watched my feet.

"I used to work here," she explained. "It's like getting your sea legs, you know?"

The fact that the whole building was in danger of imminent collapse didn't seem to affect business in any way. It was one of those rare places that everyone seemed to like. And I mean *everyone.* Families still dressed for church sat around the wobbly tables and nibbled their pastries carefully so as not to get crumbs on their Sunday best. Meanwhile, bleary-eyed community college students nursed their massive coffees in the corner booth, still hungover from the night before.

"What do you want?" Livvy asked, gesturing to the chalkboard sign listing the drinks. "Don't worry about getting something too fancy. It's Claire's turn to pay and she's the only one of us that has a job with actual medical benefits." She raised her voice as she said this so that Claire could overhear from the front door.

"I miss when you worked here and slipped me free drinks," Claire complained, hugging Livvy hello. Before I knew it, she'd crushed me to her in an aggressive hug. "What we need is for Ethan to have a cousin posted at every hangout in town," she mused, once she'd released me. "It'd be so much more economical that way."

"You tell him to get on that." Livvy had a mischievous glint in her eye. "I'm sure if you asked him, he'd make it happen ASAP."

I hid my snort behind my hand as Claire tossed her head. I'd only been hanging out with them for a little bit. Bu even I could see that Ethan and Claire were madly in love with each other.

"He's a pain in my butt, though," Claire sighed obliviously. She scanned the chalkboard. "Oh man, they don't have the Red-Eye anymore, that was my favorite."

"What was it?" I asked.

"Hot chocolate with a shot of espresso. My brother turned me on to it before - ."

She caught herself. Then started complaining about the mountain of work waiting for her tomorrow morning. I wouldn't have noticed she'd changed the subject, if I didn't know who she was talking about.

But I did. Her espresso addicted, hot chocolate loving brother.

Claire ended up ordering for all three of us while Livvy and I searched out a free table. We found one back in the corner, far away from the counter and sat down to wait. I shrugged off my jacket. It was warm enough that I welcomed the blast of wind that hit us every time someone opened the door. "Claire is sure taking her time," Livvy sighed.

"Ugh, sorry," Claire groaned as she hurried over and set down our drinks. "I got waylaid by the barista."

Livvy and I both craned our necks. "Wait, is that -?" Livvy asked.

"Don't say it -."

"Nose-boy?" Livvy finished with an evil laugh.

"Who is Nose-boy?" I asked, clueless.

Claire buried her face in her hands. "You're new in town, so let me give you a piece of advice. Don't try to date here. Unless you're a masochist, maybe. Then you're set for life."

"Claire is attempting to date for the first time," Livvy explained. "And it's not going well."

"But why is he Nose-boy?" There was nothing strange about the barista's nose that I could see.

Claire glared at Livvy. "Don't even say it."

"You tell it better anyway." Livvy made a 'go-ahead' gesture.

"Ugh." Claire straightened up and shook her head at me. "He brought me home the other night, and went in for a kiss."

"And?"

She shuddered in revulsion. "He missed."

"What?" I burst out laughing.

Claire groaned. "His tongue went right up my nose! Oh God, I can still feel it."

"What did you do?" I leaned in. The barista kept glancing our way. "He's watching you like a little boy who lost his balloon," I informed her.

"Ugh, I told him that I don't like kissing." She buried her face in her hands again while Livvy laughed and laughed. "Can you believe it? I just froze up! Instead of saying, 'you kiss like a fish with a nose fetish,' I told him I 'don't like kissing.' So now he thinks we're going out again, and everything will be hunky-dory so long as our lips never touch." She picked up her coffee cup. "What I wouldn't give for this to be alcohol right now. I swear, you guys, this is why I never dated before."

"No, you never dated because your brothers wouldn't let you," Livvy corrected.

"What changed?" I asked Claire. "You're allowed to now?"

She swirled her coffee cup around. "Well, the brother who had the biggest problem with it isn't around at the moment."

A little frission of something I didn't understand made me sit up straighter. "Where is he?"

Claire looked at Livvy. "Who the fuck knows?" she attempted to laugh.

"Claire's brother has been missing for a few weeks now," Livvy explained gently.

"Missing? You mean you don't know where he is?" I searched my mind, dredging up a passing mention Finn had made to a note. He'd left a note. Yes. He'd told them. Right? "What happened?"

Claire licked her lips and looked down. The usual fierce gleam in her eyes was gone, replaced by the glint of tears. "He just... disappeared. Took the guys' tour bus and..." She blinked rapidly.

My breath was coming faster now. Instantly I was back in the trailer with Finn. "Why do you think you're better off without him?" I'd shouted at him. "He's better off without me!" he'd yelled back.

We'd been talking about his brother, his twin. But here was his sister, blinking back tears in front of me, clearly showing how wrong Finn had been.

What do I owe him? He wasn't here. And Claire was, with her anxious hands and the worried bags under her eyes that I finally knew the cause of. Finn had been my friend. But now Claire was too.

Claire twisted her straw wrapper in her fingers. "Yeah, so anyway," she said, clearing her throat. "I'm finally free to fuck around Crown Creek."

"Oh please, you've been out with like two guys," Livvy scoffed. "And one of them is Nick."

"And he has the tiniest head," Claire finished, dissolving into relieved giggles that the subject had changed. "So he only counts as half."

"Does he count as half everywhere?" Livvy pressed with a waggle of her eyebrows.

"Olivia!" I joked. "You're *filthy*! My own cousin! I had *no* idea."

The girls laughed along with me but inside, I was waging a war. Should I tell her now? What if he wasn't even at the camp any more?

I looked away. Like the answer to what I should do was hiding somewhere in the coffee shop. I scanned past the people at the tables. Caught the eye of the barista who still gazed longingly at Claire. Averted my eyes from his...

And froze.

My panic about Claire and Finn vanished instantly, replaced with an entirely new panic.

"What's wrong?" Livvy asked me. She twisted in her seat to look where I was staring. "Who is... oh..." She trailed off and clapped her hand over her mouth.

"What?" Claire whipped around, more obvious than anyone in the world. "Who are we looking at? Oh *fuck*!"

I wanted to scream at her to be quiet and get her head down. But the man at the counter had already turned towards us. His dark, slashing eyebrows made his scowl look all the more fierce as he scanned our table

He looked at Livvy, then Claire. "That's not good," Claire mumbled.

And then his eyes landed on mine.

It was like looking into a mirror. It was like looking back in time to the worst day of my life. He'd stood up from comforting his sister and stared me down with those eyes as I stood near my father's coffin and felt my world drop out from under my feet. Eyes the same shade of blue as my father's. And mine.

His expression changed abruptly. Without a word, he snatched his coffee and stormed out. "Hey!" called the cashier after him. "Asshole! You forgot to pay!"

"Fuck." I took a deep breath, but I couldn't stop shaking and I had no idea why. Livvy reached over and rubbed soothing, mindless circles on my hand.

Claire leaped up. "Let's move," she ordered us. "Here!" She waved a twenty-dollar bill and slapped it on the counter. "For J.D.'s bill and ours." She turned back to my cousin and me. "Let's get out of here. I have a bad feeling."

I did too, so I was only too happy to leap up and follow my cousin and Claire. I was too confused, too scared to say anything, but I listened as they discussed me.

"Do you want to go to my house?" Claire asked as we piled into her Jeep. I sank gratefully into the back seat, happy we weren't in Livvy's car. Claire's felt less... vulnerable.

Livvy thought for a moment and then shook her head. "No, your parents have enough to worry about."

"My dad could use a new project though," she commented as she swung out of the parking lot and on to the road. "He's been getting weird since Finn... you know."

I opened my mouth to tell her about Finn. But the rev of a motorcycle engine made my spine tingle. I sat up straighter and looked out the back windshield.

There was a chopper right behind us. Another one was further behind us but gaining fast. "Is that him?" I squeaked.

"That's not J.D.," Claire said, shaking her head. "I'd much rather it was, though."

The light changed ahead of us. I held my breath as we rolled to a stop.

The two motorcycles veered apart. One pulled right up to the back window, and the other along the driver's side. Livvy squeaked in fear.

But Claire wasn't having it. "Seriously asswipe?" she shouted as she rolled down the window. "You really want to go there, Rocky?" she challenged the Knight brother next to her. "You really want me to sic my brothers on you?"

Whatever that meant to Rocky, it seemed to have the desired effect. He pulled back from Claire. But the Knight by my window wasn't done yet. He braced his bike and leaned so far in that his helmet visor tapped the glass. I reeled back. "Don't you hide," Claire hissed at me. "Don't let him win."

I nodded and sat up straighter. Then I lifted my chin at my brother.

"Atta girl, see that?" Claire roared. "You see that Maddox? Keep going, fucker! You're not scary!"

The light changed and the two Knight brothers gunned around us, forcing Claire to slam on her brakes. "Fuck you!" she shouted at their taillights.

My throat felt like it was closing. Livvy twisted around. "Sky? You okay?"

I pressed my palms to my knees to keep them from shaking. "Yeah," I said through clenched teeth. "Can we go home?"

"Yeah. Of course we can."

Claire drove us back to Livvy's house, where my cousin immediately went for the liquor cabinet and poured me a shot. Claire fired off a string of text messages and one by one the Thursday night crew arrived.

I sat in my cousin's kitchen and let my new family take care of me. But I still could not shake the fear of my real one.

Chapter Thirty-Two

FINN

It had been eight days since Adam and Esther left, and by now I was used to the knocks coming in the middle of the night.

I jolted up, fully awake, the dream of Sky floating away before I could dwell on it too long and hurried to my trailer door.

Dinah was there in her puffy jacket, her breath steaming in the cold night air. "Where?" I asked her, already pulling on my coat.

"On the road," she said, keeping her voice low even though there was no one around overhear us. "He'll know it's you if you flash your lights three times." I let the door slam behind me as I followed her out. "You got your phone? In case anything goes wrong?"

"Right here." I patted my pocket to show her I still had the burner phone she'd given me last week. "Is he staying?" Our shoes crunched on the frost covered gravel as we hurriedly worked out the plan.

"No, he needs a bus ticket," Dinah explained. "I already placed the calls. His aunt in California knows to look out for him."

"A bus? Don't you think a plane ticket would be better?"

Dinah stopped short and put her hand on my shoulder. I couldn't see her eyes in the dark, but I knew she was looking at me with that same mixture of understanding and exasperation she always wore.

"Finn. Don't forget. This child has barely ever been in a *car*. I think a plane might be too much for him. Don't you?"

I swallowed down my rebuttal and nodded. After all, she was the boss and I was the muscle in this little two-person Underground Railroad.

I'd learned about the Underground Railroad from a book about Harriet Tubman. One of the books I'd bought right after Sky left. I'd told Dinah that's what we were and she liked it so much that's what she was calling it now. The Chosen Underground Railroad.

Dinah was afraid that her station wagon had been spotted last time we used it for a pick-up. So I took one of the cars our mysterious 'secular' benefactors had dropped off, and headed out into the night.

It was dark, the kind of total darkness that can only come right before dawn. I drove the empty miles through the black, watching the odometer tick over every tenth of a mile.

Exactly eight and four tenths of a mile down County Road Twelve, I pulled over to the shoulder and flashed my lights three times.

A skinny shadow shot across the road and yanked open the door. The second he was in, I started driving again.

I knew by now that conversation with these kids was impossible until I'd gotten them far enough away that they could breathe easy. So I drove through the night in silence, not even looking at my passenger's face. He'd been taught his whole life to be afraid of people like me, so I really didn't want to scare him.

Each person I picked up was different. Some needed a house, furnishings, a way to stand on their own. Others, like this kid, just needed someone to open the door for them and tell them it was okay to walk through it.

"Who's meeting you?" I asked after I put enough miles out between us and the compound that he started to relax.

He made a startled noise, but quickly pulled himself together. "My aunt."

"Was she in too?" I asked, glancing over at him for the first time.

He had the body of a man, but the voice of a confused, scared boy. I wished I could turn on the light and see his face, but I knew that would scare him. "No, she's secular," he answered me. "She's been trying to get my mom out for a long time. I guess I'm the next best thing?"

"Do you know her?"

He didn't answer. I could feel the fear coming off of him. "Hey listen," I said, launching into the story I'd told so many times now it was becoming a script. "Did you know Rachel Walker?"

"Yeah?" The familiar name made him sit up straighter.

I nodded. "She's out too. And she's family. She going to be my sister-in-law."

The kid was nodding. "She's marrying that rock music guy?"

"That's my brother." Another one of those guilty pangs. I pushed it down. "She's doing good, kid. So good. She's happy. And free." Of course, I didn't know any of this. For all I knew everything had gone to shit since I left. "She's got a new life. Just like you're going to. You've got people, they'll help you." I reached into my pocket as I pulled into the well-lighted bus station and peeled off a couple bills in my wallet. "Take it," I said, shoving it at him. "Your ticket is waiting for you right there. Under the name Finn Prince."

"Is that your name?" The streetlights lit enough of his face that I could see his hopeful smile. "I'm Gabriel."

The name sent a shock to my system. "That's my brother's name. My other brother, I mean. I have three of them. And a sister, too."

"You guys are all secular?"

Rachel had called us that too. "Yeah, Gabriel. We're secular."

He looked me full in the face. "So why are you doing this? Why are you helping me?"

"It's a long story." I lifted my chin. "Go on. I think that's your bus right there."

He rushed out, then turned like he wanted to embrace me. I looked at my hands on the steering wheel.

They tried to do that, these people we spirited it out in the middle of the night. They tried to find a way to stay in contact. Even for the briefest moment in time that we were together, they still wanted to hold on to me.

I didn't want that. Not from any of them, and especially not from

Gabriel. I didn't want him feeling obligated to me. He'd never know it, but I needed this way more than he did.

"Get going," I barked at him.

He looked frightened, and ran off. And I hated myself for having to scare him to get him away. They did this too, these people we helped. They always hesitated right before leaving. I never understood why. Because I knew, that if I were in their situation, I would rush for freedom and never look back.

That's what I told myself as I drove back through the night.

But the sun was coming up. And the darkness, which had hidden my surroundings from view, was lifting.

With a start, I realized I knew what road I was on.

If I drove for another ten minutes, I'd be home.

What would it take to step back into my old life?

Was I ready?

Was I worthy?

For the first time since I left, I let myself think about it. I let my mind be open to the idea of reclaiming my life as Finn King. Could I do it? Could I apologize? Tell my brother I thought I was doing the right thing?

Then ask him to help me find Sky?

Sky. With her big laugh, and bright blue eyes. With her fire and sass and sarcasm.

Esther had told me I was a good man. I almost believed her.

But was I good enough for Sky?

Chapter Thirty-Three

SKY

"This has been the week from hell," Claire sighed, shoving my blankets over so she could plop down on Livvy's couch. "And I'm broke as fuck to add to it."

"So what's the plan?" Livvy asked. "We skipping Thursday?"

Claire looked scandalized. "No way!" She pressed a shocked hand to her heart and pretended to hyperventilate. "How dare you blaspheme?" The doorbell rang and she stood up grinning. "No, we're just pre-gaming here first."

"She invited people over to your house?" I muttered to Livvy as Claire went to the door and let in Willa, Ruby, and Sadie.

Livvy shrugged happily. "It's Claire. I don't ask questions. I just go along for the ride.

It was one hell of a ride too. By the time eight o'clock rolled around, we were two bottles deep into the red wine. Claire declared herself 'on a mission from God,' and dragged a stool over to Livvy's newly cleaned liquor cabinet. "You have terrible taste in tequila!" she shouted from up near the ceiling.

"I have bad taste in friends too!" Livvy laughed.

"Wait." I sat up straighter. "Do you guys hear that?"

The five girls went silent, listening with me. A faint whine, no more audible than a mosquito in the room. But it was getting louder.

My hands shook so hard I had to set down my wine-glass.

Sadie shook her head. "Calm down," she instructed. "Breathe in through one nostril, then out through the other." Easy for her to say. Everything I'd seen pointed to "calm" being Sadie's default state.

"What the heck are you talking about?" I strained to listen. Was it coming closer?

"Try not to worry so much." Willa's motherly air made her seem a lot older than the rest of the girls around the table. "You've been jumping at every noise, honey.

"Have I?"

"What are you so worried about?"

"I'm not sure." I tried to snap out of it. But the feeling of impending doom was too much for me. It had been hanging around, like a dark cloud on the horizon, ever since our run-in with the Knights at the coffee shop.

I was waiting for the storm to hit. The question was.... When?

That made it impossible to pretend things were normal. But the only other option was to sit and go crazy. And I'd already done enough of that for one week.

On Monday, I'd tried to go out and find a job. But I got scared when I spotted a man who could have *maybe, possibly* been at the my Dad's funeral and rushed back to the safety of Livvy's house.

On Tuesday, I sat down with Livvy's computer and tried to put in applications online. But I wasted the entire day on obsessive searches. First, for information on the Knights. Digging through police records and incident reports didn't help my anxiety, so I stopped that quickly. Then I fell down a Wikipedia rabbit hole about the music career of the King Brothers, only to log off in a panic when I saw a picture of young, smiling Finn.

Yesterday, I'd stood frozen to the spot, watching as Finn strolled hand in hand down the center of Main Street. Until he got closer and I realized, with a sickening jolt, that it was Beau. Finn's twin.

I'd ducked into the diner. It was empty at that hour of the day, and the lights were much brighter than when I'd been there last Thursday night. I walked the perimeter of the place as I waited for Finn's twin to pass.

Which gave me ample time to take note of every single mention of my father on the walls.

He'd apparently been some kind of town benefactor. His garage even sponsored the Little League Team. Knight's Knights. They'd won the championship six times in a row, which mean there were six different plaques on the wall with my father's face on them.

I felt like I was going crazy. Finn, my father — This town was full of ghosts. "I'm a little freaked out still," I tried to explain to Willa.

But Willa wasn't listening anymore. She'd turned her head because the sound was getting louder. One whine separated out into the sound of motorcycles.

Plural.

"Guys?" Livvy jumped up, knocking her legs against the table. No one gave a shit about the wine that spilled everywhere because we all moved at once. Claire was already at the door. Willa glanced at me, a question all over her face. Even Sadie looked a little alarmed. "What is it?" Livvy called.

I closed my eyes. The storm I'd been waiting for?

It was finally here.

"It's J.D." Claire reported from her post at the door.

I looked around wildly. "What should I do?"

"Hide?"asked Sadie.

Livvy shook her head. "You're not hiding!"

"Willa! Get the phone and dial 9-1," Claire barked from the door. Willa nodded.

"I'll call Jonah," Ruby said, dashing for the back door with her phone to her ear.

Livvy moved close to me. "You don't have to be afraid of anything," she said. "We've got your back."

"I don't even know why I'm scared," I confessed.

Heavy boots on the porch made us all jump and look to Claire. She went up on her tiptoes to see out the small rectangular window at the top. "Whaddya want, J.D.?" she bellowed through the door.

"We want to talk!" came another voice.

Claire went higher up on her tiptoes. "Oh yeah? Then talk!" she shouted.

"Come on, sis!" came that same taunting, mocking voice. "Whaddya doin' in there?"

"Back off, Maddox," Claire snapped. "You want me to tell Gabe you're being a punk? You think he's gonna like you scaring his sister like this?"

"You're not scared of anything, Claire." But I heard footsteps and Claire's shoulder relaxed slightly.

Then rose again. "The fuck?"

"I have a message for Sky Clarence Knight," came the smooth, unctuous voice on the other side of the door.

"Who is it?" Livvy hissed.

Claire turned with a confused expression on her face. "Marc Auburn."

"The lawyer?" Sadie gasped.

I looked between the three of them.

"Jonah's on his way," Ruby reported, hurrying over from the back door.

"You want me to dial one, Sky?" Willa's finger was poised over the call button on her phone.

I shook my head. So many questions. And no answers. I squeezed my eyes shut. "What's the message?" I squeaked.

There was a thump and the sound of men's voices arguing. I heard "Back off," and "... little bitch." Livvy squeezed my arm.

"I'm putting it in the mailbox, Miss Knight," came the lawyer's voice over the fray.

"And then get out of here," Claire called. "Marc? My Dad's gonna hear about this."

"I know, Miss King. Tell him I said hello."

Claire scowled.

As the footsteps retreated, I felt some of the tension drain away. Wills sighed and let her hand fall. Sadie blew out a long exhale and immediately started doing some neck rolls.

"What is it?" I asked Claire, who was still watching the porch.

"A letter," she reported. We heard the sound of engines starting.

I counted four of them and then the cough of a car starting.

Claire opened the door so fast she was a blur, then yanked it shut again with a bang that made us all jump.

"Here." She handed me the embossed envelope.

My new friends craned to look over my shoulder as I opened it and pulled out a piece of heavy, embossed paper. There were a few impersonal, typewritten words on a cover letter. Words like *beneficiary, bequeath,* and *heir.* But I had to read them over five different times before I could make sense of what they were saying.

"It's the deed to his house," I said, faintly. "My inheritance."

We stared at each other.

And then jumped when the door flew open.

"Jonah!" Claire screamed.

He was out of breath and wild eyed. He looked around in a panic, and then his face crumpled with relief when Ruby hurtled into him. He hugged her tight, whispering urgently and nodding when she nodded back. He touched her face one more time before moving to Claire and giving her a one-armed hug. "Hey, everyone," he said with a wave. "I'm here."

"Right on time, too," Claire laughed. "Now that the danger is over." But she wrapped her arm around his shoulder all the same.

Everyone started talking at once. Ruby tried to fill Jonah in on what happened, with frequent interruptions from his sister. Sadie kept trying to get everyone behind the idea of burning sage on the porch to dispel the evil energy. Willa drifted over to my side and looked at the envelope that had Livvy and I transfixed. "Is this what you wanted?" she asked me.

I opened my mouth and then closed it. What I wanted was my father back so I could get some answers. "It's something?" I whispered.

Livvy squealed and hugged me tight. "That means you're really staying!" she crowed.

Willa squealed too and I couldn't help but laugh as they both sandwiched me into a hug. But then I froze and looked up again.

"What the fuck?" Claire shouted at the same moment Sadie cried, "They're back!" The paper skittered from my hands.

"Get back," Jonah ordered me. "All of you. Stay back, you hear me?"

"So bossy," Claire muttered. But I noticed she was doing what her big brother said. We all were.

It was the noise of only a single engine this time. When it cut out, the silence made my ears ring. Jonah stepped out onto the porch. Claire jumped to catch the door before it slammed shut and peered around it.

"Who's there?" Jonah called.

"That you, King?" came the answer.

"J.D.?" Jonah sounded confused. "The fuck are you doing here?"

I peered around as J.D. walked up the single stair onto the concrete front porch. The porch light over his head illuminated him fully.

His eyes were so much like my father's.

When he saw me, he held up his hands. "Sky." He breathed out. "Listen."

I shook my head. "What do you want? Leave me alone."

"You heard her," Jonah said, immediately stepping between us. "Get the fuck out of here."

J.D. sidestepped him, keeping his eyes trained on me. "Look, that was shitty, I know. I'm going to kick Maddox's ass for what just happened, you'd better believe it. He had the idea to get to you first. Before the lawyer." He exhaled. "He's never been the smartest one. Too many blows to the head."

"What do you want?" I asked shakily.

"Just to talk. Okay?"

"I've got nothing to say to you."

"Yeah. My brothers and sister say the same thing. But we've got a lot to say to each other. Don't you think?"

I opened my mouth but no sound came out.

J.D. looked down. He wavered a moment, his foot in the air, halfway into turning around. "Think about it," he went on. "Come by the garage any time. Our door is always open." He lifted his gaze back to me. "We have a lot of catching up to do." His mouth twisted. "Sis."

Chapter Thirty-Four

FINN

I answered the phone on the first ring. “You need me?” I asked Dinah.

“Just to open your door,” she answered, then hung up.

I went to the window and saw the bouncing headlights approaching. I unlocked my door and stood with my arms crossed against the cold night.

Dinah got out and hurried around to collect her passenger, holding her tight as she brought her across the gravel apron to my door. "Sorry," the camp owner apologized. "Hope we didn't wake you.”

"I'm awake," I told her. “Is she okay? Why didn’t you let me do the pick-up?”

The pick-up was a pale white ghost trying to stay in Dinah’s shadow. The older woman hovered over her protectively. "It was an emergency,” Dinah explained. “And one I needed to do. For personal reasons.” She looked exhausted, a hunted look in her eyes. “It’s kind of cold?”

"Right. Sorry." I stepped back and gestured for them to come in. The girl skirted past me, but I wasn’t insulted. I was used to these girls now. And tried to make myself as small and unthreatening looking as possible. I’d even trimmed my beard.

I smiled at the girl. "What's your name?"

"Anna." She wouldn't look at me.

"Anna, I'm Finn. You're probably tired." I gestured to the bed, and her eyes went fractionally wider.

Dinah put a hand on her elbow. "Absolutely not, honey. You can trust Finn. He's one of us."

I nodded, feeling myself stand up a little straighter. I was. Wasn't I? "You get yourself situated. I'm gonna step out with Dinah, okay? And don't worry, I'm going to sleep on the couch. I'd sleep in the tent outside, but it's a little too cold for that."

Anna shivered, and then nodded.

I stepped outside, and Dinah shut the door carefully behind her, patting it like she wanted to make sure it was secure. "Thank you," she said.

"Is she okay?" I wanted to know.

Dinah inhaled sharply. "She will be. But we have to scramble."

I nodded. "She need a plane ticket? Bus ticket?"

She shook her head. "I think it's not quite so simple this time around." She had distracted, worried look on her face. "I'm going to make a few calls, okay? Just make sure she's safe."

Dinah clapped her hand on my arm, squeezing it in her surprisingly strong grip. "Thanks," she said again.

I nodded. It was still too hard to see the gratitude in her eyes when I didn't feel I deserved it yet.

I went back into my trailer and fixed Anna a mug of hot chocolate. Then I made sure she was comfortable before curling up the couch. I told her good night. Then I laid there listening.

It took a long time for her to fall asleep. I could tell by the way she was breathing. But she finally did, I fell asleep a few minutes later, figuring tomorrow would be spent the usual way. Putting calls out to relatives, finding her new clothes, getting her a haircut. Nothing out of the ordinary.

Nothing I hadn't done before.

Why I jerked awake in the middle of the night, I had no idea. But the jolt was so sudden, I was on my feet and moving to the window before I'd even stopped dreaming.

Anna was still sleeping, curled up at the very edge of the bed. I breathed a silent prayer of thanks that I hadn't woken her. Why was I even awake, anyway? What had I heard? An owl? Hunters getting an early start to the day?

Whatever it was had me on high alert.

And there it was again. An engine. Someone coming down the road. At this time of night?

Anna flew up, and yanked the covers up high when she saw me. "Where?" she gasped.

"You're safe," I reminded her, holding out a steadying hand. "Keep quiet, okay?" I pressed my fingers to my lips, and raised my eyebrows.

She nodded, going so far as to clap her hands over her mouth to keep from screaming.

Slowly, I put one foot in to the front of the other until I was right at the door of the trailer. I pressed my ear against it, listening.

There was no mistaking it. Someone was driving around the campground. Slowly. Like they were looking for something.

Or someone.

My burner phone buzzed on the counter. I snatched it before the noise gave us away. "Yeah," I murmured into it.

"Is she with you?" Dinah's voice was thick with sleep and alarm.

"I've got her.

I heard a muffled sound , then the sharp tinkling of shattering glass. Dinah yelped. "I've got a gun!" she warned someone. "I'm not... Finn?"

I gripped the phone tighter. "Dinah?"

"Get her out of here, Finn. Get her out of here!"

The line went dead.

Then came the sound of cars. From all around us. Every direction.

I looked it Anna. She was frozen with fear. "We have to go," I told her, tossing her my jacket.

She didn't move. She stayed curled in a tight ball, her head shaking over and over again. Like her whole body was whispering “no.”

I looked out the window. "Shit," I swore as a flashlight beam swung over the trailer. I ducked out of the way.

But whoever was on the other side of the glass had seen me. I heard the shout go up.

“Anna, we gotta get out of here, now.”

She was still there, trapped by her fear. In another life, I'd been exactly where she was.

But I wasn't that person any more.

“Ah fuck, listen, I'm really sorry about this," I informed her. Then leaned in and scooped her up into my arms.

She screamed, a piercing shriek right in my ear. "Good thing I'm already half deaf," I grunted, still holding her tight. I bounded for the door, kicking it open with my foot.

It bounced back just as fast. I heard a grunt from the other side, and a man fell back into the dirt clutching his nose. "Good! Hope that hurt, fucker!” I yelled, making a beeline for my car.

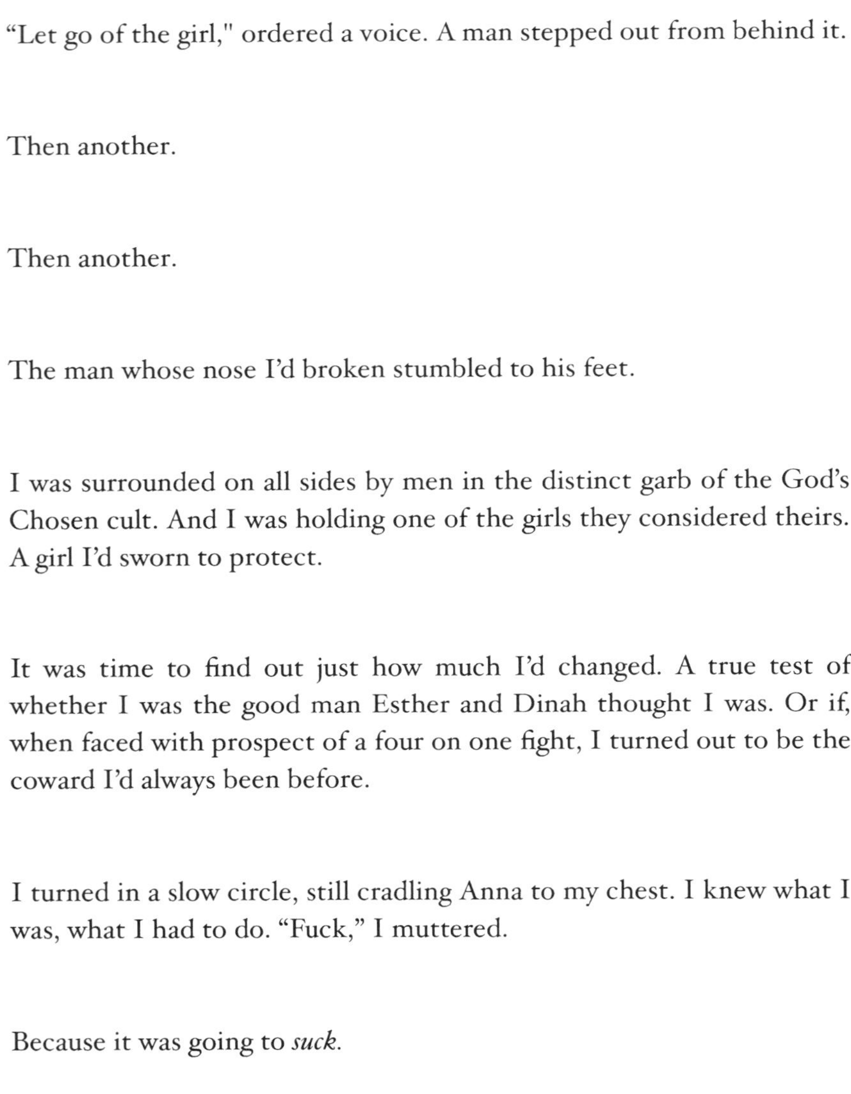

“Let go of the girl," ordered a voice. A man stepped out from behind it.

Then another.

Then another.

The man whose nose I’d broken stumbled to his feet.

I was surrounded on all sides by men in the distinct garb of the God’s Chosen cult. And I was holding one of the girls they considered theirs. A girl I’d sworn to protect.

It was time to find out just how much I’d changed. A true test of whether I was the good man Esther and Dinah thought I was. Or if, when faced with prospect of a four on one fight, I turned out to be the coward I’d always been before.

I turned in a slow circle, still cradling Anna to my chest. I knew what I was, what I had to do. “Fuck,” I muttered.

Because it was going to *suck*.

Chapter Thirty-Five

SKY

"Are you sure?" Livvy asked me one more time.

I nodded. "I'm sure."

It was close to four in the morning and by now the whole Thursday night crew knew what had happened. Willa's boyfriend Cooper showed up right after J.D. left. Now the two of them were wedged together on the loveseat, dead asleep.

Jonah stayed by the front door all night. He was now slumped with his back against it, still barricading it with his body. Ruby had her head in his lap, snoring softly as he played with her hair.

Ethan was out in the driveway, sleeping in his car so he could honk his horn if any Knights decided to make another appearance.

Ryan had checked in with Cooper a half hour ago, after doing a drive-by of the Knights' garage. All four motorcycles were parked there for now, but Naomi would check in again before she headed out to work.

And Sadie had finally gotten her hands on some sage. She'd thoroughly cleansed the front porch of all the negative energy. Then she'd made herself a nest in the corner out of everyone else's coats. She was now sleeping with her butt up in the air, just like a little baby.

I thought Claire was asleep at the other end of the couch from me, but she stirred when she heard my answer. "You're a braver woman than me." She opened one eye and shot me a tired smile. "I was scared shitless when J.D. came back."

"Me too."

"If you tell anyone though, I'll kill you," she mumbled as her eyes closed again. "Especially Ethan."

I grinned.

"When?" Livvy wanted to know. She was still sitting on the floor with her back to the couch. I had no idea how she was still upright.

"First thing," I said. "I'm tired of waiting to see what's going to happen." I licked my lips, tasting the red wine that still clung to them. "I'm ready to stop being scared and start finding answers."

She yawned and looked around at the people strewn around her house with a fond smile. "Didn't I tell you you wouldn't have to do it alone?" she asked me.

I swallowed back the tears that kept threatening to fall, and instead squeezed her hand. "Thank you," I whispered.

My head was clogged with red wine and spent adrenaline. I should have slept like a rock.

But instead, I laid there listening to the sleep noises of the people around me and tried to think about what I'd say to my brothers.

I say *tried*, because my mind kept drifting to what I'd say to Finn instead. *I get it now,* I'd tell him. *You didn't see how many people loved you, because you didn't love yourself enough to notice. I'm guilty of that too.*

But did you notice me?

Could you tell?

Was my love clear and bright? Or was it buried under too many layers of self-centered narcissism for you to see it?

Would you let me show you if I saw you now?

I stared at the dark window. Now that I realized it, I wondered how I'd ever thought it was anything else. Friends? Fuckbuddies? We weren't any of the things I'd tried to force us to be. We were soulmates, two points on the same compass trying to lead each other home.

I loved him. And I'd left him behind.

I stared at the window, adrift in that sea of guilt, until it lightened to the point where sleep was pointless. I sat up again and stretched the kink out of my back, then picked my way towards the bathroom.

I ran the water into the drinking glass as quietly as I could. But even with my best efforts, I couldn't escape my cousin's watchful eye. She appeared in the doorway, rubbing her eyes. I wondered if she'd been awake all night too.

But when she dropped her hands to her sides, she looked alert and decided. She nodded at me and grabbed her purse. "Ready to go?"

"You should stay," I tried to tell her. "If something goes wrong -."

"Then I'll be your back-up." She squeezed my wrist. "Haven't I told you all along?"

"I know," I sighed. "I'm not doing this alone."

Chapter Thirty-Six

FINN

I've been in fights. Lots of fights. I fought my way through grade school, middle school and all the way through high school. I fought with all three of my brothers. Play fights. And also vicious real ones that broke furniture and left holes in the walls.

I'd never fought for my life, though.

I'd also never fought for someone else's.

I sure hoped the same basic principles applied.

"Put the girl down," the oldest Chosen dude ordered.

"I get you're used to giving orders and all that," I laughed. "But, in the words of my little sister, 'you're not the boss of me.'"

"This is kidnapping!" shouted the youngest guy. Only I'd fucked up his nose pretty thoroughly. So it came out like, "Did id kibnabbing!"

"You should go to a hospital," I told him, as I turned in another circle, keeping my eyes everywhere at once. "Get that looked at. Also, like *fuck* it is. *She* came to *me*. I didn't kidnap shit."

"Anna!" boomed the old guy.

Anna's head snapped, jerking with the habit of obedience. She looked at him and immediately dropped her eyes.

"This is not you," he said in a soothing voice that curdled my blood. “This is not your doing. I know. I forgive you. We will forgive you."

"Father," she said. She stiffened.

With a sinking heart, I let her slide down until she was standing on her own. But I kept my hand on her shoulder. I didn’t trust these manipulative assholes for a second. Whatever happened next, I was gonna be certain it was her choice. I leaned forward. “What do you want to do?” I asked her under my breath.

She answered with a lift of her chin and looked her father in the eye for the first time. "I won't let you hurt me any more." He started to sputter, but she held up her hand and looked right in to my eyes. “Get me away from them.”

“Anna!” her father barked. “Do not get in that car!”

“Get in the car,” I shouted.

Just as he lunged for her.

I reacted on instinct, flattening him with one solid crack to the jaw. My hand stung viciously, but adrenaline made sure I didn't feel it. “Get in!" I shouted again. “And lock the doors!" I hoped like hell she knew how to do that.

Four against one is shitty odds, but I had the advantage of being young, strong, and easily pissed off. Maybe if Anna's brothers had come to fetch her - young guys strong from working the fields and lifting the wood to build houses - I might have had an issue.

But Chosen Elders, they're soft. They're used to being waited on by their wives and daughters. They lived a life of leisure at the expense of others. And it showed in every move they made.

Also, I’d been itching for a chance to fuck one of these guys up ever since I started working with Dinah. So maybe the odds were pretty even after all.

After I flattened Anna’s creeper of a dad, the two that were still uninjured hesitated. I let out a savage yell as euphoria flooded my veins. “Try it!” I urged them, beckoning with my hands. “Just try and make her come with you. I’ve been wanting to punch one of you fuckers in the face for ages now, so fucking try me!”

The one closest to me turned and spat on the ground. “You’re a demon. Hell-spawn.”

"Nope! I'm just your garden-variety asshole." I punctuated that with solid jab to his solar plexus. He reeled back, winded and I whirled on the last man standing. "You gonna try your luck, Beard-o?" I tugged at mine. "You think you're a big man pushing little girls around? You don't deserve a beard like that. Come here so I can pull it off your face!" I lunged at him.

He turned and ran.

That was my cue. I sprinted to the driver's side door and tugged at the handle. Anna fumbled at the lock until I could swing it open. I threw myself inside and hit the lock again. Then let out a long, slow breath.

I didn't have time to think about what I'd done, or even what it meant. I still had a job to do. "You wanna get the fuck out of here?" I asked Anna.

She folded her hands in her lap and primly watched the men still struggling in the dirt. She almost looked... happy. "Please," she said, as polite as can be.

"You're a bad ass," I muttered. "You're gonna do just fine."

She turned and fixed me with a radiant smile. "Thank you, Finn."

I glanced in the rearview mirror. "Don't thank me yet," I said. The Chosen Elders were struggling to their feet.

"Do you know where we're supposed to go next?" I asked her.

She pressed her lips together. "Dinah was still trying to get it together."

"Fuck."

I started the engine and floored it. We bumped over the rutted dirt road at a truly unsafe speed.

But it wasn't fast enough. Where a second ago there had been only darkness in my rearview mirror, there was now the bright, threatening beam of headlights. And they were gaining on us.

I shot out onto the main highway, the back tires skidding wildly as I cut the wheel hard to the right. In the direction of Crown Creek.

I'd been avoiding it all this time. But now my hometown screamed safety. I nudged the car faster, putting distance between us and the camp. The headlights receded. They had no chance. I knew every twist and turn of this road.

This was my home,

I whipped around a familiar turn and then yanked the wheel sharply to the left. Anna screamed as we careened off the shoulder and bounced straight into a cornfield. "It's okay!" I promised, shouting over the noise of the dead corn slapping and scratching at the car. "It's okay!"

Just as I'd known they would, the dead, drying stalks bent as we rolled over them. Then bounced right back up again, closing us in.

We were hidden, surrounded on all four sides with cornstalks. I cranked off the engine and cut the lights.

"Where are we?" Anna panted, pressing her hand to her head I wondered if she'd hit it when I took us spontaneously off-roading.

"Cutter's farm," I said with a heavy sigh. "And he's gonna have a fit about it too."

"How'd you know to come here?"

"This isn't the first time I've used his cornfield as a cut through," I confessed. "Or a place to hide from someone chasing me." I looked in the rearview mirror. "Feels weird that they're not the cops."

The darkness around us was all encompassing. I let out a long breath. Anna exhaled too, and then I heard her whispering. It sounded like praying.

Chapter Thirty-Seven

SKY

The sun was barely peeking over the treetops when we pulled up to Knights' garage. It was so early, the front gate was closed up tight. "Do you think we came too soon?" Livvy asked as we both stared at the high chain link fence that surrounded the lot. "Maybe no one is here yet."

As if in reply, the mechanical gate whirred to life. It rolled open to allow Livvy to pull in, then clanked shut again with an ominous *bang*.

"Well then!" Livvy let out a nervous laugh. "That's certainly ominous."

"Are they trying to scare us?" I wondered. Then gritted my teeth. "Because it's not going to work." I pulled my bag up close to my chest and patted it for the millionth time to make sure the lawyer's letter was inside. The deed, however, was safe with Claire.

I was scared, but for once I wasn't being stupid. Like Livvy kept saying, I wasn't doing this alone.

The office door swung open and I caught the silhouette of a man peering out at us. "And there's the welcoming committee," Livvy, sighed. "Are you sure you're ready?"

I nodded. "Let's go."

I stepped out into a day that was growing brighter by the minute and shielded my eyes. "Which one are you?" I called to the silhouette.

A chuckle was my only answer. But he was joined by another silhouette. "Sis? Is that you?"

"That's Maddox," Livvy whispered to me. "Be careful."

"Where's J.D.?" I demanded. "Where's the only one of you who's *not* a dick?"

"Here!" came the call from inside. J.D. jostled his way past his looming brothers and shielded his eyes. "You don't waste any time!"

"You want to talk? Let's talk!" I called back.

"Come on in, then." J.D. made to turn back. But when I made no move to follow him, I could hear his sigh from over here. Livvy shot me a worried look as we both heard the sounded of a fiercely whispered argument between the brothers.

"I said scat!" J.D. suddenly bellowed, lunging.

Maddox's wild laugh echoed off the building, but he and the quietly dangerous one slunk back into the building. "Come on it, then," J.D. called to me. "They won't bother you."

I looked at Livvy. "Claire's watching the clock," she murmured, reminding me. "If we don't call her in a half hour..."

I nodded and swallowed hard. "I'll go first."

Crossing the wide lot felt a lot like walking down that long, lily-lined hallway to see my father's body. Knowing that I had no idea what I would see at the end, but certain it would change everything.

I blinked as I entered the office, letting my eyes adjust to the light before going in all the way. The space was mostly taken up by a huge corner desk covered in a jagged mountain range of files. An ancient computer whirred, and the light breeze from its fan set the papers on the wall to dancing.

And there were so many papers. Every available surface seemed to have some kind of notice or invoice stuck to it. Their rustling reminded me of walking through autumn leaves. I leaned in and glanced at one of them. It was an invoice dating back over five years now.

And it was written up in my father's distinctive scrawl.

I stepped back hastily. "You can sit," J.D. drawled. "No need to be checking our books for us or anything."

"Sorry, I -." I shook my head. "I just... that's my Dad's handwriting." I swallowed and looked at him. "It just keeps hitting me, you know?"

J.D. grunted. "I know." He tapped his pen on the desk and then seemed to decide something. He pushed back in this chair and put his feet up on the desk. When he saw me watching, he gave me a small grin. "Dad never let me do this," he volunteered. "Now that he's not here to bark at me, I'm doing it every chance I get."

I swallowed and tried to smile back. "So what did you want to talk about?"

"That envelope." Livvy, J.D. and I all turned to see yet another Knight brother stepping into the office from the garage. He was broader than his brother, his hair closer cropped. "And what the hell you think you're going to do with it."

"Rocky...." J.D. muttered in warning. He swung his legs down and fixed his brother with a look. But instead of threatening him like he had the other two, he just gave a small shake of his head. Rocky wrinkled his nose, but then gave a stiff nod back.

"You want to be more specific?" Livvy piped up from behind me. I'd nearly forgotten she was here, I was so intent on watching my brothers' every move. It was like seeing my father through a warped mirror, the familiar right up against the strange. "The envelope doesn't concern you," Livvy went on. "And before we go any further, you mind telling me what's behind that door?"

I looked where she pointed. A heavy metal door that was was set into the back wall of the office. It was so papered over with my father's scrawl that I hadn't noticed it at first. But Livvy was staring at it in white-faced horror.

J.D. stiffened. He probably thought he'd hidden his reaction. But after a lifetime spent analyzing father's every movement, I was overly equipped to notice my brother's. Stranger or not, he moved the exact same way. And now he looked uncomfortable.

"That doesn't really have nothin' to do with this matter, now," he said, sounding overly casual. I caught the quick, wary glance he shot at Rocky.

I leaned forward. "Are you hiding something in there?"

"Back office isn't part of the tour," Rocky snapped.

"Why is it locked?" Livvy demanded. "That deadbolt at the top there? Why do you have it bolted from the outside?"

"So we can keep prying eyes off of it," Rocky drawled. "But it ain't working, apparently."

I sat up straighter. Every alarm bell in my head was going off at once. "You know this is fucking creepy, right?" I looked directly at J.D. "This isn't helping your 'I just want to talk' case. Scary doors that lock from the outside? Is that your murder room, J.D.?"

"Jesus fuck!" he spat. "Can we just -?" He paused and licked his lips, then spread his hands out in appeal. "Look. I just want you to understand where we are coming from."

"Oh, I understand just fine!" I rolled my eyes. "I understand you've been threatening me." I glanced at Livvy. "And my friends. And my family. Motorcycle drive-bys? Late night visits? You're all a bunch of bullies, aren't you? But it's not gonna work." I pulled the envelope from my bag and waved it at them. "I have the paperwork right here. The house is mine."

"No it ain't!" Rocky spat. "That's not -." J.D. silenced him with another shake of his head.

I stood up. I'd had enough. "Look. You might not have known about me. Hell, I sure as shit didn't know about *you*. But I *do* exist. I *am* his daughter. And I have a right to a piece of him." The word got locked up in my throat and I was suddenly crying. "You guys had him," I shouted, angry that my tears made me look weak when all I wanted was to take what was mine. "You had all that time with him, and I had to be happy with whatever scraps were left over." I brandished the enveloped. "Well this is it. This is my scrap."

J.D. had been watching me during my whole tirade and when I finally fell silent, he sounded almost sad. "But it's a pretty important scrap," he said gently.

"Whether it's important to you or not doesn't matter," I spat. I was feeling selfish and mean and I wanted to hurt them because my Dad wasn't around to yell at instead. "Your opinion really doesn't fucking matter because it's all down in the will. In black and white and fancy fucking insignia. The house belongs to me."

This time it was Rocky who sounded sad. "So maybe? Maybe we come to an agreement." He looked at J.D. "We 'll buy it from you."

"I'm not selling. It's my goddamned legacy."

He tented his fingers and pressed his lips together. The room was silent as tension filled it. So silent I could hear the flutter of papers on the wall.

And the loud clang of an alarm bell.

"What the hell?" I yelled, leaping to grab Livvy. "What was that?"

J.D. looked at Rocky. "Is there a drop today?"

"Not supposed to be." Rocky shoved past me and went to the door. "I don't recognized the car!" he called. "Check the cameras!"

"Is everything locked down?" J.D. yelled into the garage. Maddox bounded into the office and handed his brother something. "Is that a gun?" Livvy shrieked.

"Are we locked down!" Rocky bellowed. And turned to look at the bolted door.

"What the hell is in there?" I gasped.

Rocky ignored me. "Check on them," he ordered Maddox.

"There are people in there?"

Rocky still wouldn't look my way. "Tell them they're okay, you hear me? Hey Aaron!" he called when Maddox opened the door. "Don't worry, okay?" he called to the unseen man inside. "Just don't talk. We'll do the talking." He nodded at J.D.

J.D. nodded back and then pressed his finger down on a a call box next to the phone. "Who the fuck is this?" he snarled.

"Hey! Dinah sent us!" came the garbled, staticky answer over the intercom. "Don't fucking shoot me!"

J.D. shook his head and backed away. "That's not him," he warned. "That's not the usual guy."

"But he said Dinah sent him," Maddox pointed out.

"I've never in my life heard someone from the Chosen say 'hey'" Rocky mused. "Or drop f-bombs. It could be a new guy?"

"You want to risk it?" J.D. snarled. "What would Susanna say?"

"She'd say let's see what he wants." A woman I hadn't seen until just now stepped into the office. Her long hair was so blonde it was almost white. She moved like a dancer, all floating limbs and careful motions. But the look in her eyes was pure steel.

Rocky swore when he saw her. "Baby, we're on lockdown, get the fuck out of here. Please. No women allowed."

"And them?" she gestured to me and Livvy.

"That's my new sister," Rocky sighed. "She doesn't count."

Susanna stared at me. "Have you asked her yet?"

"We were getting to it," Rocky grunted impatiently. "And then got interrupted by an unscheduled drop."

She walked over to him and touched his face. "You'll keep me safe though."

"Always," he promised, and pressed a desperate kiss to her lips.

Then he swallowed and nodded to J.D. "Do it," he said. "Open it up."

J.D. looked at his brother. And then looked at me.

"Welcome to the family, Sis," he laughed.

And then he pressed the button.

Chapter Thirty-Eight

FINN

I jerked awake again, checking the passenger seat with my heart in my throat.

Anna was sleeping slumped against the window. I blinked when I saw her and realized *why* I could see her.

The sun was up. We'd stayed hidden in the cornfield the whole night long and no one had found us.

I'd kept my promise to keep her safe,

But I had no idea what to do next.

I shifted in the seat, trying to roll the stiffness out of my neck. Anna stirred and then stretched.

And then we both jumped a mile when my phone buzzed in the pocket of my jacket. "Jesus," I muttered, dragging my hand down my face. "Talk about a wake-up call."

Anna gave me a shy, delighted grin. "That was funny," she said.

"I'm not usually," I informed her, then pressed the call button. There was only one person who had this number. "Are you okay?" I asked by way of greeting.

"Finn?"

"Dinah? Are you hurt?"

"Do you have her?"

"I do." I looked over at Anna and smiled. "She's safe."

Dinah blew out a long exhale and then laughed. "You're something else," she marveled.

"I'm not."

"I'm too tired to have this argument with you, Finn. I've got an address for you, are you ready?"

"Is it safe?"

"The safest I can manage at this hour." She sounded worried. "I'm still trying to get things final with them. But they have a fence and guard dogs, and knowing this crew, they have a lot of guns on hand too. If they're there, and God willing they are, they're the best people to make sure she's protected." She paused. "Next to you, of course."

"Guard dogs and guns?" I stared at Anna again. Her hands were still folded, but her knuckles were white. "Who is she, Dinah?"

Anna cleared her throat. "I'm the daughter of the Prophet," she declared in a clear, cold voice.

I blinked. "The Prophet?" I rubbed my knuckles. "The guy whose jaw I broke?"

"No."

"You called him Father, though," I pointed out.

"That man is my husband," she sighed. Then unclenched her hands and looked at me. "*Was* my husband."

"They were married last night," Dinah explained over the phone. "I took her before it could be consummated."

I gripped the steering wheel tighter. Then looked at Anna. "How old are you?" I asked.

She lifted her chin. "Thirteen."

I saw red. "I should have broken more than just his jaw," I growled.

"You see why we're taking extraordinary measures?" Dinah asked. "Finn?"

I pulled my thoughts away from slow murder. "Yeah?" I barked.

"Take her to this address. They'll know what to do next."

"You got it, boss." I ended the call. "Shall we get the fuck out of this cornfield?" I asked Anna.

My wayward past came in handy again. I alternately rocked the car and gunned the engine and dug Cutter's field all to shit to get us out of there. I promised myself I'd send a Cutter a check for the damage I was doing, and then cut a wide U-turn back out onto Highway twelve.

Mud and broken pieces of cornstalks covered the windshield. "After I drop you off," I muttered. "I'm heading to the car wash."

Anna didn't find that joke quite as funny.

We drove in silence to the address Dinah had given me. I slipped past the still sleeping houses with my eyes straight forward. *If I can't see them, then they can't see me* the irrational part of my brain insisted. But then I turned and snuck a glance out the window anyway. After the night I'd had, I was almost hoping I'd run into Beau. Or Claire. Or... *dare I even hope it?*

Sky.

My thoughts were tangled up in her, so I drove without thinking. I took the turns out of town on instinct, passing by the old warehouses and the mills that stood empty but had once taken their power from the creek. We were out of the pretty part of town and entering the part where the pawn shops and the used car lots hunkered in front of a backdrop of more dead corn.

I'd thought the address sounded familiar when Dinah told it to me.

But when I rolled in front of the Knights' garage and double checked it, I swore for a long, long time.

"What's wrong?" Anna whispered as I cursed.

Her voice was quivering. I'd scared her. And she didn't need any more scaring for the day. "Nothing." I swallowed down the impulse to rage at the irony. I fought the need to jump from the car and rain down justice on the people who'd scared the woman I still thought of as mine. Hell, I'd flattened three guys for Anna's sake. I'd gladly take on one hundred for Sky.

But if Dinah had sent us, that meant the Knights were somehow involved in the Underground Railroad. I couldn't punch them.

Yet.

"Let's get you inside," I told Anna. "Get you safe."

I pulled up to the gate and heard a faint alarm ring out from the low slung building. "Dinah was right," I told Anna. "This place has security." I didn't tell her it was because the Knights were a bunch of lowlifes with plenty of people after them wanting to settle scores. Me being one of them.

The speaker hanging on the gate crackled to the life. "— fuck is this?"

It was J.D. Even over the tinny speaker, I recognized the voice of the most reasonable of the Knight brothers. "Hey!" I greeted him. "Dinah sent us! Don't fucking shoot me!"

I sat back and tapped my fingers on the wheel. Then caught a glimpse of myself in the mirror and wondered why I was suddenly smiling. I wasn't at all happy to see J.D., or any of his idiot brothers. I had no idea how they'd gotten mixed up in the Underground Railroad Dinah and I were running, but I suspected their motives weren't exactly pure of heart.

But I knew them. And that had me almost whistling with relief.

And then, like an anvil dropped from on high, it hit me.

I was ready. Ready to come back. To make my amends and ask for forgiveness.

I was ready to be a King again. I was ready to show how I'd changed.

When this was over, I would call Dinah and let her know Anna was safe. Then I'd thank her for giving me the purpose I'd spent my whole life searching for. But I wasn't coming back to the campground. She'd probably be relieved to hear it.

The gate slid open with a terrible screech that made Anna clap her hands to her ears. Sliding through it felt like turning a page in the book of my life.

Ready to start a new chapter.

"I'll go first," I told Anna, then jumped from the car. The day was the warmest we'd had in a long while, and the sun was now beating down from a brilliantly blue sky. I shielded my eyes and inspected the low white building. "Ready?" I called. "Stay close to me."

I held out my arm to guide her behind me. But she grabbed my elbow instead.

"King?" There was a shadow in the doorway. "Is that you?"

"Rocco?" I called out. "What the fuck is going on? Why'd Dinah send me to you?"

He opened his mouth to answer, but turned his head, distracted by a sudden commotion from inside. There was a shout and then a chorus of voices, and then Rocky was suddenly yanked from my view.

A familiar silhouette took his place. A jolt went through my body before I even saw her face. Because I'd know her body anywhere. She hadn't changed.

But I had.

"Sky?" I called.

"Finn?" she cried.

"The fuck?" Rocky yelled, muscling his way back out the door again. "How the fuck do you two know each other?"

Chapter Thirty-Nine

SKY

I heard his voice out in the lot and turned so quickly I made myself dizzy. Without even thinking, I grabbed Rocky by his beefy forearm and yanked him out of my way.

It took several blinks before the backlit silhouette resolved itself into a familiar shape.

He was here. Standing right in front of me, his arm around a frightened young girl. "Sky," he said my name again.

All around me was a frenzy of action. Susanna appeared at the girl's elbow and gently coaxed her inside. My brothers all surrounded Finn and demanded to know what had happened - why did the drop go bad? what was Dinah doing? and a whole lot of other questions that made no sense to me. My cousin emerged from the office and her mouth fell open when she saw Finn standing there.

I was aware of all these things. But I couldn't tear my eyes away from the hazel ones I'd missed do much. "What are you doing here?" I whispered.

"Missing you," he murmured, brushing his finger under my chin.

His kiss was as soft as a feather, hardly the soul-searing assault I craved from him. I pulled back and stared at him, thrilled that every single gold fleck I'd remembered still glinted in his eyes.

And then I socked him in the chest. Hard.

"What the fuck?" I demanded. "Your family didn't *know*! You said you left a note, but you *didn't*, Finn! They had no idea why you left!"

He blinked at me.

"It's true though." Livvy shot me a significant 'we'll talk about this later, cuz' look, and then turned to Finn. "Claire's been a mess. What the *fuck*, Finn?"

"How do you?" He pointed from me to Livvy. "Are you -?"

"Cousins," I said flatly. "I have family too. And I didn't leave mine to think I was dead in a ditch somewhere."

"No, I -." He shook his head. "I left a note. I told them. I did, Sky. I swear I did."

"Why are you *here*? What are you *doing*?" My voice was rising because, like always, I was skipping right over the thing that was too difficult to deal with and focusing on the tiny details. "What were you doing with that girl, anyway?"

"Sky." Susanna's voice cut through my questions like a knife. She smiled and gestured for me to follow her. "I want to show you something."

I glanced at Finn who was still looking down at his feet. His mouth was working silently, but I thought I caught the words, "I swear."

"Sky," Susanna called again. "Come on." She paused. "You too, Finn."

I had no fight left in me to protest. I followed Susanna back into the office. I stood in the middle of it, surrounded by my cousin, my brothers and --- whatever Finn was. It was like having every moment in my life happen simultaneously.

Susanna sat down in the chair J.D. had abandoned. "Tell her," she ordered Rocky. "She's family." She cocked her head at Finn. "And he's involved too."

"Tell me what?" I asked, twisting around to stare at Finn. "Is this about the girl?"

"Anna," he supplied. "Her name is Anna."

Susanna let out a whoosh of breath and sat back in her chair. "So it *was* her. She's sure grown."

"You know her?" Finn asked.

But Susanna was looking at me. "You're not for around here, are you?"

"No shit," I replied testily. This secrecy was setting my teeth on edge.

"You though." She turned to Livvy. "I've seen you before. And you too, Finn."

Livvy was shaking her head. "I'm sorry... I don't..."

"My hair was longer," Susanna said crisply. Rocky moved to her side.

Livvy widened her eyes.. She looked from Susanna back to Rocky. "You're Chosen?"

"Not anymore," Rocky said, a possessive gleam in his eye.

"And there are others like me too," Susanna added. "We help them. We give them a place to stay."

"You run the safe houses?" Finn demanded.

"House. Singular," Rocky corrected. "Only one safe house." He turned and glared at me. "Our Dad's place."

"He was always gone," J.D. piped up. "He was too selfish to even notice we'd started doing this behind his back. He didn't need it."

"Not like we do," Rocky added.

"You mean... my house?" I gasped.

"Our Dad's house." J.D. looked at me then swiveled his finger in a circle. "*Our* Dad..."

"No." I shook my head. "But it's mine."

"Sky." Finn spoke softly.

But I shook my head. "It's mine!"

"Don't be selfish," Rocky snapped. Susanna laid a finger on his wrist and he immediately calmed at her touch.

"Sky," Finn said again. "These people need help."

"How do you know?" My brain was swirling. "How do you know they need help?"

"Because I've been helping them."

The silence was so immediate that it was like the sound cutting out of a movie.

It was Livvy who finally spoke. "You, Finn?"

Her surprise didn't anger him. He seemed to accept it as fair. He raised his head and looked at each person in the office in turn. "Since Sky left the camp, I've been working with Dinah. She called it the Chosen Underground Railroad. I've moved -," he counted on his fingers. "Seven people by myself, and helped Dinah relocate two other families." He leaped forward and planted his hands on the desk. "Adam and Esther, were they in your safe house? Are their girls okay?"

"They are." Susanna smiled up at Finn. "Charity just said her first word, too."

His face crumpled with happiness and relief. "Thank you," he whispered, and stood back up again.

I stared at him. "Finn?"

He turned and looked at me.

"Finn? You've been helping -," I swallowed. "These people?"

He ducked his head. "I know that probably surprises you, but I've changed, Sky. I hope that..."

His words were swallowed up when I kissed him again. "How did I miss this?" I whispered against his mouth. "Where were you hiding?" I reached up and pressed my hand to his chest, over the space where the heart he kept hidden from everyone beat huge and good.

The corner of his mouth tipped up. He'd just started to smile when the clang of the alarm bell made us all jump again.

Susanna was the closest, so she pressed the button on the intercom.

"*WHERE ARE THEY?*" came the shrieking bellow from the call box. Susanna clapped her hands over her ears.

I swallowed and looked at Livvy. "Did we forget to call her?"

Livvy looked like she was going to faint. "We forgot to call her."

"Shit, uh, Finn?" I looked down as he came back over to me. "Hey uh, you know the reunion you need to have? With the family who has no idea what happened to you?"

"I get it, Sky," he sighed. "I got a little distracted, sorry." He touched his finger to my lips again.

I shook my head and pulled back. “No.” I pointed to the call box. “It’s about to happen.” I looked at the man I’d thought about every single day since the day I’d left him. He said he’d changed. I’d soon know how true that was. “Get ready,” I warned him. “And I’m really sorry.”

I reached over the desk and pressed the button to let Claire in.

Chapter Forty

FINN

There are three things I hope I never have to face again.

The inside of the hospital room where I was held on suicide watch.

The sight of Sky's car pulling away from me as I stood helplessly in my trailer.

And my baby sister's face when she saw me standing in the lot outside Knights' garage.

Claire rage was white hot. Incandescent. And I got exactly nowhere with her before she got back into her beloved Jeep and went squealing out of the lot.

The last thing I saw was her shoving her phone against her ear and I knew the moment of truth was at hand.

I had to go home.

"Sky," I said, turning back to the woman I had to lose to realize I loved her. Every cell in my body screamed to stay here with her. But I swallowed hard and said what I had to say. "Can we start over?"

Sky tipped her face up to mine. Her wide blue eyes were heavy-lidded with a sadness I didn't understand. "Again?"

I took her hand in mine. "I know. We've done this before."

"What are we now, Finn? Are we friends again?"

I shook my head. "There's no way I could be your friend."

She looked stricken. "Why?"

"Because I'm in love with you." I pressed my lips to her knuckles. "I'm sorry."

Her eyes widened. She gave a little squeak. She reached up to pull me to her, but I gently caught her wrists in my hands and lowered them back down. "I love you," I repeated. "So that means I'm going to do this right." I checked her face. "If you'll let me," I amended.

She searched my face. "How do we do it right?" she whispered. Like she genuinely wished to know.

I did too. "I'll see you," I kissed her hand again. "I'll see you again, really soon. Okay?" I nodded. "I have to do something now, and it's going to suck, but it has to be done."

Her eyes filled with tears but she nodded. Cupping my face with her hands, she pressed a sweet, gentle kiss to my cheek. "Go see your family," she whispered. "And then come back to me."

I straightened up and squared my shoulders. Taking a deep breath, I nodded again. "How do I look?"

She touched my shoulder. "Like a new man."

Her words echoed in my head the whole drive across town. Thankfully. Because the closer I got to the moment of truth, the harder I had to fight to keep from turning around.

I never meant for it to be like this. That was the hardest part. The old me would have raged about the injustice of it. How could they even think I would have left without at least telling them why? What right did they have to be angry with me when my intentions were so good?

I finally understood that my intentions meant nothing. Not if my actions were those of a callous, unfeeling asshole.

The wind caught the fallen leaves and blew them across the long driveway that wound back to the house I shared with my twin. When I'd left, they were still on the trees that surrounded it, forming a green curtain that hid the house away.

Now, the bare branches meant that I could see the house the whole time I approached. And for some reason that made me laugh.

Even the house we shared was sick of secrets.

I pulled in to my usual spot, took a deep breath and reminded myself that I had changed. "A new man," Sky had told me.

Hopefully one who could be with her when this was all over.

I climbed out of my car and stretched, rolling my neck from shoulder to shoulder.

"You're here."

I looked up sharply. Beau stood on the deck with his arms folded across his chest. A stranger might think he looked calm and composed.

But the crossed arms betrayed him. Beau didn't close himself off unless he was trying to keep from getting hurt.

He was closed off from *me*... That little whisper left of the old voice in my head told me to get defensive. To wonder aloud what his problem was. To sarcastically needle him about being happy to see me.

“I’m back,” I said instead. And then cleared my throat because that wasn’t enough. “And I am so, so sorry.”

He stiffened slightly in surprise and I wondered if I'd ever truly apologized to him before. Not the fake ‘sorry you got your panties in a twist’ apologies. But sincerely admitting I was wrong. “I’m not trying to make an excuse,” I went on, holding up my hands in surrender. He kept his eyes on me as I walked up the stone steps to the side yard. “Just telling you that I, well, I didn’t leave without saying goodbye.” I lifted my foot and placed it deliberately on the first step that led from the yard up to the deck. When he didn’t stop me, I took another step. “I left a note. Explaining.”

“Yeah, there was no note,’ Beau sniffed.

I climbed the last step and suddenly we were face to face. Eye to eye. Mirror images. The face I knew better than my own. “Claire told me,” I sighed. “I don’t know what happened to it, but I’m sorry Beau. You must have been losing your mind.”

His Adam’s apple bobbed and he ducked quickly away. “We called the police.”

“Shit.”

“They opened a missing persons’ case.”

I let out an explosive breath.

"Mom cried every time she said your name."

I staggered back and gripped the railing.

"Finn. Note or no note, why the fuck would you ever leave?"

I dug my nails into the wood of the railing. "I wrote it all down," I told him. "And I'd need to find it to be able to explain." My voice caught. "Because to be honest with you, I don't even know why anymore. Other than I felt I had to."

Beau glared at me, the only evidence of his anger the rapid rise and fall of his shoulders. Then he brought his palm down on the railing with a loud *smack*. "Okay then," he said roughly. "Then let's go find this fucking note."

I nodded and followed him, half mortified to be doing this. And half relieved that he was even letting me in the door.

He stopped short in the living room and made a 'go ahead' gesture.

I took a deep breath. "The refrigerator." I walked over to the kitchen and glared at the stainless steel appliance like it had betrayed me.

"Right here." I lifted the magnet with the library hours printed on it. "I put it right under here."

Beau shook his head.

Panic rose in my throat and I fought the urge to throw up my hands and demand to know what else he wanted from me. Instead I closed my eyes.

An image of Sky flashed across memory, her quick, capable hands stitching up the hole in my shirt. Finding a solution for the problem I'd wanted to give up on.

"Maybe it fell," I said slowly, still keeping my eyes closed. "When I opened the door?"

I opened my eyes and Beau was still watching me, expressionless.

I went down on my hands and knees. "Somewhere. It's gotta be somewhere."

"I know this is surprising to hear, but we've actually cleaned a few times since you... left. And we didn't see anything."

My brother's sarcasm cut me deeper than his silence. I pressed my lips together and redoubled my search. I slid my hands along every crack and crevice in the kitchen. The space between the counter and the oven. Under the dishwasher. Behind the toaster.

Nothing.

"Fuck," I whispered and whirled around to stare at the fridge again.

Seized with sudden inspiration, I yanked open the junk drawer. I rummaged around until I found a penlight printed with the King Brothers' logo. Then I dropped to my knees and shone it under the refrigerator itself.

"It's there!" I called. "Way back in the back. See it?"

For one terrible moment, I thought Beau wouldn't come. That he'd stay standing with his arms crossed, refusing to believe I was telling the truth. That I'd used up my last chance and lost him forever.

And then he was there, dropping down onto his knees next to me. He bent his head to the floor right next to mine. "Where?"

"There." I jiggled the penlight. "Caught in the coils."

Beau jumped back up again. "We need like, a coat hanger or something. Or maybe... I know! Tongs!"

As my brother fashioned a tool to fish the note out from under the fridge, I closed my eyes and tried not to cry like a fucking baby. But when he knelt down again, ready and willing to help solve a problem he didn't even create, I actually did cry. A little. One tear hastily wipe away before anyone could see it.

"Got it," Beau grunted. He sat back up again, dragging out the note I had written what felt like a lifetime ago. It was covered in dust bunnies, and a smear of something that might have been oil.

I had a distinct urge to reach out and grab it from him. Snatch it away before he could read those old words from a man I barely recognized as myself anymore.

But I held still, keeping my hands by my sides. It was hard to watch him read it - to see the combination of disbelief and sadness on his face - so I looked away.

I knew he'd finished by the way his breathing changed, and waited for him to say something. Anything. But when the silence stretched out long enough for my knees to start aching, I couldn't help trying to break it. I turned back to my brother. "So?"

He was still staring at it with his lips pressed into a thin white line. After another heartbeat, he flicked the edge with his finger. "So yeah." He exhaled long and hard. "Yeah, this might've changed a few things. I mean, I'd still say you were fucking stupid for doing it, obviously." He looked up. "And I would have come after you and told it to your face." He swallowed. "But I wouldn't have, well -," he coughed and looked away, blinking rapidly. "Maybe I wouldn't have felt like you'd carved open my chest with a butter knife." I winced. "Maybe I wouldn't have walked around the past month feeling like I was missing a limb."

It hardly made sense to me anymore. It was like explaining something I'd done in a dream. "In my head, I was doing it for you."

"You are such an asshole," he said on an exhale.

"Believe me, I'm well aware."

"It's got your kind of twisted logic all over it though." He flicked the paper again. “But if you’re okay with it, I’m going to burn this fucking thing.”

I clapped my hand on his shoulder. "I am so sorry. For everything. For all the things I did to you that I wasn't even aware of. You know? While I was away? Any time I wanted to be a better person, I pretended I was you. You're the best man I know, and, well, you deserve better than a brother like me."

"What I deserve has nothing to do with it,” he said flatly. “You're my brother.” He stood up and pulled his phone from his pocket and checked the notification on the screen. Then held it out for me to read. “And you’re theirs too.”

I leaned in. It had been sent eight minutes ago, and we were exactly eight minutes out of town.

Jonah: I’m with Gabe. We’re on our way.

Chapter Forty-One

FINN

Beau stood next to me. Not closely. But close enough that I felt strong enough to look my two older brothers in the face.

"Well then," Gabe finally cracked. "No one's gonna punch him in the face? Now I *know* we're going soft."

Jonah sniffed. It might have been a laugh.

And then we collapsed back into an awkward silence.

"You good?" Jonah checked in with Beau.

My twin shrugged. "Getting there."

"*You* good?" Gabe narrowed his eyes at me.

It was my turn to shrug. "Getting there," I echoed.

Gabe looked at Beau. Beau looked at the ceiling. And Jonah mumbled a long string of curse words before throwing his hands in the air. "Welp! I don't know about you three, but I am way too fucking sober to be having this conversation right now." He turned to the door. "I'm headed to the Crown," he called over his shoulder. "If you dipshits want to have this out, then meet me there."

Gabe set down our beers, then turned back and grabbed his drink.

I stared at it. And then him. "What the fuck is that?"

Gabe looked down at the luridly pink concoction in front of him. "Virgin strawberry daiquiri," he declared.

"Did you hand over you cock and balls to get it?" Jonah wanted to know.

"Hey fuck you. It's delicious and I'm secure enough in my masculinity to enjoy a fruity pink drink." He sat back. "Plus if I have to be sober during this conversation while the rest of you get to drink, then I deserve to enjoy myself." He punctuated this tirade by taking a prim sip from his straw - pinky elevated.

"This is what happens when you leave, Finn." Jonah was looking at Gabe with exaggerated concern. "I'm afraid we've lost him."

I leaned forward, figuring this was my invitation to start explaining, but as I did so, I caught Beau's eye.

It's a twin thing. I can't pretend to understand how I know what he's thinking. It's that connection that formed in the womb.

And fuck, I really missed it.

"We good?" my raised eyebrow asked.

"Getting there," the slight tension at his jaw replied.

"Good enough I can fuck around with Gabe again?" the tilt of my head wondered.

"Have at it," his lifted chin agreed.

Gabe looked at Jonah. "They're doing it."

"I know," Jonah sighed, drumming his fingers on the table. "Can't you two use your mouths to talk like the rest of us normal people?"

"You might not like what it has to say," I shot back. Beau smirked.

"Why, what the fuck were you just saying about me?" Jonah's ego was his Achilles' heel and the three of us exploited that mercilessly.

"I was saying," I leaned back and closed my eyes. "I was saying... I'm sorry. I don't know... I can't explain why I thought what I was doing was the right thing. I just...." I let out a long breath as my brothers watched me closely. "There's something in my head that hates me." I nearly choked on the admission. "And it had me convinced you were all better off without me in your life."

"What changed?" Jonah asked after a beat. His tone was cool and neutral. Business Jonah, our oldest brother and leader. I recognized it as the same wary tone he used to sniff out bullshit. If he detected a single whiff of it, you were toast.

I pressed my hand flat on the table. Talking about her made my stomach clench. “I met someone.”

“Sky,” Beau supplied.

“Wait, you have girl-?” Gabe started, but I held up my hand. Because if I didn’t tell them this now, I wasn’t ever going to say it

“No. I don’t.” I took a deep breath. “Not yet, anyway.” Gabe gave an approving nod. “I fucked it all up because I thought I knew how it would end. That voice, it had me convinced that there was no way I was good enough for her. But the thing that was different was that I -.” I rubbed my temples vigorously. “I didn’t’ want to hear it this time. Instead of agreeing with it, I finally started to argue.” The buzz of the bar slid away as I heard myself saying things I’d been too afraid to express in words. “And then I set out to prove it wrong. *Fuck you, voice.* Right?” I opened my eyes and looked at my brothers. “You probably aren’t surprised that I wanted to get in a fight. The difference was - ."

“You were fighting for yourself.” Gabe was nodding like this made sense.

I suddenly needed to reach out and grab his hand. He looked startled, but closed his hand around mine in an awkwardly bent handshake. “Yeah. Exactly. I didn’t recognize it at the time," I told him. "Like I said, I really thought I was just finding another new and delightful way to be a dick to myself. But somewhere along the way I started to think I might actually be wrong about myself.”

“You are,” said Beau.

The corner of my mouth jerked up involuntarily. I felt naked. Stripped down and bare. My fists were clenching, fighting still. Fighting the feeling of being vulnerable. “I don’t believe it. Yet. But the difference is, now I want to.”

“For her.”

“For me,” I corrected. “For you.” I nodded at Beau. “And then, maybe... someday...” I trailed off, for the first time allowing myself the fantasy of knocking on Sky’s door. Bringing her flowers, taking her to dinner. Something healthy.

And normal. Could I do that?

I looked around the table at my brothers. All three of them had found love already and all three of them had gone through their own unique hells to find it.

If I felt vulnerable before, now I felt downright pathetic. But it couldn't be helped. This was an emergency. This was... Sky.

"Guys?" I asked. "How the fuck do you... date?"

Chapter Forty-Two

SKY

Yesterday, I'd stopped by the lawyer's office and gotten my Dad's house officially transferred to my name. Today, Livvy was meeting me after she got off work and taking me furniture shopping before I moved in on Saturday.

"See what you need," she'd told me before leaving this morning. "Swing by and make sure all those people didn't like, destroy the place. Last thing you want after all of this is to move in and and find out the bed is missing."

So that's what I had set out to do.

But now, as I stood on the sidewalk in front of the house that was now legally mine, I couldn't bring myself to even walk up to the front door.

I looked up and down the street. It was a nice enough neighborhood, all boxy two-story colonials with identical rectangles of green front lawn. Very middle-class pride gone frayed around the edges. I could hardly picture my train-crash of a father fitting in here. They must have hated him, and I bet he relished the chance to hate them right back.

His house - my house - was sided in white with black shutters around the windows. It looked so normal from the outside that it seemed familiar. But that was only because I'd seen houses jus like it all over America. There was nothing about it that said, 'This is where Bill Clarence Knight lived, this is where he raised one family while keeping the other one a secret.'

In fact, out of all the places in Crown Creek, this felt the least touched by his hand. There was nothing of him here. No ghosts lurking around corners ready to ambush me with his handwriting or his face on a plaque. I looked at it and felt nothing.

And that scared me.

I closed my eyes and squeezed the key so tightly that it dug into my hand. And I tried. I tried to summon him. I tried to call up those old, faded memories, those moments I had relived so many times they now ran like movies in my head. I watched them, but I didn't recognize the girl in the starring role. She loved her father with a blind devotion that was almost religious. And what about him? Had he loved her?

He must have. In his own way. Because he left this for her... for me.

I opened my eyes. I hadn't been forgotten or discarded, no matter how many times I'd been convinced of that fact since the funeral. He'd remembered me and wanted to give me a piece of him.

But now the question was, did I want it?

I swallowed hard and unclenched my fist, feeling the sting of the blood returning to the crevices the key had dug into my hand. This gift wasn't actually for me, though. It was for him. A way to absolve himself before dying without telling me the truth. If I walked into this house, I'd be tying myself to him. I'd be beholden to his memory. I'd be accepting just another scrap of his love instead of the wholeness I deserved.

I stepped back. I didn't want to be tied to bad memories any more. I didn't want to live in the shadow of his betrayal, or accept his token acknowledgement. Accepting it would mean I accepted what he'd done to me. And to everyone who loved him and who he supposedly loved.

I'd thought it was my legacy, but it was just one more bribe to keep me on his team.

I blinked rapidly, but I didn't need to. I was done shedding tears for my father.

———

I drove back across town. The gate was actually open since it was during business hours.

It felt strange to pull in to Knights' garage and walk up to the office door without any drama or hesitation.

But there was no need for that anymore.

J.D. looked up from his books and scowled when he saw me. "You came alone? No posse?"

"Do I need one?" I challenged him.

His scowl lessened. "It's your call. But *I* don't think so."

I squeezed the key in my hand until the teeth sank into my palm, digging into the flesh until the mark was left there. It hurt.

Then I let it go.

J.D. jerked back when I slapped my hand down on his desk. "What's this?" he stared at the key like he'd never seen one before.

"I don't want it."

He snapped his head up. "You're serious?"

I let my shoulder lift in a shrug. "I don't want to owe him."

J.D. was my brother. With eyes so like mine that if I held his gaze and looked nowhere else, it was like looking right into a mirror. He shared those eyes with my Dad.

Our Dad.

Something was happening to his face. The grim, serious set of his jaw softened.

And for the first time I saw my brother smile.

That was just like mine too.

"Damn," he said, chuckling as he shook his head side to side. "Damn." He reached over and covered the key with his hand. "You know? It took me nearly a whole lifetime with him before I figured out what a fraud he was. You sure caught up quick."

"I must be the smart one in the family," I quipped.

He laughed. Big and loud and full-throated. It caught the attention of Rocky and the silent brother whose name I still didn't know. They came to the office door in their coveralls. When they saw me, they both stepped back, but J.D. held up his hand. "Hey guys, c'mere.

There's someone here you gotta meet. This is Sky..." he paused and waited for me to supply the name.

"I dunno." I shook my head. "Sky Knight? If you go last name first, that reads Knight Sky and I don't know if I can live with that kind of pun."

"Lennon here was almost named Ryder." Rocky socked his silent brother in the side. I finally knew his name.

"Knight Ryder?" I pinched the bridge of my nose. "Oh God, he loved that show. He used to make me watch the reruns when he was home."

My brothers stiffened a little when I mentioned "home," but for the first time, I didn't let that bother me.

"So this is Sky Clarence," J.D. went on, giving me a nod. "She's our sister, as you know. But she's also sort of a badass." He gestured to the key.

"Sort of?" I protested as the two men stared at it. "Only sort of?"

Rocky was the first to come forward. He rushed to me, paused, then held out his hand. "Sky?" He rested his hand on my shoulder, then let it slide down my arm like he wasn't sure he was allowed to touch me yet. "Is this what I think it is?"

I nodded. "I want a fresh start. You guys can put it to way better use than I can."

Rocky looked at J.D., who nodded and picked up his phone. As he stalked out of the office, I heard him greet the person on the other end. "Yeah Dinah? You can send them. We've got a place all ready."

"This is awesome, Sky," Rocky said. It sounded like he was choking up. "This is more than I ever...." He blinked and then coughed.

"More than you thought I'd be capable of?"

"I'm sorry," he said quickly. "We didn't know you."

"It's okay," I said. "I didn't either."

Chapter Forty-Three

SKY

That evening, I stayed close to the window, waiting for Livvy's gray hatchback to pull in. I'd spent the afternoon searching out a list of rentals, but needed her help to figure out which ones were a good fit. Small as it was, I was still learning my way around this town.

Finally I heard the squeal of tires turning in to Livvy's driveway. Which was weird, because Livvy was a pretty cautious driver and I'd never heard her tires squeal before. I went up my my tiptoes and saw the reason why.

It wasn't Livvy's gray hatchback pulling in to the driveway. It was Claire's white Jeep.

She honked the horn until I locked the door behind me, then rolled down the window. "Get in! If we move fast, we'll have time to see all four places before we meet everyone."

Livvy emerged from the passenger seat. "I couldn't stop her. When I told her you wanted to see apartments, she showed up five minutes later to pick me up from work." She shook her head. "Honestly, I don't think Superman himself could have stopped her."

"Come on!" Claire shouted. "Get in, we're on a schedule here! Give me that list. Livvy! Sit in the back so she can see better."

She was bossy and bratty and a pain in the ass. And I was really glad to have her on my side. I grinned at my new friend, then slid into the passenger seat of her Jeep. It was pristinely white, polished and waxed on the outside.

The inside, to my surprise, was filthy.

Claire looked up from scanning my lists of addresses and caught me looking at the drift of trash on the floor. "Sorry," she said. "I've kind of been living out of my car lately."

"Why's that?" I wondered.

"Working a lot of hours and stuff."

"And going on a lot of dates," Livvy piped up from behind us.

"That's between you me and the wall," Claire snapped. "Good Lord, don't let my brothers find out."

I sat up little straighter. "How are your brothers doing?" I asked innocently enough. I hoped.

She gave me a withering look. "Which one?"

"All of them?" I squeaked.

"Heh," was all she said.

She turned down the road where my father's funeral had been held. The church seemed like something out of a case of deja vu. I knew it had happened, but it felt like it'd happened to someone else.

Then Claire hit the gas and we slid past it and it was gone. "Wait, isn't that the address?" I cried as we flew past the first house on my list.

"Oh we're not going there. I found you someplace better."

I looked at Livvy who just laughed and mouthed "Sorry," again.

"It was close to the middle of town," I protested.

"It was close to the Crown," Claire corrected.

"That's not a bad thing!" I was so excited when I found the listing for the second floor apartment in an old general store right at one of the Five Corners. When I looked at a map, I had immediate visions of walking down from my place and meeting everyone on Thursdays. "I loved it."

"No, it's no good. Might get loud in the summer."

"I don't mind."

"Now this." Claire ignored me. "I love. Right on Main Street, but down at the quiet end. Look!" She parked and pointed up.

It was a two story red-brick building, plain but solid looking. The street level was taken up by a florist called Best Buds.

But it was the upper level that made my breath catch. “Is that a porch?” I asked. “On the second floor?”

“And your neighbors are the florist and the pet food store,” Claire added smugly. “Much quieter.”

I rolled down my window. After a stray car shushed by, all was quiet except the rustle of the leaves still clinging to the branches above us. And further off was the quiet murmur of the creek. Like a reassuring voice whispering that everything was okay. I was home now.

An old woman walked by on the sidewalk in front of the building, cradling a small white dog dressed in a tartan sweater. I'd seen her before. “I wonder if Mrs. Gaines knows that walking your dog involves actually putting it down?” Livvy mused.

And now I knew who she was.

My heart felt like it was going to burst out of my chest. I was home. “I love it!”

“Wait ’til you go inside!” Livvy laughed. “You don’t know that yet!”

“I do!” Claire said. “Let’s go in.”

There was a wide drive running between the two buildings that led to a small parking area in the back. A small grassy space, no bigger than a passage stamp, was dotted with white wicker furniture. “Too cold now,” Livvy said. “But in the summer?”

“Who cares about a tiny yard when you have a huge porch?” Claire wanted to know. “Come on!”

We entered from the back, following the sharp left turn up the narrow staircase. “Should be open!” Claire called up to me when I reached it first.

I pushed in to a wide open living room, with gleaming hardwood floors. A kitchenette lined one wall, but the rest of the space could be set up any way I wanted. I spun in a circle. “I feel like a ballerina in here.”

“The porch is off the bedroom,” Claire instructed. “Through there.” Then laughed when I took off running.

“This is so nice!” I breathed, stepping out onto the porch. I was high enough that through a gap in the buildings across the street, I caught the play of light on the rocks that lined the creek bed. I perched at the edge, ignoring Livvy's panicked gasp, and leaned out. "I can just imagine sitting out here with coffee in the morning."

"We'll need to get you some porch furniture." Livvy had her phone out and looked to be making a list of furnishings for me. I loved her for that. "You could get a rocking chair, or one of those swinging things you could hang from the roof here."

"No, I want a whole set," I declared. "A table with two chairs and a swing that we could rock on too." I looked out. "We're facing west, right? We could watch the sun set."

"You planning on having parties?"

I blinked out of my reverie and widened my eyes. Heat was climbing up my face. The way Claire was watching me, I was almost sure she knew who I pictured sitting in the swing next to me.

I blinked and looked away before I started crying. The future. I was looking to the future. "This is it," I said, nodding. "This is home."

Chapter Forty-Four

FINN

It was early enough on a Saturday morning that I was trying my best to be quiet. But not quiet enough. Rachel jumped out of bed and caught me putting my boots on.

"Where are you going?" my future sister-in-law asked, a sharp note in her voice.

I sighed. "You don't have to worry every time I leave, you know."

"I'll work on that." She crossed her arms over her chest.

I stood up. "Actually, do you want to come with me? I'm going out on a coffee run."

"We *have* coffee," she pointed out.

"Yeah, but my friend Dinah doesn't."

Rachel's expression changed immediately. She moved her lips, rubbing them together and then dragging her teeth across the bottom one. "I remember Dinah," she said, with a far off expression in her eyes. "Want to know the funny thing?"

"What's that?"

She looked at me. "I never liked her. Can you believe that?"

"Dinah? For real?"

She nodded. "I thought she was selfish."

"She's not."

"Well, yeah!" she exploded, sounding exasperated. "I see that *now*." She shook her head. "I can't believe what she's doing for them." She touched my arm. "You either."

"Dinah said you're the reason people started," I told her, hoping to stop the tears that were gathering in her eyes. "That you gave them hope it was possible."

Rachel swallowed hard. "Have you heard anything about Rebecca?" she asked in a tiny voice.

Her sister. I shook my head. "I'm sorry, Rach."

She looked away for a moment. Then nodded her head. "Hang on a sec and let me get my shoes. I'm coming with you."

The Chit Chat Cafe was packed as usual. "Is this place ever not busy?" I wondered aloud. "It's like 8:30 in the morning."

"What does Dinah drink?" Rachel asked, leaning up against the counter. "I'm buying it for her."

"I got it."

"I said I'm buying," Rachel snapped, showing the same fire that had driven her to take an overnight bus to New York City to find my brother again. I would always love her for that.

"Fine! She likes espresso," I laughed, holding up my hands in surrender. "But I'm paying for my own cup, thank you." I shoved my hands back in my pockets and waited while Rachel put in her order, idly looking around the place. I turned to read the chalkboard sign with the specials on it...

And came face to face with my sister.

"Claire!" I started to smile and immediately stopped when her expression went icy. "You've been avoiding me."

"I'm busy," she snapped. "And if you're planning on badgering me into talking with you later, forget it. I have plans."

Rachel turned and smiled at Claire, then frowned when she saw our stand-off. "I'll be over here," she said, sliding out of the way.

Claire snorted and turned to put in her order.

"Plans?" I asked. "What are your plans?"

God bless her, Claire was terrible at the silent treatment. “If you must know,” she declared, tossing her hair. “I’m picking up these up before I go help a friend move in to her new place. And then I have a lunch date.”

I blinked and decided to go with the lesser of two evils. “Who’s moving? Sadie?”

She turned to face me completely. “Sky,” she said, tossing the name at me like a grenade.

“Sky’s moving?” My throat felt like it was closing.

“I found her a place right on Main Street, down at the quiet end.” Claire bragged. “She loves it.”

“What about her house?”

She shrugged. “Didn’t want it.”

My brain was spinning. “Where? Where is it?”

Claire blinked and then laughed way too loud. “What, so you can show up and ruin my morning with your half-assed apologies? No thank you.”

“I wasn’t going to -.”

“You know? I was in a good mood too,” she complained. “Here I was looking forward to spending the morning with my friends before letting a hot guy take me out to lunch...”

If she was trying to rile me up, it fucking worked. “What guy?”

She gave me smug smile. “None of your business.”

"I think I have a right to know."

"Do you? Do you really?"

“Is he at least a good guy?”

"I don't know, Finn.” I couldn't remember the last time Claire had called me by my actual name and not some bratty variation on it. It used to drive me crazy, the nicknames she'd come up with. Doll-Finn was the worst of them.

But now I missed them.

“I'm gonna find out at lunch, though," she went on.

"What's his name?"

"Aloysius Percival Winterbottom the Fourth."

"Claire."

"Fuck *off*, Finn."

“Claire. Just... Be careful, okay?”

"Oh, you care now?"

"I've always cared."

"You have an odd way of showing it."

"I know. I am well aware. But I'm back now, right?"

“And now that you’re back I’m suddenly not allowed to go on dates any more?”

"It's not that you're not allowed, I just... I want to know, you know, if he's good for you." Even as I spoke, I realize what a hypocrite I was.

Claire lifted her tray of coffees and looked me in the eyes. “You lost any right you might have had to intrude on my love life when you stepped out of my real one. Fuck off, Finn.” Then she nodded at Rachel. “Bye sweetie! We’ll talk later, okay? I’ve got some ideas about bridesmaids' dresses I want to run by you. Lots of wedding planning to do!”

My sister glanced back at me to see if her words had been the gut-punch she wanted them to be. Whatever she saw on my face must have been the effect she was going for, because she nodded and walked out the door.

“Finn,” Rachel said softly. “Nothing has been set in stone yet. We haven’t even set a date.”

I swallowed and nodded. “Okay.”

“She’s just mad.”

“I know.”

“You’re her favorite brother, you know. I think it hit her hardest. But she loves you and she’ll come around.”

I nodded again. My sister’s trust was something I’d still need to win over, but I had to thank her as well. Because, without realizing, she’d given me the path back to Sky.

“Come on,” I said to Rachel. “Let’s get Dinah her coffee real quick, because there’s something I need your help with.”

“What’s that?”

“How good are you at shopping for housewarming gifts?”

Chapter Forty-Five

SKY

I grabbed a tall glass of ice water and headed out onto my porch.

My porch.

It was an unseasonably hot day and I'd spent much it moving boxes and building furniture. It had left me with that floppy, boneless feeling that comes from sweaty exhaustion.

I was aiming to collapse onto the swing that Claire and Livvy had hung for me.

But got distracted by my new view.

I perched on one leg with the other resting on the railing and rested my water glass on my thigh.

And then I just... *breathed.*

The chaos of moving was over. The chaos of... my *life?* I couldn't say that was done, not for certain. There was always the possibility I'd slip into old, bad habits. But for right now, I had a place I could call my own. I had friends willing to clear their Saturday morning just to help me move. I had a family I was just starting to get to know.

For the first time in my life, it was quiet inside of my head. There was nothing to distract me from the moment. It was almost scary. It felt like the universe was pausing to take a breath before speaking to me.

And it said, "Hello?"

I spilled my water right onto my thigh. "Shit!" I yelled jumping up and brushing at my wet crotch. "What the hell?"

"You okay up there, Sky?"

I froze. It wasn't the universe speaking to me right now, but it was almost as improbable. I leaned way out over the railing. "Finn?" I couldn't see him. "Where are you?"

"I'm at your door!"

I skidded across the hardwood - I still needed to put a rug down - and thundered down the stairs to the ground level. I threw open the door with a wild, "Hi!"

He was fiddling with the trunk of the car he'd parked in the drive, but when he heard me he straightened up. "Hi," he said.

Seeing him at my front door like this knocked something loose in my head.

He was dressed in a button down shirt. The sleeves were rolled to his elbows because of the strange heat, exposing the deliciously corded strength of his forearms. In one breath I was knocked backwards in time to our fishing competition and that strange span of time when he was my whole entire world. "You look good," I said.

He did. The button down was fitted enough to see that he'd put some muscle back onto his range-y frame. His beard was clipped close to his face now and his cheekbones were no longer so sharp and feral.

But his eyes had changed the most. Instead of darting every which way, never resting on any one place for long, he held my gaze like he owned it. But the hazel fire of them hadn't changed, and it still felt like it was going to burn me if I let him look at me for too long.

"It's good to see you," I said, looking down and studying my fingernails.

"My sister let it slip that she found you a place."

"Yeah?"

"She still thinks she's giving me the silent treatment." He was smiling but the pain in his voice was palpable. "But she's pretty terrible about it."

"I would imagine."

"It's nice." He let his glance flick up the stairs.

"You want to come in?" I asked.

He shook his head. "No, I was just stopping by."

"Oh."

"I wanted to give you housewarming gift."

"You don't have to..."

"It's not much. More of a joke, really. But Claire said you didn't have much of anything yet, so I figured you needed one."

He went to the trunk of his car and pulled out a slim box.

I smiled so hard I thought my face would crack. "A DVD player? Thanks, but you have heard of streaming, right? You weren't living like a hermit for *that* long."

"Yeah, but without a DVD player, you wouldn't be able to watch all these."

He pulled out another box.

"*Cat On a Hot Tin Roof?*" I breathed, running my hand over the spines. "*A Streetcar Named Desire*. Wait, *Goonies?*"

"My sister in law helped me. She asked me what you liked and I said old movies. I figured these would keep you occupied a while."

I traced my fingers over the spines. "Have you watched them yet?"

He licked his lips. "I actually bought some of them the day after you left."

"What?"

"I thought... I wanted to... I wanted to continue my 'cultural touchstone education.' Or whatever you called it." He rubbed the back of his neck. "So I went online and made a list of the Top Hundred Most Important Movies."

I gripped the doorframe to keep upright. I had to. My knees were trying to give out. I was going to swoon right to the floor like a Victorian lady. He touched one of the spines and I held my breath. "Is that my copy?"

He held out *My Fair Lady*. "I watched it seven times."

I didn't dare hope. "You're going to watch it the eighth time with me, right?"

"I'd love to." He leaned in and pressed a kiss to my cheek.

"When? Tonight? Tomorrow?"

"Saturday. After I take you out to dinner."

"Like a date?"

He nodded.

"Aren't we sort of past that?"

"No."

"That's kind of silly don't you...?"

"I want to date you, Sky," he interrupted forcefully. "I want to come to your door with flowers and buy you a steak and all that shit. I want to do things right with you." He ran his hand through his hair as I held my breath. "Fuck, I don't know what I'm doing, but I'm doing it. Your Dad... well... I can't ask his permission and shit, so I did the next best thing. I think."

"What?"

"I asked J.D.."

"Jesus Christ, Finn."

"I know Rocco's the oldest, but I didn't feel like dealing with him."

"You asked my brother's permission?"

"Nah," He looked sheepish. "I mean I *meant* to. But it came out wrong."

"How'd it come out?"

"'Hey Knight, I'm taking your sister out this Saturday, and if you have problem with it you can kiss my ass,'" he quoted. As I laughed, he blew out a sigh. "I'm working on it."

"You are. And honestly, if you'd done it any other way, I would have told you no and slammed the door in your face." I ran my hand down his cheek and he closed his eyes. "Okay, Finn," I said softly. "See you Saturday?"

His eyes gleamed with pleasure. "Yeah. It's a date."

Chapter Forty-Six

FINN

Joey's Pasta House was as fancy as it got around here, and they did a surprisingly good steak. I called to make a reservation and Joey laughed and told me to say hi to my Dad.

I really hoped that meant I had a table.

I did every single thing my brothers had rattled of that night at the Crown. "Bring her flowers," was Jonah's best advice. "Shave that thing on your face," was Gabe's. But Beau's advice wasn't as easy to follow.

"Give her something she doesn't even know she needs."

I'd thought I had that covered with the DVD collection. But when I picked her up that Saturday night and saw the way her eyes were shining when I bent down to kiss her, I knew it wasn't enough.

"Should we order a bottle of wine?" I asked her, once Joey himself had made sure we were seated.

Sky looked down at her hands and her shoulders started shaking.

"What's wrong?" I asked, alarmed.

"We're on a date!" She was laughing. Thank God.

"I told you. I wanted to start over."

"You did." She took a sip of her water. "And then you disappeared for two weeks."

"I had to figure out how. You deserved the absolute best I could do."

"Joey's Pasta House?" There was a dimple on her cheek. I'd just noticed. It seemed I would never run out of things to learn about this girl.

I raised my water glass. "Only the best for my girl."

"Am I your girl?"

"I really fucking hope you will be." The candle light made the pink in her cheeks look even more delicious. I leaned over and covered her hand with mine. "Tell me three things you fear the most."

"What the hell?"

"It's from a dating website," I sighed. "'Conversation starters for first date success.'"

She looked impressed. "You really are trying to do the best you can do."

"You deserve it," I promised her.

She tapped her finger against her top teeth. And then launched into a passionate speech about how she didn't care how silly it sounded, whales were fucking terrifying. "They could swallow you whole!" she cried.

Her fear of whales led us to all the things we knew weren't going to happen, but were on the lookout for anyway. "I'm waiting for the day my parents' dog sits up and reveals that he could actually talk this whole time, but was too polite to interrupt. He had to wait to get a word in edgewise," I sighed. "I swear that dog has seen some shit."

Sky laughed and started wondering what would happen if animals could be credible witnesses to crimes. Which led to me imagining a squirrel detective with a 50s-noir accent. "She had these amazing gams, and walnuts to make a man weep," I sniffed, miming taking a drag from a cigarette, then nibbling.

And then we were off, trading animal voices and arguing about whether cats had squeaky voices or super chill surfer dude ones.

We were so wrapped up in our discussion that it took a second for us both to realize someone was standing over our table. Sky trailed off her 'kangaroo cop punches a suspect' impression and looked up at the intruder with a polite smile. "Hello? Can I help you?"

I felt frozen to the spot. And then I was angry as fuck that out of all the people in the world to show up on my perfect date, it was Grace Knight.

"You don't remember me?" she asked Sky. I glanced around and saw Ethan Bailey sitting at a table, watching, and wondered if my sister knew about this.

But there was no time to think of that now. Because, judging by the way Sky's expression was changing....

She remembered.

Chapter Forty-Seven

SKY

"Yeah. I remember." I cleared my throat and looked into my sister's eyes. "Last time I saw you, you were cursing me out. And preventing me from going to see my Dad's grave."

Grace seemed to be expecting that, because she only pressed her lips together. "I - I'm sorry for that. It's not your fault. None of this is any of our fault. The only person who's fault it is is lying in Crown Creek Cemetery."

Just as quickly as my anger blazed up, it drained away again, leaving me feel hollowed out inside. "Yeah. You're right."

"You've met all my - our - brothers already, I know. And I'm sorry it took me so long to say anything. I was just... I was pretty fucked up."

I felt my smile tug upward. "Same."

Grace laughed. "J.D. told me you were a little badass. He's the only one I listen to." She sighed a world weary sigh. "I love that giant group of knuckleheads. But it gets to be a little much sometimes. And somehow, with all this hate I have for Dad over what he did, I have to be grateful to him too. He gave me something I always wanted."

"What is that?"

She smile sadly. "A sister."

I clenched my fists, and then released them. I was ready for her hate. I didn't know what to do with her understanding. "He gave me a family," I said slowly. "I just - had to find them myself."

Grace shook her head. "I'd love to sit him down and find out just *what* the fuck he was thinking."

"Me too," I sighed. Out of the corner of my eye, I could see Finn watching us both intently.

Grace caught the direction of my glance. "Well I'm sorry for interrupting," she said, stepping back. "I just - I guess I wanted to say," she lifted her fingers. "Hi?"

I laughed and lifted mine in return. "Hi!"

She waved one more time. And then scurried away, looking relieved.

I turned back to Finn. "Well!" I heaved a huge sigh. "So that happened." He looked pensive and far-off. I leaned in. "Are you okay? Sorry if that ruined our date."

He shook his head. "It didn't ruin anything. In fact, it gave me an idea."

"Yeah? What kind of idea?"

He grinned. "You're going to have to wait and see."

I leaned in, making sure he was watching as I played with the neckline of my dress. "What if I don't want to wait?"

He threw down a credit card. "Let's go," he ordered as he grabbed my hand.

"Don't you want to wait for the check?"

"Nope!"

Finn broke every rule of the road, but it still took forever to get back to my apartment. I fumbled at the lock as he peppered kisses down my neck, and finally burst through the door in a tangle of limbs. I stumbled up the stairs trying to kiss him while climbing backwards, and he growled and swept me up into his arms before going up them two at a time.

"Nice place," he murmured against my lips. "You need a rug though. This floor is way too hard to fuck you on."

I pressed my hands to his chest, curling my fingers just to feel him solid and real under my touch.

Then I raked them downward. "I'm not waiting until I get a rug delivered, Finn. I've been waiting long enough. I've been playing it your way, with the waiting and the dating. Now I want it mine."

Chapter Forty-Eight

SKY

The curve of his mouth tipped up into a dangerous smile. "That sounds perfectly fair to me."

I'd missed his kisses. The ones that bruised my lips and made my limbs go weak. That all consuming assault on my senses that canceled out anything that wasn't him. I'd been so afraid of it, but now I welcomed it because I knew I could handle the oblivion.

"Sky." His mouth made the shape of my name against my lips, and then his hands were in my hair. Tugging back to expose my throat, he bit down on the sensitive place where my neck met my shoulder. I squirmed, then retaliated, pulling his shirt up and over his head in one quick motion, and dragging my nails down his back.

"So glad that part of you hasn't changed," he growled appreciatively before walking me backwards until the back of my knees caught the bed.

He landed on top of me, crushing me under his weight. And I gloried in it because I suddenly realized something. "Finn, this is the first time we're going to do this face-to-face."

He paused a moment, the emotion on his face crystal clear.

Then he smiled again. "Being face-to-face with you sounds so good, baby. But I've really missed being face-to-pussy."

My shocked gasp at his crude language dissolved into a gasp of pleasure when his tongue found me. I was just as primed for the explosion as I was the very first night he'd done this to me. But instead of losing myself, and pulling away, I stayed connected to him, sinking my fingers into his hair, and grabbing at his shoulders and hands. Any bit of skin, any part of him that I could hold onto was enough.

"Missed this," Finn murmured between my legs, moving his tongue in slow lazy circles. "I could do this the rest of the night."

I arched up onto my elbows. "Don't you dare," I chided him.

He chuckled, and those hazel eyes peering up at me from between my legs nearly knocked me flat back on my ass. "Then you'd better come for me, sweetheart. I'm not stopping until I can feel your greedy little pussy grabbing at my fingers."

"Oh my God, it does that?" I gasped.

Then Finn did something with his tongue that made my world explode.

I panted, and bucked, and swore until I could speak again.

Then looked down at him sheepishly." "Well then. I guess it does."

"God, I fucking love you," he sighed. "Come here." He yanked me upright, and claimed my mouth.

He tasted like me, my scent lingering in his beard, and it drove me out of my mind. "Now, Finn. Don't make me wait any longer."

"I don't think I could," he panted against my mouth. "One more second, baby girl, just hang on one more second." He fumbled with the condom wrapper, and rolled it down his length at light speed. I spread my legs wider, urging him on.

He sank into me. And finally, *finally,* Finn King and I were completely connected.

"Shit," he mumbled against my skin. "You feel... shit." He seemed incapable of words. His hips moved in a slow rolling rhythm that touched every part I'd known about myself. And some parts that had still been secret.

"Finn." My breath was coming faster now... desperate... keening. "Finn, oh my God, I love you. I love you!"

He groaned, gathering me up into his arms and holding me so

tightly I could barely breathe, but it was so overwhelming that I lost control anyway. "Sky, you're it. I love you, I love..." His words dissolved into a long animal groan.

And he gave himself to me. Completely.

Chapter Forty-Nine

FINN

"Jesus!" Sky fell back, collapsing in a tangle of hair and limbs.

I studied her, still panting. But not satisfied. Not even after an orgasm so powerful I almost blacked out.

Because it hadn't been how I'd envisioned it. It had been too fast. Too rough.

It seemed like I'd always need to start over with her. Try again and again. Until it was perfect... like she deserved.

Luckily, with her, I knew that I could.

"Come here," I said, gathering her to me.

She closed her eyes and tilted her head to kiss me. Her fingers wandered over my chest and down to -.

Her eyes flew open. "Again? Seriously?"

"Over and over again. Until I get it right."

"That felt good enough for me."

I pressed her back onto the bed, already wanting her so badly I was shaking with it. "Can't hurt to practice though, right? You make me a better man, Sky. I need to get better at... everything."

"What are you talking about? You're good, you're incredible you're...oh!"

I'd finally figured out how to get her to stop asking me questions.

After I'd worn her out a second time, she looked up at me with a sleepy smile. "You're the only one," she murmured, her voice thick with sleep.

"The only one who can make you come like that? Good to know."

"No!" she pouted. "I'm being romantic."

"I am too."

"*Finn.*"

"Sorry. You were saying?"

She heaved a sigh. "I feel like, there's this break in my life. Like it's got these two parts. The before. And the after." She yawned. "The before? That was my life on the road, with no roots and no family. And the after?" Her smile was the most beautiful thing I'd ever seen. "Well now I have an apartment, and friends. And a family."

"And a boyfriend," I reminded her.

"Yes, but, that's what I was saying." She pressed her lips together. "I don't have anyone from the before anymore." Her fingers brushed down my cheek. "You're the closest I've got." She smiled. "You're actually the person who has been in my life the longest."

I blinked. And then blinked again. The germ of the idea that had come when I watched her with Grace took shape and was suddenly fully formed.

"I'm honored," I told her, leaning in to kiss her eyes shut. "Now go to sleep."

"Are you in a hurry for me to shut up or something?" she mumbled.

"No, I'm in a hurry to make a phone call."

"Who-mmmm?" She was asleep. I kissed her gently and slipped from the bed. I'd taken my brothers' advice. I'd brought flowers and shaved.

Now, I hoped I could give her the thing she didn't even know she needed.

A history.

When Dinah picked up on the first ring, I had to smile at her excitement. "What, are you bored without me?" I teased her.

"It's sure quieter," she chuckled. "But I'm not saying that's a good thing."

"Well, if you're looking for something to do, I have a favor to ask."

"You know you can ask me anything, Finn," she said firmly. "Anything."

I smiled. How had I ever thought I had no one who cared? "Hey," I said, lowering my voice so as not to wake Sky. "Remember how you told me you have a lot of people?"

"I do."

"Do you think you could help me track someone down?"

"I'm your girl," she bragged.

"Even if it's someone from Reckless Falls?"

"You just leave it to me." Dinah promised.

Chapter Fifty

SKY

Growing up, I learned that love can survive long separations.

I'd yearned for my father to stay home, to be with me every waking moment. The long droughts between the times he visited me weren't healthy.

I'd done the opposite with Finn at the campground. I'd gorged myself on spending every second with him that I could.

That hadn't been healthy either.

Now I was learning how to love someone without letting it take over my life.

"Have a nice day," I murmured, as he kissed me goodbye. I could smell the cup of espresso he'd already prepared for me.

He was really good at coffee. We already knew that. But we were finding out that I was a much better cook. Willa had made good on her promise to teach me.

Finn had acted as my taste tester as I tried out a menu for my first dinner party. On the day of, he'd helped me chop the veggies for the appetizer tray, pour the drinks and wash the dishes.

And then he'd kissed me goodbye and left so I could have time with my friends.

We weren't together every moment. And I didn't even think about him every single moment.

I knew he was there, and I knew I'd see him again. He was my constant now.

And our love was the lived-in kind I'd always dreamed of.

"Hey!" I laughed into my phone. "Since when do you *call* me?"

Finn chuckled at the other end of the line. "Since I need to make a date with you."

"One date was plenty," I grumbled. "We covered that already, I think."

"Okay, but what if I'd showed up to your house and you weren't there? Better to call you first and make sure, right?" His voice softened. "For real though, I'm not sure. You know I'm still new at this."

My heart felt too big in my chest. "I love you. And wait, you're on your way over? Why?"

"Isn't wanting to see you enough?" he exploded. Then waited a beat. "I'm just fucking with you, Sky. No, remember the surprise?"

"The one I had to wait and see about?"

"Yeah. Come on down and see me. The wait is over."

I grabbed my purse and thundered down the stairs so fast I almost ran right into him. "Oh! What the hell are you doing waiting for me here?"

His face was solemn. Almost nervous. "Do you trust me?"

"Of course!"

"Do you know that I'd never willingly hurt you, and if I ever do it's because my intentions were good?"

"Finn? You're freaking me out."

"And wait." He held up a finger as if remembering something. "You're not supposed to be going anywhere the rest of the day, right? Shit, I knew I should have made this a real date."

"Why? Is the surprise going to take long?"

"We have to drive a bit." He swung open the door. "And we're going to have company too."

I stared at the back seat of his car. "Grace?" I hissed.

He looked down at his feet. "I thought... you both could use some answers."

Chapter Fifty-One

SKY

We drove for almost an hour before things started to look familiar. All the while, I peppered Finn with questions about where we were going, what we were doing. “What the hell, are we going to the waterfall?” I asked when we made the turn that wound down from the mountains and into Reckless Falls. “Did you plan a picnic or something?”

It took right up until the moment he turned on to my old street for me to fully comprehend what he’d done.

“She’s -.” I clapped my hand over my mouth. “You... Finn? You found her?”

He licked his lips. “Hope so,” he murmured. Then twisted to look at me. “I figured you - the both of you,” he gestured to Grace. “Needed some idea of the ‘before.’”

I clasped his face in my hands and kissed him desperately. “I can’t believe you,” I murmured.

“Are you sure you want to do this?" Finn’s huge hand closed over mine, squeezing in silent worry. Now that he'd made it happen, he seemed uncertain if it should.

I turned and looked into the backseat.

Grace looked ill. She was staring at the shabby ranch house with her lips pressed tightly together. "You okay?" I asked.

The side of her mouth curled up in an ironic sneer. "I've been here." She looked out the window again. "I can't remember why but he brought us here."

"He did?" The thought stuck in my throat like I had swallowed a toothpick. I wracked my own brain. A fuzzy picture formed of playing with kids my own age. Kids with dark eyebrows and light hair. Half remembered. as if in a dream, it slipped past my memory before it was gone forever.

"Maybe he was testing us," Grace supplied. "After all, loyalty was something he expected. No, demanded."

"But he didn't expect it from himself," I finished slowly.Then tapped the window. "Whatever we want to know, she'll be the one who knows it." I reached for the car door handle, and looked back again. "I can go alone, if you guys want me to."

"You're not going alone," Finn corrected. And then smacked my hand. "And you're not opening your own door either, so stop that."

Some of the tension eased as I laughed, and then teased him by locking the door before he could open it for me.

But it came back with a vengeance as I walked up the familiar pitted walkway to the front door.

It was yellow now, not the faded robin's egg blue of years past. But the brass knocker was the same and I lifted it, feeling like it weighed a thousand pounds.

The sound of it dropping made all three of us wince.

The murmur of the television on the other side of the door ceased. I heard shuffling footsteps, and then saw gray hairs at the top of the window before I heard the sound of door latches opening.

She swung it open..

And there she was.

It was like someone had poured hot liquid into my chest. My heart melted at the sight of the woman, now frail, but whose iron gray hair still advertised her iron strength. This was the woman who had loved me when she had no reason to. I gasped her name. "Janet!"

She blinked. Blinked again. Her mouth opened, then shut tight. I watched her steely eyes soften, and then fill with tears. "Sky!" It came out as a warm exhale.

She pushed the door open and I caught it, flinging it back and then throwing my arms around her neck.

I was crying. But I was also laughing too, and between her exclamations of surprise, I kept interrupting her with the only thing I could think to say. "I'm sorry, God I am so, *so* sorry."

"Where did you come from?" she asked. "And who are these two?"

"Finn is my," I paused and looked at him

"Boyfriend," he supplied crossly.

Biting back a smile I nodded, and then turned to Grace. "And Grace is my sister."

I turned as I said it, checking Janet's reaction when she heard me.

Just as I thought, her eyes widened before she could catch herself. Her pale face went bright red. "Oh my," she said. "You found each other."

"So you did know?"

She stepped back. "Why don't you come on in, darling?"

Chapter Fifty-Two

FINN

I loved her. I knew that with more certainty than I knew anything else

But if I hadn't known before, I would have been certain right now. In this moment. I would have fallen in love as soon as I saw her sit on the faded couch of the woman who had the power to devastate her, and still hold her head high.

“That man could have you believing the sky was green just by his say so," Janet started, after she'd fetched us all mismatched mugs of weak tea. "We were neighbors, your folks and I. My Edgar had just died, and while he left me set with his postman's pension, the taxes were killing me. I needed to go back to work, but raising kids was all I knew.”

She looked at Sky with such love I wanted to hug her. “So when your mom left, I guess I felt pity. Here was this poor Daddy left trying to make do for his little girl. And it was so tough for him, especially with him being on the road so much."

She set down her tea on an end table, and folded her hands in her lap. Sky didn't ask anything, but waited patiently for Janet to continue.

She was finally getting her answers.

Janet cleared her throat. "It didn't take long for me to figure out the truth, because he really didn't bother to hide it. But he had a way -

as you know - of making you disbelieve what you saw with your own eyes." She blinked hard. "I confronted him. You have to believe I did. More than once, too. I told him I didn't judge him for his mistakes. bBut it wasn't right for him to be denying his little girl the stability of a real family."

"That's how he was," Grace spat through clenched teeth. She was taking this worse than Sky was. "None of us saw it for how it was, of course. But asking questions? That was the worst thing you could do in my house. And everyone *loved* him."

She bit that off bitterly, then turned and looked at Sky. "All I wanted growing up was a sister. But I never had the courage to ask for one. What I wouldn't have given for somebody to share my secrets with." She grimaced. "Someone that wasn't going to hold me down and fart in my face for my efforts."

"See now, we tried that with Claire," I spoke up.

Sky shot me a smile. "I'm not trying to figure out *why* he did it," she said gently. "I'm more trying to figure out *how*."

"Well now," Janet twisted her hands in her lap. "I suppose, that's on me. I covered for him." She looked at my girl. "I told you stories of him out on the road, you remember? That truck of his, it was my idea to have him come home in it. Soften the blow. And give you a story to hold on to." She closed her eyes as Sky's filled with tears. "Darling, I'm so sorry. You worshipped your daddy. And I never minded that. It was right that you loved him, that you thought the sun and moon orbited around him. That's the way of the world. And I knew I was never going to be your mama." Janet opened her eyes again. "If I told you the truth, back then, would you have believed me?"

Sky shook her head slowly. Then faster. "No. And I would've hated you for even mentioning it."

Janet nodded sorrowfully. "Yes honey, and I knew that too. And maybe I couldn't make you love me the way I loved you. But I definitely didn't want to make you hate me."

"Janet. I do love you," Sky blurted. "I don't know why... I can't say... God it was so selfish of me not to see what you did for me. I owe you."

Janet shook her head. "You owe me nothin', darling. But I'm grateful that you've got some love to give back."

With a hoarse sob, Sky fell against Janet's shoulder. The older woman closed her arms around her in a tight embrace. And even though my girl was sobbing like her heart would break - and the mere sound of it made my fingers itch - I was able to hold still.

Because I knew, thanks to her, that wounds can't heal if you keep them bandaged up tight.

You have to let the air in.

Chapter Fifty-Three

SKY

We'd dropped Grace off with plans to take her to Reckless Falls with us next time we went. I'd promised Janet I'd be back next Sunday. I intended to keep that promise.

Finn pulled up to my house and threw the car into park. "Are you good?"

I looked up at him. "I can't - I'm speechless."

"For once," he laughed.

I stared up at him and knew, with more certainty than I'd ever felt in my chaotic life, that he was the one. I didn't want him for *my* sake. I didn't want to *lose* myself in him.

I wanted *him.*

I had fled. I didn't realize that's what I was doing, but now I knew. I'd run away from him before I understood my feelings.

But he followed me. He'd just given me a history, a gift I couldn't ever put a price on. And he hadn't let me go.

And now I knew, I'd never let him go either.

I was putting down roots now. I had a family, a brand new family, and friends too. I was no longer seeking the chaos. In the day-to- day, hour-by-hour, I found an order, a structure in my life. I was building a solid foundation.

"You're it," I told him solemnly.

His hazel eyes searched mine . I nodded. "I'm done," I told him. "I'm not searching for anything anymore." I pressed my hand over his heart. "Because it's right here."

"Are you sure?" he whispered against my lips.

I wanted to laugh. I was sure I could fly, but I wrapped my arms around him anyway, thinking maybe we both could fly together. "I finally trust myself," I told him, loving the eager hopeful look that spread across his face. "I finally know myself well enough to know what's true and what isn't true. And what's true is that I love you, Finn. I want to kill you, I want to throttle you, and I want to be with you."

"I want to be with you too. Forever, for a start. But I'm going to do this right, Sky. You're not proposing right now, you hear me? I'm going to propose to you!"

"Are you trying to one-up me?" I laughed.

"Hell fucking yeah, girl, and get ready. It's going to be epic."

"Mine was first, though. So I win."

He laughed, and then his eyes grew solemn again. "I'm going to be worthy of you," he murmured.

"You already are."

"But I'm going to keep working at it too. Every day. I'm going to wake up each morning ready prove myself all over again. And I'll happily do that for the rest of my life, if you'll let me."

I laughed even as giddy tears streaked down my face. "We're doing this? This is forever?"

"This is forever," he echoed. "And I can't wait to start."

EPILOGUE

Finn

My phone went off at midnight.

Sky rolled over and stretched. "Another one?" she murmured.

I checked the text from Dinah as I pulled on my shoes. "A road pick-up. It shouldn't take long. I know we have my parents over for dinner tomorr -."

Sky pressed her finger to my lips. "Ssh," she whispered. Then sat up and pressed her lips to mine.

"Maybe I won't," I groaned, deepening the kiss. "Maybe I need to stay right here."

Sky pulled back. "Go," she said. "There's someone out there who needs you more than me right now."

I groaned theatrically, but headed out into the night, grateful even if it took me away from Sky. I wanted to do this. I needed to do this. I needed to have something to do that was entirely outside of myself. It kept me sane. Even my brand new therapist approved of this strange hobby of mine. "It's good you have something that proves it's always possible to start over again."

Sky had taught me that. I didn't know what I'd done to deserve her. But I intended to keep her. I'd keep doing everything I could to deserve all of the people I loved.

Claire in particular. My sister's anger was still a weight on my shoulders.

But I couldn't think of that now. Not when I was pulling off to the side of the road at the meeting point.

I switched off the headlights. Now the wait would begin.

Sometimes it only took seconds. Sometimes I waited for hours only to learn that my contact had lost their nerve. This moment, when the blackness of the night enveloped me in a silent shroud, was always the most tense.

I'd moved almost twenty people now. But each one got harder and harder as the Elders cracked down. They'd even approached the courts, alleging kidnapping.

And if they did, fuck it. I'd spend my life savings to make sure that everyone got the same second chance I'd been handed.

I leaned forward. Was that a shadow there, moving in the thicket of bushes by the roadside?

I rolled down the window. "Hello? Do you have any jumper cables?" I called into the night. It was the codeword for tonight's pickup. We had a new one every night now.

The shadow moved, separating from the dark undergrowth. The streaking along the road and into my back seat.

I drove. That's what came next, getting enough miles between us and the compound that we could be sure no one had seen us. "You did good," I said to the shadow behind me. "Good work."

A tiny mewling cry was my response.

I yanked the wheel, sending us onto the shoulder. "Is that a baby?" I hissed. "No! That's not safe!" I turned on the interior light and twisted around. "I'm *driving*. You can't be holding a baby in your arms when I'm dri- ."

My voice died when she lifted her face from her infant. I sat back in my seat. "No way."

Her eyes widened. "Beau?"

I shook my head. I didn't have to pretend to be my brother any more. I didn't have to pretend that I was a good man. "No, I'm Finn. And I know you. You're -."

"Rebecca," she finished. She jiggled the baby on her lap and closed her eyes with a sigh. “I’m Rachel sister."

THE END

BOOKS BY THERESA LEIGH

The Crown Creek Series

The Kings

Sweet Crazy Song

Jonah and Ruby's story

Cocky Jonah never wanted to come home to Crown Creek. But a chance meeting with kindergarten teacher Ruby has him wanting to stay forever.

Lost Perfect Kiss

Gabe and Everly's story

A risk taking bad boy. A girl-next-door nurse. And the kiss that never should have happened. Gabe has to convince Everly to take the biggest risk of her life. Him.

Soft Wild Ache

Beau and Rachel's story

Growing up in a repressive religious cult meant that Rachel always believed the outside world was evil. But when sensitive rocker Beau opens her eyes to life outside the compound walls, she learns that he's the sweetest sin she's ever seen.

His Secret Heart

Finn and Sky's story

Sky was certain she knew everything she needed to know about volatile, unpredictable bad boy Finn King. But when her world turns upside down, she realizes everything she thought she knew is wrong.

Crown Creek Standalones:

Last Good Man

Cooper and Willa's story

Willa hates Cooper. But when she wakes up in a hospital room, he's the one who's there waiting - rumpled, frantic... And swearing she's his fiancee.

Coming soon:

Ryan and Naomi's story

Sadie's story

Visit theresaleighromance.com for more.

ABOUT THE AUTHOR

Theresa Leigh is a romance author whose love of reading is so intense, she sometimes injures herself by walking around with her nose in a book. She loves writing stories that have you feeling every emotion... sometimes all on the same page.

Theresa lives and writes in the beautiful Finger Lakes region of New York State (not the city) (that distinction is important to her), where she lives with her husband, twin sons and twin orange cats, Pumpkin and Jackie O'Lantern. When she's not writing or reading, she enjoys eating too much Thai food, walking around barefoot, and cooing baby talk at her cats.

Get in touch!
www.theresaleighromance.com
authortheresaleigh@gmail.com
facebook.com/booksbytheresaleigh

Made in the USA
Lexington, KY
29 November 2019

57862016R00142